COWBOY
heaven

CHERYL BROOKS

Copyright © 2015 by Cheryl Brooks
Cover and internal design © 2015 by Sourcebooks, Inc.
Cover design by Dawn Adams
Cover image © Rob Lang

Sourcebooks and the colophon are registered trademarks of Sourcebooks, Inc.

Published by Sourcebooks Casablanca, an imprint of Sourcebooks, Inc.
P.O. Box 4410, Naperville, Illinois 60567-4410
(630) 961-3900
Fax: (630) 961-2168
www.sourcebooks.com

Library of Congress Cataloging-in-Publication Data is on file with the publisher.

Printed and bound in the United States of America.
VP 10 9 8 7 6 5 4 3 2 1

For my pal Angela.

She wanted me to write a story about cowboys.

I gave her a whole bunkhouse full of them.

Chapter 1

THERE HE WAS AGAIN. That same cowboy I'd seen on the drive into town, still walking, still carrying a big green duffel bag on one shoulder and a saddle slung over the other. He'd been traveling in the opposite direction and hadn't bothered to look up as I'd passed him earlier. I'd barely glimpsed his face then, but I saw it quite clearly now. A glance over his shoulder revealed his bleak, exhausted expression. He might have been near the point of collapse, but he obviously wasn't prepared to admit defeat.

Not yet, anyway.

I couldn't believe no one had picked him up in the three hours since I'd last seen him. He hadn't looked very fresh even then. I had no idea where he was headed, but in the middle of Wyoming, there wasn't much within walking distance, no matter where you were going.

He turned toward me, sticking out a halfhearted thumb as I came closer, his face streaked with dirt and sweat and what might have been tears. A black Stetson shadowed his eyes, and his boots and jeans were dusty and worn. His sweat-soaked denim shirt clung to his chest, unbuttoned halfway to his waist, the sleeves ripped out. He probably wasn't trying to look cool, even though he did. No, he was likely trying to *get* cool, in any way he possibly could. My truck was air-conditioned and comfortable, and there was plenty of room for him and his meager belongings. I could no more have left him there than I could have ignored a starving child.

As I pulled over to stop, his eyes closed and his lips moved as though uttering a prayer of thanks. His knees buckled slightly, and for a moment, I thought he truly would collapse. Instead, he took a deep breath and stood up straight. Lifting his chin, he aimed luminous blue eyes at me and flashed a dazzling smile. His silver belt buckle suggested this man was no ordinary ranch hand but a down-on-his-luck rodeo cowboy who, unless I missed my guess, was heading for Jackson Hole.

A real heartbreaker of a rodeo cowboy, too. Up close, he was even more handsome than he'd been from a distance. Long and lean with tanned, muscular arms, dimples creased his cheeks and black hair curled enticingly from the open edges of his shirt. Several days' growth of dark beard surrounded full, sensuous lips, darkening a jaw that my fingertips ached to caress. More ebony curls peeked from beneath his hat, making me long to yank off that Stetson to discover what else it was hiding. Oh yes, there was enough gorgeous cowboy to sway a much stronger woman than I ever claimed to be. Tears stung my eyes as something in his expression reminded me of Cody.

My dear, sweet Cody… He'd been gone for two years now, but I hadn't forgotten that look, and I doubted I ever would.

Determined to mask my roiling emotions, I searched for something amusing to say as I rolled down my window. "Lost your horse?"

My clever tongue was rewarded with another heart-stopping smile. Cody used to say funny things just to make me giggle—which wasn't difficult since I tend to find humor in nearly any situation—but brushing up on my own repertoire of one-liners to keep this guy smiling seemed like an excellent idea.

His grin was sheepish as he tipped up the brim of his hat. "He sort of drove off without me."

"*Drove* off?" I scoffed. "Somehow I doubt that. Seems like he would've needed help."

My handsome cowboy gave me a grim nod. "Oh, he had help all

right. My girlfriend dumped me on the highway and took off with the truck, the trailer, and the horse—all of which were actually hers, by the way. She was kind enough to leave me my saddle and my clothes, although a cell phone would've been nice."

I shook my head. "Nice, yes. Helpful, no. They don't work very well around here. Which kinda makes me mad—I mean, where would you need a phone more than if you were stranded out in the middle of nowhere?"

He glanced around at the vast expanse of sunbaked rangeland. "Is that the name of this place? Nowhere?"

"Sure is." I couldn't help giggling. "Want to get out of nowhere?"

"Yes, please," he replied. "And as quickly as possible."

"Throw your stuff in the back and hop in," I said. "We'll leave nowhere and go…somewhere."

He did as I suggested, and suddenly the interior of my truck was filled with the pungent aroma of hot, sweaty, dusty—but cologned—cowboy. He'd most likely showered that morning, but it had been one helluva day. The forecast called for the upper nineties—quite a heat wave even for mid-August—and though the humidity was low, some temperatures are best avoided no matter how dry the air.

"You're a lifesaver," he said. "I thought that sun was gonna roast me alive."

"As hot as it gets in these parts, I never go anywhere without water, enough food for a couple of meals, and an umbrella in case I'm ever forced to hike. Want a sandwich?"

"You bet."

I tossed a nod over my shoulder. "The cooler's on the backseat. Help yourself. There's plenty of water." Although, at that point, a cold beer probably would have been his first choice.

He pulled out two bottles of water and a sandwich, downing the first bottle in three swallows.

"Better now?"

"Much."

"Let's see now…" I said as he unwrapped the sandwich. "A cowboy dumped in the middle of nowhere with a saddle and no horse. There's got to be a country song in that."

"If you mean a song about a guy bein' picked up by a girl in a flatbed Ford, I think the Eagles already did that one."

"I love that song," I said wistfully. "Guess I always wanted to be that girl."

"Well, now you are." He took a bite of the sandwich, chewing it quickly. "How does it feel?"

"Not much different." This wasn't entirely true. I wasn't in the habit of picking up gorgeous cowboys—and this particular cowboy's presence had me feeling strangely excited. Oh yes, I was very aware of him, and if my brain hadn't noticed him, my erogenous zones were there to remind me. "For one thing, this isn't a flatbed Ford, and I'm not what anyone would call a girl anymore."

He paused in mid-bite. "Why? Have you had a sex-change operation?"

"Nope," I replied with another giggle. "You can't call a forty-two-year-old a girl. Well, maybe you could if you happened to be eighty-two yourself, but I'm pretty sure I outgrew the girl category a long time ago—about the time that song was popular."

Despite the fact that I never once took my eyes off the road, I was aware of his prolonged scrutiny—an assessing gaze that left delightful tingles in its wake.

"Some things improve with age." He turned toward the window. "You don't seem like the type to dump a guy in the middle of nowhere."

Having heard the catch in his voice, I did my best to keep my tone light. Bursting into tears in front of a perfect stranger probably wasn't on his bucket list. "True—unless he was really obnoxious."

This particular cowboy would have to have been homicidal or, at the very least, abusive for me to throw *him* out. He was the most adorable cowboy I'd ever laid eyes on, including the one I'd married.

"I wasn't being obnoxious." He fairly bristled with indignation, which seemed to have won out over heartbreak. "I was *asleep*. I thought she was stopping for gas when I felt the truck slow down. She asked me to take a look at the tires on the trailer, said she thought one had gone flat. While I was checking the tires, she dumped my saddle and duffel bag on the side of the road and drove off. I found this tucked into the saddle." Reaching into his shirt pocket, he handed me a torn, sweat-soaked scrap of paper.

It's not working out. Sorry.

"Ouch," I said with a sympathetic wince. "That's pretty hard."

"Yeah." With an absent nod, he stuffed the note back into his pocket. "I don't even know what I did wrong. Don't guess I ever will."

He seemed nice enough, and he certainly wasn't ugly. Maybe his girl had breakup issues. As irresistible as he was, I couldn't imagine breaking his heart while gazing into those eyes of his, and I didn't even know his name.

She'd probably gone about it the best way possible—a quick, clean break before losing her nerve completely. One glance, one smile, and she'd have forgotten why their relationship wasn't working. I wasn't looking forward to dropping him off at the crossroad to the ranch, myself. I had a sudden, overwhelming urge to take him home and wash him, feed him, and tuck him into bed—*my* bed, to be precise.

I had my doubts about that part. He couldn't have been more than thirty, and young men generally didn't seek solace from older women—not that kind of solace, anyway. Consoling him seemed impossible, so I changed the subject.

"Where were you headed?"

"The rodeo in Jackson Hole," he replied. "I'm a rodeo cowboy."

"No shit," I drawled. "I'd never have guessed that. I don't suppose your girl left you with any money, did she? I mean, I'm not going to charge you for the ride or the lunch, but I'm not going all the way to Jackson Hole, either."

"I didn't figure you were." His downcast expression suggested his hope that he'd been wrong about that. "But at the time, I didn't really care."

"Neither did I. I wouldn't have left you there no matter where you were going. It was…well, let's just say it was something I couldn't bring myself to do."

"Pick up lots of strays, do you?" Turning sideways, he leaned back against the door, a move that not only drew my eye, but also gave me a full-frontal view that made my breath catch in my throat. Oh yes, I'd taken in lots of strays, but none that were anywhere near as attractive.

I shook my head. "Actually picking them up usually isn't necessary. They all seem to know where I live."

"If you don't mind my asking, where *do* you live? I mean, are we close?"

Obviously, he hoped I lived somewhere near Jackson Hole. I hated to disappoint him. "It's about another twenty miles—most of which are *not* on the main highway. I'll let you out at the turnoff, if that's okay with you."

His face fell, but he nodded, apparently resigned to the fact that this ride wasn't going to be more than a brief respite. "Not much choice, is there?" He gave a fatalistic shrug. "I don't have enough money on me to pay you to take me to Jackson Hole. I really should pay you for what you've already done."

I caught myself wishing that he *did* have enough money—or that he would ask me to run off with him and follow the rodeo circuit, never going home at all. I would have loved to throw caution to the wind and do just that, but I had too many responsibilities. Not only did I have a ranch to run, but I also had my father and my kids to look after.

No, scratch that. Chris and Will were both in college. I had a hard time remembering that except when confronted with the sight of their empty rooms as I passed by them every day. Out on the highway I could pretend they were both there at home waiting for me—and Cody, too.

No, regardless of how much money this man might offer to pay me, I couldn't shirk my duties and simply up and disappear. Nor would I accept his money. He obviously needed to hold on to what little he had stashed in those jeans.

"I couldn't possibly take money from you," I protested. "I wouldn't be much of a Good Samaritan if I did, would I?"

"I suppose not."

He shrugged again and we drove on in silence. Remaining slouched against the door, he draped his left arm across the headrest and bent up one knee, stretching his legs apart enough that my eyes were continually landing on that section of blue jeans due south of that big, silver belt buckle. From time to time he shifted his hips as though my glances made him uncomfortable, and while I *did* try to keep my eyes on the road, every once in a while they would stray back to him—and that enticing bulge in his jeans…

"What would it take to get you to drive me all the way to Jackson Hole?" The hint of suggestion in his voice startled me almost as much as the abrupt nature of his query.

Suddenly, my mouth was as dry as a gulch. Reaching for my bottle of water, I took a sip and stole another peek at him. Those luminous eyes peered at me from beneath lids that were heavy with sensuous intent.

His lips curled into a provocative smile. "I'd be willing to bet there's *something* I could do for you that would pay you back—or at least make it worth your while."

I'll just bet you could. Something quite remarkably wonderful...

Aloud, I said, "Such as?" hoping that my voice sounded more innocent than my thoughts.

He shifted his butt on the truck seat with a slow pelvic thrust. "Pull over and I'll show you." Glancing over his shoulder at the road ahead, he nodded toward the big cottonwood that was as much of a landmark for the turnoff as the road sign. "There. Under that tree."

My brain told me to keep driving, but my hands and feet ignored that directive, choosing instead to follow orders from my more primal body parts. I parked the truck in the shade and turned to face him. "This is where I let you out." Despite having cleared my throat before speaking, my voice still sounded a tad hoarse.

"You're not dumping me, are you?" His tone was teasing, but at the same time he managed to sound rather hurt that I would ever do such an awful thing to him. "I couldn't possibly get dumped again. Not twice in one day."

"No, this is where I make the turn toward home," I replied with a trace of regret. "This is where I said I'd let you off."

He nodded slowly, tipping his hat back with a finger to the brim. "Mind if we sit here and talk for a minute?"

"I suppose not. I'm not in any big rush to get home." Quite honestly, I could have sat there gazing at him for at least another hour or two. He was candy for the eyes, and I was starving to death.

He nodded again, reaching for that huge, shining belt buckle. "Let me show you something. Since you plan to leave me here anyway, I don't have much to lose."

I gasped in surprise. "You're not thinking about trading your belt buckle for a ride to Jackson Hole, are you? I can't imagine you'd want to part with something like that." Closer scrutiny proved it was no ordinary belt buckle, but a trophy buckle—the kind you can't buy, but have to win at the rodeo.

"I don't plan to." Releasing the buckle, he flipped open the button on his jeans. "What I intend to give you I can easily afford to lose." He unzipped his fly and pushed the fabric back away from his briefs. I could see the reason for the bulge now. His dick was rock hard and oozing all over his underwear. "You've been staring at this for miles. I thought you might like a better look." With that, he pushed off his jeans and briefs in one long, slow sensuous thrust. His stiff rod escaped its confinement and stood erect, taunting me—daring me not to look, not to touch…

I believe I gasped, and I know my jaw dropped in amazement. His handsome face, incredible eyes, and terrific body had already rendered him irresistible. The addition of a fabulous dick—thick and long with a tight, shiny head—created a truly lethal combination. All I could do was stare, breathlessly waiting to see what he would do next.

Pulsing his cock, he pumped out rivers of pre-come that poured over the head and down the shaft like hot fudge over vanilla ice cream. With a wicked smirk, he slid his fingertips up and down the shaft. "Want a ride?"

I let out a pent-up breath as my tongue swept involuntarily over my lips. I'd never dreamed anything like this would happen when I picked him up—would've bet money he was too exhausted for any funny business—which only goes to show how much a sandwich, a bottle of water, and air-conditioning will do for a guy. Not to mention a place to sit down and rest.

Or some strong incentive.

He obviously wanted a ride to the rodeo badly enough to sell himself for it—and to me, of all people. I had to be at least ten years his senior, and I probably outweighed him—although he *was* a good bit taller than me. Perhaps he was heavier than he looked.

Not having enough spit in my mouth to lick a stamp, I swallowed with a great deal of difficulty.

"Maybe you'd rather have a drink." His voice was a seductive purr as he pumped out more fluid. "You look a little on the dry side."

My hand flew to my lips, and I tried to swallow again but couldn't. Every ounce of excess fluid in my body had gone south, along with my reason. I couldn't help it. Powerless to resist and ignoring the protests of my normally reasonable brain, I leaned forward and kissed his cockhead, sliding my tongue over the slick surface while inhaling his intoxicating scent. Salty to the taste and smooth as silk to the touch, he robbed me of every inhibition I had. I went down on his cock, capturing as much as I could inside my hungry mouth.

Laughing softly, he stretched out his right leg and jacked off his boot using the stick for the four-wheel drive. Then he slid his leg out of his jeans. "Maybe you'd like some ass too." Raising his leg, he pushed me away with a foot on my shoulder before bracing it against the seat to flip himself over onto his knees.

Damn. Somehow, this man—this stranger—seemed to know my every weakness. His tight cheeks waved back and forth in front of my face as an orgasm struck, doubling me over. Falling forward, I kissed his sweet buns, giving myself sufficient recovery time to move on to lick his succulent balls.

He'd certainly chosen the right currency. For a little more of this, I'd have driven him all the way to California, given him my truck, hitchhiked my way back home, and considered myself the lucky one. I devoured him, licking my way underneath him before turning onto my back. His tasty cock dangled above my waiting lips.

"Fuck me in the mouth," I whispered. "I want you to come in my mouth."

"How far is it to Jackson Hole from here?" Groaning, he slid his thick head past my parted lips. How in the world he thought I was supposed to answer him, I have no idea. I couldn't possibly be expected to carry on a conversation with a cock that size in my mouth.

"Not that it matters," he went on. "I'll fuck you every twenty miles and twice when we get there. You can have it any way you want."

Giggling around his penis, I pushed it aside on the upstroke. "You are *such* a slut."

"Yeah. Doncha just love a slutty cowboy?" He came down on me again, sliding his wet cock across my cheek. "And you're just the kind of sweet little woman that brings out the man-whore in me. As cute and round as a robin, with big, brown eyes and long, dark braids like an Apache maiden." He groaned again and pressed his cock to my lips. "Suck me, baby. I'm ready to fill you up with my cream."

He punctuated those words with a push past my lips. His hard cock filled my mouth, and I licked the underside of his shaft as he pumped in and out. Cupping his swinging balls in my hand, I fondled them gently, massaging them while tugging on the long, curly hair adorning his scrotum.

"You like my nuts, baby?" he asked breathlessly. "I like what you're doing to them. It makes me feel like I'm gonna explode all over you."

That prospect was too much for me. Moaning, I came again, grabbing his ass in a desperate attempt to pull his dick farther into my mouth. My fingers crept to the cleft of his buttocks, seeking his soft, velvety hole. Putting a hand to his mouth, he spit on his fingers before reaching back to lubricate himself.

My massage of his slick, tight hole made him fuck even harder until at last, a sharp exhale heralded his climax. His body tensed as his breath hissed back in through his teeth. Semen shot straight down my throat, filling my mouth with spurt after spurt of warm juice. As he slowly withdrew, I sucked the cream from his cock, savoring its tangy sweetness before swallowing every last drop.

"That was payment for the ride so far." He twisted around to land heavily in the passenger seat. "To get more, you have to keep driving. I'll be hard again in another twenty miles."

I stared mutely through the windshield at the highway stretched out before me, that huge cottonwood tree a mere speck in the distance. Barely visible on the horizon, it moved closer with each passing moment. Breathing deeply in an attempt to restore harmony to my riotous emotions, I fixed an unwavering gaze on the tree—the familiar landmark steadily bringing me back into reality.

I blinked as a hand passed up and down in front of my eyes.

"Hey." His voice was overly loud, as though I hadn't been listening and he was trying to recapture my attention. "Are you always this quiet?"

As I glanced in his direction, I noted that, unlike the man in my fantasy, this cowboy remained fully dressed, his cock still an enigma, well hidden behind stout layers of blue denim.

Not quite trusting my voice, I cleared my throat. "Sometimes."

"Thought I'd lost you there for a minute." He smiled, seeming somewhat relieved. "Do you know how far it is from here to Jackson Hole?"

Chapter 2

IT'S AMAZING HOW LOST in thought I can become when the right subject steals my attention. Cody used to accuse me of daydreaming—and he was right—although he usually benefited from my woolgathering. Over the years, I'd come up with some pretty wild stuff while my mind was elsewhere, things from which he seemed to derive tremendous enjoyment, so he probably shouldn't have complained.

Dear, sweet, sexy Cody. I missed him more with each passing day. My hitchhiking cowboy could have no idea that such thoughts ever crossed my mind. I knew for a fact that my imaginings never showed themselves in my face, which meant that he could have no inkling that I might actually want to live out that fantasy. If he did, I was pretty sure he wouldn't have wanted to drive another yard with me.

I thought about all the cowboys—some quite young, some older, some cute and some not—who had worked for us on the ranch over the years, none of whom had shown the slightest romantic or sexual interest in me, either before or after Cody died. Not even the foreman, who was nearly sixty and was still a rather attractive man, seemed to consider me to be a female worth pursuing. To him, I was nothing more than a silly little woman who needed to be kept out of trouble.

Rufus had worked for us for a long time and had been a good foreman. Neither I nor my father—or Cody, for that matter—ever had any complaints about the way he managed the ranch, even though he'd always seemed to be somewhat lacking in personality. Far from being interested in me in the romantic sense, he seemed to disapprove of me. He was always considerate and respectful, but I couldn't help feeling there was something about me he didn't like. I could almost see it in his eyes.

Cody must not have told any of the other men about the fun things we'd indulged in while we were alone, for none of them had ever stepped forward to take his place. Dad had made no secret of the fact that he thought my marrying Rufus might not be a bad idea, but it didn't look as though there was much chance of that ever happening. Besides, I didn't love Rufus, and he sure as hell didn't love me.

Cody had spoiled me. I knew what a marriage could be like with the right man, and I wasn't about to settle for anything less. I had my memories and my fantasies, and for the rest, well, let's just say I wasn't willing to compromise. After Cody's death, my friends had told me I couldn't afford to be choosy—especially at my age— but we weren't talking about their lives. This was *my* life and my decision. Just as it had been my decision to pick up a startlingly handsome cowboy who had gotten my mind working along erotic lines again, much the way Cody had when I'd first laid eyes on him as a junior in high school.

I glanced over at the cowboy, noting his anxious, wide-eyed expression. No doubt he expected that someone who could withdraw so completely wouldn't be able to drive safely, but it had never been a problem for me, and it helped to pass the time I spent on the road.

"Sorry," I said. "I was thinking about something else. Jackson Hole is about two hundred miles from here." With a fuck every twenty miles and two more when we got there, that made twelve times he would have to get it up. I doubted there was a man alive who could actually do that.

So much for fantasy.

He blew out a pent-up breath. "I was afraid of that. Like I said,

I was asleep—I had no idea where I was when I started walking. I'm not sure I can walk that far."

"Not in those boots, anyway," I agreed. "Not made for walking, are they?"

With a rueful shake of his head, he glanced toward his boots, then back at me. "Not at all. I've probably got blisters on top of blisters by now. Would you mind if I took them off?"

No, dear, you can take off anything you like, starting with your boots and working up to your hat. The mere thought made my nipples tingle.

"No," I said aloud. "But I should warn you we're almost to the point where I have to let you out."

He swore softly under his breath. "I was afraid of that, too." He looked so miserable at the prospect of getting out and walking again that I had to think of something, some other alternative we hadn't considered yet—or maybe I had, somewhere in the midst of my fantasy.

"Tell you what," I said, doing my best to sound as though I were doing him a bigger favor than he would be doing for me. "Let me take you back to the ranch. You can rest for a while—take a shower, even spend the night if you like. Then you can call someone to come and get you. You must have some friends on the rodeo circuit who would do that for you."

"I guess I could." He chewed his lip thoughtfully. I had to turn away from him for a moment as another wave of desire washed over me.

No, I wasn't the one doing him any favors. The pleasure of his company would be all mine, and if he couldn't find anyone else to give him a ride, I would do it myself. I just wouldn't do it today—after all, I had supplies in the truck that were needed at home, and I'd have to at least unload them before I could make a run into Jackson Hole. It would, at the very earliest, be ten or so the next morning before I could start out.

In the meantime, I could wash him, feed him, and tuck him into bed.

Unfortunately, it wouldn't be my bed he slept in—it would be one of my sons', or more likely a bed in the bunkhouse—but, hey, it was better than nothing.

"If you can't get a ride, I'll take you there tomorrow myself. Would that be too late?"

"Oh, no," he replied. "I just need to get there before the weekend. I don't know where I'll go after that. Maybe I can ride with some other guys. The trouble is I don't have a horse."

That could be a problem for a cowboy if he happened to be more into calf-roping and steer wrestling than he was bronc or bull riding. I glanced pointedly down at the belt buckle—noting that it was indeed a calf-roping medal.

"You'd be handy at the ranch," I said with a nod at the buckle. "Our guys are all pretty good, but they've never won any competitions." Of course, a working ranch hand was better all-around than most rodeo cowboys. There wasn't much call for bull riding on a ranch, but roping required skill and practice as well as talent—and it was useful.

Tipping his head to one side, he studied me carefully. "Are you offering me a job?"

This was an even better excuse to keep him around, although if he worked for me, I'd be in continuous heat for the duration of his employment. I wasn't sure I could keep my hands off him. As it was, my palms were itching for a chance to touch him. I swallowed around the lump forming in my throat. "Maybe. We're short a man right now. One of the guys has a broken leg and can't do very much. It would only be temporary, but—"

"If you could give me a day or so for my feet to heal, I accept." He said it so quickly I had to wonder just how much money he actually had stuffed in those jeans, if any. "Besides, I think I'd like working for you. I feel like I owe you something."

Damn. I really was looking forward to that ride to Jackson Hole. With a fuck every twenty miles, it might turn out to be the high point of my life. Then I remembered he'd never promised me anything of the kind. That particular offer was merely a figment of my horny little imagination.

"You don't owe me anything," I assured him. "Really, you'd be doing me a favor. In fact, you already have."

"How's that? I haven't done anything for you at all."

His quizzical expression nearly made me laugh out loud. "Oh, yes you have. Trust me on this one."

I seriously doubted he understood what I meant by that, but he nodded as though he did. "How far did you say it was?"

"About another ten miles." With two fucks at the end of the road, I added silently. Now, if only that were true…

"I'll keep my boots on, then," he said. "I might not be able to get them back on if I take them off."

"Your feet might swell up," I agreed, thinking that I'd like to see that third leg of his swell up a little. I chuckled to myself. Men really had no idea what women were thinking about most of the time, which was probably a good thing. My adorable cowboy would have run all the way to Jackson Hole if he'd known what had been going on in my head.

I realized then that I didn't even know his name. "By the way, my name is Angela McClure. If you're going to get a paycheck from me, you'd better tell me yours."

"Troy." He leaned forward and held out his hand. "Troy Whitmore."

I placed my hand in his warm, firm grasp and was instantly lost. When he grinned, I nearly drove the truck into the cottonwood tree as I tried to take the turn too fast. Momentarily blinded by his smile, I'd almost missed it.

His response to sliding off the seat and onto the floorboards of the truck was to laugh. I liked that he could find the humor in that small accident, rather than cussing a blue streak as so many men would have done—not to mention the fact that his laughter sent a rush of tingles racing up and down my spine.

No doubt I would regret my impulsiveness eventually—tomorrow perhaps, or maybe even for the rest of my life.

But not today.

Troy didn't have to know what I was thinking about, and if I didn't tell him, he never would. It would remain my dirty little secret. Besides, I wouldn't have to keep that secret for long. Dusty's leg wouldn't take more than a couple of months to heal, and in the meantime I could certainly enjoy my eye-candy cowboy.

"Guess I should be more careful. I don't need two cowboys with broken legs." Bringing the truck to a stop, I reached over to help him up. "Then again, you should've been wearing a seat belt, young man." My firm, scolding tone was one sure way *not* to entice him into my bed. I might've been talking to one of my kids.

He shook his head. "I've had worse falls off a horse. That was nothing."

"Put your seat belt on anyway," I advised. "It gets pretty bumpy from here on. I try to avoid the potholes, but there are so many, I can't miss them all. I was twelve years old the last time this road was actually paved, rather than patched. You'd think with all the property taxes we pay they could do better than that, but I've gone way past the point of expecting miracles." A freshly paved road truly would be a miracle. Right up there with hell freezing over and handsome cowboys letting me suck them off.

Troy fastened his safety belt without protest and eyed me expectantly. His expression was so innocent, I nearly laughed again. By this time, if he'd had any idea what I'd been thinking, he would have been in a state of sheer panic.

I hesitated before continuing down the road. "You're sure about this? Ever work on a ranch before?"

"I grew up on a ranch," he replied with a nod. "I know it's not as glamorous as the rodeo, but I think I can handle it."

"I hope so."

For more reasons than one.

Chapter 3

TRAVELING ALONG SUCH A rough road made conversation difficult, which left my mind free to consider what to do with my new stray.

My first thought was that offering Troy a job might have been a mistake. As an employee, he would live in the bunkhouse with the other hands and be out working all day. If I kept him in the house, I'd see a lot more of him.

I reminded myself that he still needed a few days for his feet to heal. During that time, I could indulge myself by nursing him back to health before I had to break down and actually make him work for his keep. Realistically, I couldn't expect his blisters to heal up overnight, nor would it take a week before he could walk without pain.

On the other hand, he might think there was something funny about staying in the house with Dad and me after he'd accepted the job. Dad might think there was something odd about it too.

These and other points to ponder kept my mouth shut and my mind occupied during most of the drive. Fortunately, Troy had figured out I was the quiet type and wouldn't assume I was ignoring him. I couldn't decide how to relate to him. I wasn't old enough to be his mother, nor was I his contemporary. Being employer and employee wasn't much better. Thinking of us as friends was the best alternative I could come up with. I would be friendly with him—perhaps more so than with the other hands because I...

Because I *what*? Liked him more? Thought he was cuter? There had to be some explanation as well as a reason for allowing a total stranger into my home. I could say he was a distant cousin of a friend of mine, but that would be too easy to disprove if anyone decided to check into it.

I waited until we'd reached one of the smoother sections of pavement before I broached the subject. "Troy, I feel sort of weird about this. I really don't know you from Adam, and it's going to seem strange when I tell everyone I picked up a hitchhiker and brought him home. I need some sort of…justification."

"What, my being a handsome devil isn't reason enough?"

He was laughing when he said it, but I doubted he was kidding. Chances were good that his looks were the reason he'd acquired his previous girlfriend. It was also the conclusion almost anyone would reach for what I'd done—no matter how pitiful he might've seemed at the time.

"Really, Angela, you don't need an excuse to hire me. I'm a cowboy—not a con artist or a serial killer. I know there's no reason for you to believe that, but it's the honest-to-God truth."

I ignored the crack about the serial killer and focused on his first question, which was first and foremost in my mind. "So you think I picked you up because you're a gorgeous hunk, huh?" If that was the case, then he already knew me too well. I wouldn't get away with much.

He arched a brow. "Am I wrong?"

"Maybe. I'm not sure. But even if you *are* a real cowboy, there must be something wrong with you, or your girlfriend wouldn't have left you stranded on the highway."

Troy didn't answer me right away. Whether he used the time to fabricate a lie or search for the truth wasn't clear, but if I'd had to guess, I'd have said he was genuinely puzzled.

"I dunno," he finally said. "Maybe I waited too long to ask her to marry me."

"Were you planning to?"

"Nope." With a sheepish shrug he added, "Actually, it never

even occurred to me. I haven't got what you'd call a shining future as a rodeo cowboy, and I never have any money to speak of. I can't afford a wife."

In my humble opinion, he could have sold his body on the street corner and been rich enough to retire in a month.

I didn't say that, of course. Instead, I suggested he model Levi's.

His grimace led me to believe he'd heard that line before. "Maybe. But I couldn't do that forever. Maybe it's time I admitted to myself that a ranch hand is all I'm cut out to be. There are worse things a man could do for a living."

The streetwalker notion came to mind again, but I modified the idea slightly—feeling him out, as it were. "Like being a boy toy for a rich socialite with a thing for cowboys?" I hoped my accompanying giggle would encourage him to assume I was joking, but I wasn't. His viewpoint on sex with older women was a topic I had a considerable interest in at the time.

Obviously not a man to speak without thinking—a trait I found quite appealing—he took his time to reply. Either that or he was stunned speechless. "I don't believe I'd like that," he said slowly. "I wouldn't have much to talk about with the socialite type. Rich people are too...*different* from the rest of us."

At least he hadn't rejected the boy toy suggestion out of hand, only the rich socialite part—which was a good thing, since I wasn't rich. Perhaps I still had a chance to recruit him. "So it's not the boy toy thing you object to, just the rich socialite part?"

"I'm not sure I'd make a very good boy toy, either," was his cautious reply. "I think I'm too old for that."

He still seemed to be skirting the issue. Searching for a slightly different tack, I chose the most obvious. "Aha! Now we're getting somewhere. I know why your girlfriend dumped you. Viagra is too expensive." My cowboy fantasy was already beginning to fade into oblivion. He wouldn't be hard in another twenty miles—it would be more like another twenty hours, or twenty days, or twenty weeks, or—

"That isn't the problem," he said, interrupting my dismal appraisal of his sexual stamina. "Trust me, everything works fine. I just think a guy would have to be younger and not have much of a mind of his own for that sort of occupation. I'm not what you'd call submissive."

Damn. Clearly, none of my fantasies about him were going to come true. He was too old and so was I. At least I *assumed* that was the problem.

Back to the drawing board.

On the other hand, I didn't think I'd care for a totally submissive man. I liked a little sexual aggression now and then—liked the idea that a man could be so strongly attracted to me that he might get carried away sometimes.

"Bullheaded, huh? Is that what your girlfriend didn't like?"

"Maybe," he said with a shrug. "Although, now that I think about it, for all practical purposes I probably *was* her boy toy. We were roughly the same age, but she did have money. I guess you could say she sponsored me, buying the horse and trailer and paying my entry fees when I couldn't come up with the cash. She probably got tired of wasting her money on a cowboy who didn't win all the time. Maybe she figured she'd have a better chance of finding a new guy without me tagging along."

He was making me wish I'd never brought it up. "She couldn't have found one who was better-looking, that's for sure." I tried for a teasing tone but didn't quite make it. The conversation was getting a bit deep for that.

My pathetic attempt at humor drew a mirthless chuckle. "Nothing more than a pretty face, huh? Lots of women complain they aren't taken seriously because they're beautiful, but I can relate to that in a way. No one seems to think I have a brain—that I'm the male equivalent of a dumb blond."

I was beginning to feel guilty about my fantasy but consoled myself with the knowledge that he didn't and—if I kept quiet about it—wouldn't *ever* know I'd had such erotic thoughts concerning him. I was regretting the "slutty cowboy" part, too—until I remembered it was all in my head.

"Why is it that so many people feel the need to categorize others? You know what I mean—the whole 'he's a geek, she's a brain, he's a hunk, or she's an airhead' thing, when the truth is that everyone has more than one defining characteristic. Some people have it all—brains and beauty and money and talent—but most of us don't, and we always seem to want what we can't have. You wish people wouldn't look at you and see only a pretty face, whereas I, on the other hand, would like very much to have a problem like that. Too bad we can't ever be satisfied."

"Being satisfied might not be a good thing," Troy said. "If you were satisfied, you'd never do anything different or strive to be better at what you already do, would you?"

This was a much deeper thought than I would have given him credit for having, which made me as guilty as anyone who'd decided he was all beauty and brawn and no brains. I peered at him out of the corner of my eye. "Now, there's a deep, insightful comment if I've ever heard one. You're absolutely right, Troy. Point made." I gave him a quick once-over. "There's certainly more to you than a pretty face."

"And you're a lot prettier than you think you are."

"Bless you for that," I whispered. Tears stung my eyes as I focused them on the road again. I didn't want him to see me cry any more than he'd wanted to shed tears in front of me. We'd come to another bumpy stretch of road, so I concentrated on that for the time being, but in truth, all I wanted was to simply stop the truck and hug him. Pain swelled within my chest as I realized I would probably never get the chance to do that. I never seemed to get hugs from anyone anymore.

"Hey, now, don't cry."

Only then did I realize I *was* crying. Tears slid down my cheeks in salty little rivers, puddling in my eyes and fogging up my contact lenses until I could barely see.

"Why don't you pull over for a minute?" he suggested.

I did so without protest, having no other choice since I couldn't see well enough to avoid the potholes. I put the truck in park and dissolved into tears, leaning on the steering wheel as it struck me exactly how alone I felt. My husband was dead, my sons had gone off to college, and Dad hadn't been himself lately, though he'd never been what you'd call understanding and supportive. Mom had been gone for years. I had no one to turn to but—

"Come here." Troy raised the fold-down console between us and popped the release on my seat belt. Pulling me out from behind the wheel and across the bench seat, he took me in his arms and held me as I added my tears to the sweat already staining his shirt. It seemed I'd gotten my wish, for I'd pulled over to the side of the road and hugged him. Too bad I was crying my eyes out at the time.

At that point, I didn't care *what* he was. He could have been a killer, a thief, a rapist, or any kind of creep you could think of. All I knew was that for the moments he held me in his arms I felt safe, cared for—possibly even loved. Believe me, it was heady stuff for a lonely widow. That, on top of all the fantasizing I'd been doing, may have been responsible for what happened next. But somehow I didn't think I was entirely to blame.

"I'm sorry," he whispered. "I didn't mean to make you cry, but you really are pretty, Angie. Didn't anyone ever tell you that? Not even your husband?"

Sobbing harder, I held tightly to the open edges of his shirt. "Yes, he did. But it was such a long time ago, and now he's dead. No one's paid the slightest bit of attention to me since he died, and I *miss* that. He couldn't be the only one, could he? I mean, there's got to be someone else on the planet who would feel the same way. Maybe I need to get out more or something. I tried going out with some friends once, but I only got ignored, so I never tried it again."

He gave me a squeeze. "Not much of a flirt, huh?"

"Only with my husband. Cody and I used to flirt outrageously with each other, but we were so slick about it, no one ever realized what we were doing. We had a sort of code. One of us would catch the other's eye, or I would touch him in a way that didn't mean anything to anyone but us. I miss the closeness, the contact—this sort of thing." I hugged him even harder than before. "Someone to put my arms around. My dad isn't much of a hugger, and my sons are both in college—the only ones who get hugs from me are the dogs and the horses, and they never hug me back."

"You can hug me anytime you like." He stroked my back, his hands gliding up and down. Soothing yet stimulating. "I'm feeling a little unloved, myself. I could do with a few hugs."

"I'm sorry." I sat up, sniffling as I wiped away my tears. "I'd forgotten. You should be the one crying, not me."

"Yeah, well, I did that already," he said. "I might do it again, but I'm okay for now. What about you? Are you all right or do you want me to drive?"

"I can drive."

"Are you sure? Is there anything I can do to help?"

I shook my head, but a moment later I found myself staring at his mouth. I hadn't kissed him in my fantasy. What would it be like to taste those succulent lips? To feel their heat, to linger over their soft fullness…

I glanced away, knowing I shouldn't even think about kissing him. Hugs were good—certainly better than nothing—and he'd said I could hug him whenever I wanted. Any form of physical contact was an improvement over my previous situation. For now, hugs would have to do.

In a vain attempt to defog my contacts, I blinked several times. He must've thought I was batting my eyelashes, flirting with him, because when I looked up, he had this peculiar expression on his face. I can't describe it exactly, but it was a mixture of emotions—uncertainty, puzzlement—and then it changed, as though a light went on in his head and he suddenly knew the answer.

Reaching out, he took my face in his hands and leaned toward me. His kiss was whisper soft on my lips, which were parted in surprise. Tentative at first, he seemed to be asking for permission, seeking reassurance that this was indeed what I wanted.

I replied to his unspoken question the best way I could. Laying my hands on his shoulders, I slid them slowly around to his back, enfolding him in my arms.

Obviously needing no further encouragement, Troy deepened the kiss. Slipping one hand to the back of my head and the other to my waist, he pulled me closer until I was practically in his lap. I didn't think about the fact that only a few miles down the road, we hadn't even met. Didn't think about whether he minded kissing a woman older than himself and, comparatively speaking, far less attractive.

No, what I thought about was the maleness of him, the intoxicating combination of scents. His warmth, the strength of his arms, the tantalizing feel of his tongue as it teased its way into my mouth. He might have been wondering just how far he could go with a lonely widow, how much he could get. I didn't give a damn what he did as long as he didn't stop. Looking back on my fantasy, if I'd only known then what a great kisser he was, I would have added kissing to that scenario. *Lots* of kissing. I would have driven him to Timbuktu for one fabulously, deliciously enthralling kiss…

"I love your braids." His murmur vibrated against my lips as he allowed one braid to slide through his fingers. "But I'd really like to get my hands in your hair when it's loose. So soft, so…" A deep sigh escaped him as he kissed me again. Shifting off the seat, he leaned into me, pushing me flat on my back, kissing me all the way down until he was on his knees straddling my hips. I felt him tugging on my braids, realizing after a moment that he'd pulled the bands off the ends and was unbraiding my hair, combing it out with his fingers. I kept waiting for it to end, waiting to come to my senses with him waving a hand in front of my glazed eyes, saying, "Earth to Angela!"

But it didn't happen. This was no fantasy playing through my mind. This was really happening. I was making out with the hottest, sexiest cowboy this world has ever seen, and it was real. It wasn't a fabrication of my love-starved mind.

Jesus, what a concept… What a totally mind-blowing concept! I'd been virtually ignored for two years and now this. It's a wonder I didn't pass out from the shock.

Somewhere along the line I noticed his hat was missing, and I clutched at his head, reveling in the texture of his soft, springy curls between my fingers. After that, I figured, what the hell, anything was fair game, and I ran my hands down his back and slid my fingertips beneath the waistband of his jeans.

With that tiny scrap of encouragement, he reached down and unbuckled his belt and unzipped his fly, then rocked forward on me, moving his hips higher up on my body, allowing me to reach them more easily. I shoved those jeans down as far as I could and went for his bare buns. I sucked in a breath as my hands made contact with his hot, smooth skin. Grabbing his cheeks with both hands, I squeezed hard enough to leave fingerprints.

"Angie likes ass, huh?" His whispered question tickled my ear.

All I could say was, "Mmm…"

"Well, Angie baby, you can grab my ass all you like," he growled. "Do anything to it you want, although what you're doing now feels so damn good, I just might come all over you."

"Guess I'd better stop, then." I was surprised I could even form the words, let alone carry them out. "You know…save some for later?"

He groaned as though that thought might be the death of him. "No, don't stop. Keep going, Angie. Keep playing with my ass."

"I could do it better if it was a little closer," I said. "Let me scoot down some."

As he released me and raised his right knee, I slid across the seat underneath him until I was in almost the same position I'd been in during my fantasy. A glistening droplet of fluid dripped onto my lips from his rock-hard penis. I was just about to suck that puppy into my mouth when we were rudely interrupted by the honking of a horn as another vehicle rattled past, reminding us that we were parked on the shoulder of a public road in broad daylight.

No one in a small car could've seen us, but Troy's bare butt may have been visible from another truck. Also, since my truck was fairly well-known in those parts, it was a safe bet that whoever had passed us probably knew I had to be there as well, whether they'd seen me or not.

So much for being discreet.

Troy burst out laughing. "Maybe this wasn't such a good idea after all. No, let me rephrase that, maybe this wasn't such a good *place* for it. The idea itself was excellent."

Needless to say, I was in complete agreement. "No shit. Are they turning around to come back for another look?"

He rose up to peer through the windshield, giving me a full frontal view of him that was even more breathtaking than the one I'd imagined. His shirt was hanging open, completely unbuttoned, revealing black, curling hair on his chest that tapered down across his stomach only to flare out again to surround his stellar cock and balls. I had to bite my lip to keep from gasping out loud.

"Nope," he replied. "All I see is a car driving on down the road. Don't see anything heading in this direction."

"Great. Give me just one more second…"

"For what?"

"This." Pushing up from the seat, I ran my tongue over the head of his engorged penis, lapping up the juice oozing from his slit. That endeavor got me more, but instead of the hot fudge on vanilla ice cream analogy, it was more like maple syrup from a squeeze bottle, although salty rather than sweet. I painted my lips with the slippery sauce before sucking him in like a Popsicle.

"Oh, Angie," he groaned. "You wouldn't happen to need a slightly used boy toy, would you?"

I pushed his dick aside to reply. "I thought you said you wouldn't make a good boy toy. That you were too bullheaded. And you are, aren't you?"

"Well, yes," he admitted. "But I'd try to be good." He rubbed the tip of his cock on my cheek. "I'd be *very* good. No nasty diseases. No strings attached."

"Troy the Boy Toy." I couldn't help giggling. "I like the sound of that, but my dad probably wouldn't. We'd have to be sneaky."

"Your dad?" he asked with surprise. "I thought you said you'd be the one writing my paycheck."

"That's right, but technically, Dad owns the ranch. I just pay the bills."

"Damn."

I giggled again. "You'll probably end up actually having to do some work to earn your money. The boy toy thing would have to be a perk."

"That would be quite a perk. Of course, if you work me too hard, I won't have enough energy for my boy toy duties."

"Yes, but you're young. You'll adjust." To demonstrate how much fun a job like that could be, I tickled his nuts and slid his cock into my mouth again, sucking him hard and deep. The surge of heat in my core served as a reminder of how good his fabulous dick would feel if he ever got around to actually fucking me with it.

"Well, yes, I probably *could* do both," he agreed after a moment's reflection. "I've done it before for my, um, girlfriend."

I paused in my efforts to comment. "Whose name you seem to have, um, forgotten?"

With a nod, he let out a groan of pure pleasure. "I don't think I even remember what she looks like. All I know is she never made me feel as good as you have in the past hour or so—not in the whole time I knew her." He sighed deeply. "And not only by what you're doing right now—which she didn't like to do, by the way—but by making me feel like I can talk to you, tell you things about myself and you don't judge, you just accept me for who I am."

Actually, it was the way anyone's mother might make them feel, but I chose not to mention that. Instead, I followed his comments with one of my own that put me clearly out of the mother category.

"Which is what? A tasty cowboy with a brain and a dick to die for?" I punctuated my sentence with a kiss on the end of said dick, and slid out from under him. Settling myself behind the wheel, I flipped my hair back over my shoulders. "What do you say we get you back to the ranch before someone else drives by?"

With a pained expression, he nodded his reluctant agreement and pushed up from the seat. After easing himself upright again, he looked down at his groin. "This is gonna be worse than if I'd taken off my boots. I don't know if I can get into my jeans."

"Think of something that would make your dick shrivel up," I advised. "Like going for a swim in the North Atlantic."

"Or getting left behind on the highway in the middle of Wyoming." The note of irony in his tone was impossible to miss.

"That might do it—or not. Hmm…" I reached over and cupped a hand beneath his cock, lifting it up for a closer inspection. "It doesn't seem to be getting any smaller. Maybe I need to suck you off, after all."

Having said that, I was pleased to note that his penis didn't shrivel in the slightest, but turned to granite in a matter of seconds.

"I don't think you're helping matters any," he gasped. "Do you think you could…?"

"Suck your dick? Tickle your balls? Play with your ass?" I stared at his stiff shaft, giggling. "Troy, this is amazing! It seems to grow a little more with everything I say."

"Keep talking and it's gonna fire off all by itself." He was moaning now. "Please, Angie. Help me."

His pleading expression would have swayed a much stronger woman than I'd ever claimed to be. "Pretty pushy for a boy toy, aren't you?" Scooting closer, I took his cock in my hand and coated my palm with the slick fluid pouring from the head. "I think I'll do it like this the first time. That way I'll be able to tell whether you can shoot straight."

"*Anything.* Just do it."

I'd never seen a man look quite so desperate before. Grinning hugely at the effect I seemed to have on him, I put a stranglehold on his swollen member at its base and pumped up and down on the shaft with my other hand. It took longer than I thought it would, but suddenly…

"Wow, Troy! Looks like your first job is going to be cleaning my windshield—along with the dashboard, headliner, seat, floor mat, and"—I aimed the last shot in a different direction—"my mouth." Licking my lips, I swallowed. "Never mind, I took care of that one. And, yes, you shoot pretty straight. Quite a range too."

His head had snapped back against the headrest as he came, his mouth flying open and his eyes rolling back in his head, but he still managed a smile. "I can do better if I'm not dehydrated."

"Well, then…" Lowering the console, I reached between the seat backs and flipped up the lid on the cooler. Grabbing a bottle of water, I slapped it into his hand. "Drink up. If you don't mind my asking—although since you're my boy toy, I feel I have the right to know—what's your turnaround time?"

Twisting off the bottle cap, he shrugged. "I dunno…twenty minutes, maybe?"

At sixty miles an hour, that was twenty miles.

Damn. Maybe there really *was* at least one man alive who could actually fuck all the way to Jackson Hole—and out of all the people who must have passed by him as he trudged along the highway, lucky me, *I* had been the one to pick him up. For the first time in my life, I had an idea of how that girl in the flatbed Ford might have felt—and it was a very nice feeling—just as I'd always known it would be.

"Sounds good." I patted his bare thigh. "Put your pants on and we'll head for home."

"How much farther did you say it was to the ranch?" He took a long swig from the bottle before pulling up his jeans. I'll admit to being slightly disappointed when he zipped his fly and buckled his belt. I could hardly wait for his rampant penis to escape again.

"About twenty minutes."

With two fucks when we get there.

Chapter 4

FUNNY HOW THINGS NEVER seem to work out quite the way we think they should. For one thing, Troy didn't clean my truck—well, maybe he did, but it only took a quick hit with a Kleenex to remove the evidence. With no one at the house to question where my stray cowboy had come from, all I had to do was show him in and direct him to the nearest shower. I helped him undress, of course, but a thorough examination of his feet only uncovered a few small blisters. This discovery, while fortunate for him, made my plan to keep him in the house for a few days unnecessary—which was *un*fortunate for me.

While he was in the shower, I made use of the time to fabricate a better story to explain his sudden appearance. Although he wouldn't have been the first cowboy to show up at the barn door looking for work, I figured I could say a friend had recommended him for a job while I was in town—perhaps even dropping him off at the ranch. That way there would be no need to explain why I'd picked him up on the highway. Whoever had driven by and honked must have assumed there was no one in the truck when I didn't wave back. If asked, I could always say I'd dropped something and pulled over to the side of the road to retrieve it.

At any rate, by the time Dad came back to the house, I was in the office discussing employment with a freshly showered and perfectly respectable cowboy. That I had stolen a few more kisses from him wouldn't have been obvious to anyone. I'd wanted to watch him in the shower—perhaps even help him out. Unfortunately, I had no idea when Dad might be back, so I figured it was best not to get caught with him right off the bat. Alas, I was forced to let him shower alone.

Sitting across the desk from Troy while we went over the paperwork was an exercise in self-restraint the likes of which I hadn't experienced in quite some time. Knowing what he had hidden in those jeans and what thoughts lurked behind those fabulous blue eyes was enough to make me want to leap over the desk and do *something*.

Since I wasn't going to pay him any more than what the other hands were paid when they hired on, no one could accuse me of paying for sex. I only wished we'd had the opportunity to go over the ground rules more thoroughly. Beyond deciding that sex would be a perk rather than a requirement, the precise terms of our verbal agreement were never discussed in detail. Although they probably would have been if Dad hadn't arrived when he did.

The back door slammed, instantly altering what I was about to say as Dad stomped down the hallway.

"Angela! Where the hell are you?"

"In the office," I yelled back.

Dad had gotten a bit hard of hearing in recent years, which meant our conversations took place at a fairly high volume. Even though lengthy discussions tended to give me a sore throat, he refused to admit to that weakness. God forbid I should ever mention he might need a hearing aid. I had toyed with the idea of using flash cards to make my point but decided it would only tick him off, which happened often enough without any encouragement from me. Warning him that his high blood pressure was going to make his head explode someday wasn't a good idea, either. Especially since I was pretty sure he didn't take his meds like he was supposed to.

Dad's face was purple when he stormed into the office, proving that this was one of those days when he'd conveniently forgotten to take his pills. "Where the hell did that saddle and duffel—? Oh, I see, it must be his." He glared at Troy. "Who the hell are you?"

"This is Troy Whitmore," I explained. "He's looking for work. I thought he could fill in while Dusty's leg heals up."

Dad's bushy white brows knit together as he peered at Troy, almost as though he might have been able to tell by looking at him that I'd had my hands on his—

"Looks too clean for a ranch hand," he announced after a moment or two of careful scrutiny. "But I guess he'll do. Any good at roping?"

"Yes, sir," Troy replied. "I don't miss very often."

"Well, just don't get your leg broke doing it," Dad advised. "How that damned Dusty managed to fall off his horse and break his leg beats the hell outta me."

Dad's memory wasn't much better than his hearing. "The girth on his saddle broke, remember?"

Actually, it was a wonder Dusty hadn't broken more than his leg. In one incredibly spectacular fall, both he and the saddle had soared into the air only to slam into the corral fence upon landing. I'd been one of the witnesses and nearly came unglued when I saw how badly he'd been hurt. I had already hopped the fence and was running toward him when Rufus grabbed me and insisted that I go up to the house to call an ambulance, saying that Dusty would rather I didn't "coddle" him.

I doubted Dusty would have said anything of the kind. He was such a sweetheart, not to mention being my personal favorite among the hands, and I'll admit to having had a few fantasies about him. He'd never seemed anything other than friendly and respectful—although I did catch the occasional smile that might have meant something more. For the most part, I dismissed those smiles as a figment of my overactive imagination. Still, he was very nice to look at, and a woman can always dream, which was all I'd been able to do for quite some time.

At least until Troy showed up.

I cleared my throat. "I'm sure Troy will take good care of his tack."

"See that you do," Dad told Troy in a stern tone. "Too many accidents around here and no one will work for us anymore."

"It's not *that* bad," I protested. "There are always accidents on a ranch." I certainly didn't want Dad scaring Troy off, even though we *had* seen more than our fair share of mishaps in recent months.

"I'll be very conscientious," Troy promised. "I don't much care for trouble myself."

The meaningful glance he gave me from beneath his thick, dark lashes told me he would be very careful about more than the condition of his saddle. I had no desire to watch him fly through the air the way Dusty had, nor did I want Dad ripping his balls off if he caught us together.

The fact that I didn't subscribe to my father's antiquated notions of propriety didn't count for much as long as I lived under his roof. No doubt he was the reason none of the hands ever so much as tapped me on the shoulder, which was probably why I'd been so willing to be comforted by a stranger. Granted, Troy was nice and sweet and handsome, but I'd also been alone when I met him. We hadn't been introduced under the watchful eye of my father—or Rufus.

Rufus was almost as bad as Dad, and though he'd been very supportive after Cody died, he hadn't exactly encouraged me to go out and find another husband. I sometimes wondered if he wasn't interested in taking on the task himself. Although if he was, he was being damned subtle about it. Or maybe he'd needed two years to come up with the idea.

It made me feel *so* attractive to think it would take a man *years* to realize that if he could only stomach being married to me, he might actually inherit the ranch one day. I'd pretty much decided none of the men of my acquaintance wanted the responsibility of a ranch. Surely I wasn't *that* hard to take. Cody had never complained about the way I looked, but he'd actually loved me. I'd come to believe that bit about love being blind really was true. In which case, the rest of the men in the world all had perfect vision.

On the other hand, I didn't need to be blindly in love to be attracted to a man like Troy. Even someone who hated him would have to admit he was gorgeous. My only hope was that I wasn't getting into something I might regret.

"Trouble is something we try to avoid too," I told Troy. "You won't be any trouble, will you?" For my father's benefit, I made it sound as though I meant fighting or getting drunk or stealing cattle.

Troy obviously knew exactly what I meant because another of his smiles nearly blinded me. "I'll be good, ma'am. I won't cause you any problems. I can promise you won't regret giving me a job. I'll give you my best."

I'm sure he sounded very impressive to Dad, but he impressed me even more since I knew what he was actually talking about. No regrets and no trouble. Only his best.

Oh *yeah*...

"That's good enough for me." Dad held out his hand. "I'm Jack Kincaid. Welcome to the Circle Bar K. I presume you and Angela have already introduced yourselves."

Troy aimed a subtle wink in my direction as he shook my father's hand. "Yeah, we've met. Thanks for the welcome, Mr. Kincaid. I'm sure I'll be happy here."

"Okay, then," I said with a nod. "If you'll gather up your gear, I'll show you to the bunkhouse."

Unfortunately, I was already dreading the time when he would leave our employ. The job was, after all, a temporary one. In a few weeks, Dusty would be back to a full workload and we wouldn't need Troy anymore. At least, not as a ranch hand.

What if I fell in love with him before he went on his merry way? What then? I'd have to get over losing another one.

Shit. Maybe this wasn't such a good idea after all. Already, the thought of watching him ride off into the sunset was making me sick. How on earth would I feel when it actually happened?

My regrets must've shown in my face because Troy asked me about it on the way to the bunkhouse.

"Are you sure you're okay with this? You looked like you were having second thoughts back there."

"Maybe," I admitted. "I was just thinking about this job being temporary—about how I might feel when you leave."

A grimace marred his perfect features. "A week from now, you might *feel* like kicking me out. Did you ever think of that?"

"No," I replied. "That was just about the last thing on my mind."

What was actually running through my head was Kix Brooks singing about how I'd better kiss him because I was gonna miss him when he was gone. I was pretty sure I'd miss Troy—even if he made me mad enough to throw him out—because I was *already* missing him, and we'd only known each other for a few hours.

We crossed the driveway and started toward the stable yard in silence, and during that time I came to the conclusion that it might be best to let him off the hook. If our affair never got started, I wouldn't miss it so much when it was over.

"It might be tough for us to, um, get together," I began. "I won't hold you to that boy toy thing. It was a silly idea, anyway."

"You mean you don't even want me to try?" I thought he might've sounded sort of disappointed, but it was hard to tell.

"I don't know, Troy. It seemed like such fun when we talked about it on the drive home. But now…" I shrugged. "You know how it is—everything changes in the cold, clear light of day. What with Dad living here and so many other people around, it might not be as easy as we thought. I certainly don't want you catching any flack over it."

"Wouldn't be first time I'd taken a little heat."

"Maybe not." I stopped as we neared the corral, chewing my thumbnail as I focused my thoughts. "Tell you what. I'll leave it up to you to decide what you want to do. It's your call. I honestly don't expect anything, and I'll understand if you figure it's not a good idea. Like I said, it has nothing to do with whether you work for us. That wouldn't be right. Do you know what I'm saying?"

"Yeah. You don't want to end up getting accused of sexual harassment." Tipping up the brim of his hat, he aimed that mesmerizing blue-eyed gaze at me. "I wouldn't do that, Angie. Honest, I wouldn't."

"It isn't so much the accusation as the feeling guilty—not to mention wondering how I could have sunk so low that I—" I broke off there, reluctant to put my painful thoughts into words.

"—was willing to pay for it?"

I nodded in reply—which was all I could do at the time because tears threatened to overcome me if I said anything more.

"Imagine how it would feel to be the one getting paid," he said. "Which, by the way, you are *not* doing. You aren't paying me any extra, and I have to work for my wages just like the other guys. You are *not* hiring a prostitute, so you can get that idea out of your pretty little head right now."

Pretty little head. Did anyone actually *mean* that when they said it, or was it only a figure of speech?

I believe I nodded or smiled or something. Whatever I did, Troy must've taken it as acknowledgment because he kept right on talking.

"If I do anything it's because I *want* to. Nothing more. No gratitude for picking me up or giving me a job or anything like that. It's a free country, and you're fair game—and pretty enough not to have to coerce someone into paying you some attention. I don't understand why there hasn't been someone else before now. It seems sort of…unnatural. You're as lovable as anyone, Angie. You had me so hot back there in the truck I thought I was gonna spontaneously combust. But it left me wanting more—and believe me, I'm gonna take all I can get. You just be ready for me."

Chapter 5

Wow! Can I pick them, or what?

A few choice words from Troy and I was ready to pounce on him right there in front of the bunkhouse—and I would have if Calvin hadn't come strolling out of the barn.

"Hey, Calvin," I called out in greeting. "This is Troy Whitmore. He's going to fill in for Dusty for a while. Have you got time to show him around?"

"Not unless you want me to burn the men's dinner," he replied. "I'm heading over to start cooking now."

Calvin Douglas was primarily a ranch hand, but he was also a damn fine cook, although you wouldn't have guessed it to look at him. A tall man in his sixties with iron-gray hair, he was about the skinniest man I'd ever seen, but that didn't mean he wasn't strong. I'd once seen him pull a wooden fence post out of the hard, dry ground with his bare hands.

"Anyone else around?"

"Naw, they're all out—but I'm sure they'll be home in time for supper."

Having been an Army cook in Vietnam, Calvin was kinda particular about how the meals were served. If the men weren't on time they might not get anything to eat, and the guys knew that. I glanced at my watch, noting it was four thirty. The others wouldn't be back until around six.

Hmm… That meant the bunkhouse would be empty—except perhaps for Dusty. That is, if he was taking it easy like he was supposed to.

"What's Dusty doing?"

"He went out in the truck to drop off that fencing you brought home," Calvin replied. "Don't think he's back yet."

"He really shouldn't be doing stuff like that," I said. "Almost makes me wish he'd broken his right leg instead of his left. At least that way he wouldn't be able to drive."

Calvin shrugged. "Can't say as I blame him. He's probably bored stiff with nothing to do but feed the stock."

"I suppose you're right," I admitted. "I don't like the idea, though."

I hadn't known where Dusty was when Troy and I arrived at the ranch, and I couldn't help wondering whether he'd seen us drive in together—although he had to have known I was back if he'd taken it upon himself to deliver those supplies. I'd already decided it wasn't terribly important that no one knew I'd brought Troy home. The problem was his having been a hitchhiker. I didn't care much for all the secrecy, but I figured I'd have to get used to it if I was ever going to get to play with my new toy.

"Bunkhouse is empty, huh?" Troy murmured. "For how long?"

Clearly we were operating on the same wavelength.

"An hour at least," I replied, keeping my voice down. "Maybe an hour and a half, unless Dusty gets back before dinnertime." I shot Troy a knowing glance before returning my attention to the cook. "Okay, Calvin. I'll show Troy around myself."

I would give him the grand tour, all right. We just wouldn't get much farther than one of the bunks.

Calvin waved good-bye and headed for the kitchen, which was on the far side of the mess hall, well away from the bunkhouse and showers. Only the cook's quarters and Rufus's office and bedroom were farther away…

"You weren't really going to hand me off to one of the other guys, were you?" Troy asked.

"No, but I figured I should at least make the attempt. Don't want anyone getting suspicious. How's your equipment?"

"Raring to go," he replied. "How's yours?"

"Are you kidding? I've been in heat all day."

"Nice of you to say that," he said. "Seems like most women won't ever admit to wanting a man—like it's the farthest thing from their minds anytime you mention it."

"Aw, they're just trying to be coy," I said with a grin. "Trust me, it's never far from our thoughts—not far from mine anyway. There've been times when I'd have loved to catch Dusty in the bunkhouse alone—with or without a broken leg. He's a cute little bugger."

Troy's eyes narrowed, and for a moment, I caught a glimpse of steel in his gaze. "You mean I've got competition?"

"Not really. I mean, I think he's adorable, but he's never so much as hinted he might be interested in me—although he *is* kinda shy. Maybe he thinks it wouldn't be appropriate since he works for us."

"Aren't you glad that minor detail doesn't bother me?"

"Yes, but I'm the one who hired you," I reminded him. "You haven't met Rufus yet."

"He's the foreman?"

I nodded. "He's a good man, but I wouldn't want to cross him if I were one of the hands. They don't call him Ruthless Rufus for nothing."

"Ruthless Rufus, huh?" Troy chuckled. "I promise I'll be careful. I'll only speak of you with the utmost respect. He'll never get so much as an inkling that I'm your, um, boy toy."

"Just don't be calling him ruthless to his face," I cautioned. "I'm not sure he knows the men call him that, and I doubt it's a term of endearment. He can be pretty tough. Not mean or unfair, but he doesn't take shit from anybody. Shiftless cowboys don't last long around here."

"He won't have any complaints about me. I'll work very hard." He paused, giving me an impish smile. "At both of my jobs."

"Dammit! Don't call it a job! You'll give me a complex and I won't be able to participate effectively."

"We can't have that, can we? How about we refer to it as my extracurricular activities?"

"That's better." I opened the bunkhouse door and ushered him inside. "Here's your new home. It's not much, but it's air-conditioned and clean. The roof doesn't leak and there aren't any mice or snakes or anything creepy—although you won't have much in the way of privacy."

Originally built for a much larger group of men than it currently held, the bunkhouse was a long, low building with windows at regular intervals along both sides. The extra beds had all been shifted to the far end, but there were a couple of mattresses that weren't in too bad a shape. If Troy complained, I'd buy him a new one.

"You can gather up any of the extra furniture you like for your space," I said. "Most of the guys have their own things, but you can use what's already here for now. You might want to clean the cabinets out before you put anything in them, though. This stuff hasn't seen much use for a while."

"I haven't got much to put in them anyway," he said. "I'll take care of that later. Right now though, I'd like to try out the bunk." Sliding his arms around me, he pressed a bone-melting kiss to my lips.

Somehow or other, I managed to retain a smattering of common sense. "Want to put sheets on it first?"

"I will if you insist."

My knees were still weak as I selected a set of sheets from the linen cabinet and handed them to Troy. "The sheets and towels are kept in here, and there are plenty of extra pillows. Take whatever you need. It's all community property. I think Rufus makes everyone strip their beds and wash the sheets once a month—might even be once a week. He's pretty strict about keeping this place clean."

"I've got no problem with that," Troy said. "Just as long as no one strips the bed while we're in it." His eyes flashed as his eyebrows rose in a highly suggestive manner.

Honest to God, I hadn't seen an expression of his yet that wasn't charming. How could anyone dump this guy on the highway? Simply being able to look at him on a daily basis was worth putting up with any shit he might dish out—and I *still* hadn't figured out what sort of shit that might be. He had me so distracted I had to give myself a mental slap before I could figure out what to say next.

"No chance of that happening." Not that spending that much time in bed with him sounded bad. "I don't come out here very often, and when I do, it's to check the supplies to see if anything needs replacing. I don't do that when the guys are here."

He took a step back in mock dismay. "What? You mean you've never been gangbanged in the bunkhouse? You don't know what you're missing."

"Yeah, right. You haven't met the other guys yet. Dusty's about the only one I wouldn't kick out of bed. I had a bit of a crush on Rufus when I was a kid, but that died a long time ago—and he doesn't strike me as the gangbanging type. Like I said, I don't hang out in here much. Dad would probably throw a fit if I did. He's always been pretty strict with the men, which is one reason he and Rufus get along so well. If Cody had been one of the hands, I'm not sure either of them would've let him near me."

"Protective, huh?" Troy purred. "Me too. I won't let any gangbanging ideas get started. You're mine, Angie. I'm not going to share you."

Those words reminded me of Cody. "*Mine,*" he would say. "*No one touches what's mine.*" Troy's claim gave me the same shivers of desire that Cody's had.

Damn, I miss him.

I liked the idea of a man staking a claim on me and demanding exclusivity. In return, I expected the same from him. I wasn't the jealous type, but I'd made it perfectly clear to a number of women that my husband was off-limits. No conniving harpy was getting her claws into *my* man.

On the other hand, Cody had never given me any reason to be jealous. I wasn't sure about Troy. What did I really know about him anyway?

I stole a peek at him, and what I saw in his face made me forget what I'd been thinking about mere moments before. He leaned down for a kiss, and we didn't even get the bottom sheet on the bunk before falling onto it in each other's arms. We were both naked in a few breathless, frenzied moments. I didn't even have time to wonder how well he thought I looked without my clothes.

Cody had always claimed to like my body. In fact, the description I gave of myself in the fantasy with Troy was the sort of thing he used to say to me. Whether he'd only said it to be kind didn't matter. I was no airbrushed cover girl, and I had no illusions that I was—or had ever been—the kind of woman men lusted after.

Troy, on the other hand, gave every indication he believed I was precisely that sort of woman. He might have been pretending, but he certainly seemed out of control with desire—and not at all like a man who had already had a hand job once that day. No, he behaved as though he hadn't been near a woman in ages while I was acting like a woman who hadn't gotten laid in years—which happened to be true...

I took him in without hesitation—like he'd done me a million times before and belonged there—but it was more akin to being invaded than welcoming him home. There was nothing warm and comfortable about it—nothing romantic—only urgent need screaming at both of us to give it all we had. We might have had an hour or so to play with, but Troy didn't seem interested in taking it slow. Perhaps it was due to the fear of getting caught, but whatever the reason, from the moment he threw my feet up over my head and slammed into me, I knew it was going to be memorable.

My orgasm was nearing detonation when he gasped, "Do I need to pull out?"

"No, and don't you dare." Seizing him by the hips, I pulled him in deeper. "Don't stop."

My mouth flew open and I nearly slid off the side of the narrow bunk as he doubled his efforts, sending my brain spinning wildly off into space. My groans were loud enough that Calvin might have heard me from the kitchen, but I didn't give a damn. I glanced up as Troy fired off inside me, catching his openmouthed expression of pure, ecstatic release. I damn near came again simply from watching him do it.

I'd never had a more intense sexual encounter in my life. Brief perhaps, but satisfying, leaving me to wonder how much better it would have been if we'd had more time. Then again, if he intended to fuck me every twenty miles, he would need to be fast or we'd have spent more time stopped than driving.

I reminded myself that the every twenty miles thing had been a figment of my own fertile imagination. Nevertheless, I had a sneaking suspicion Troy probably could've done it.

When Dusty hobbled in a short while later, I was putting sheets on the bunk and Troy was stowing his clothes in a cabinet at the foot of the bed.

Good thing he'd been quick.

Chapter 6

DUSTY MUST NOT HAVE spotted Troy right away because the warm smile he gave me morphed into a scowl the moment his gaze landed on Troy. Had he assumed I was alone in the bunkhouse? If so, he'd seemed delighted to see me—and not at all pleased to discover Troy there with me. Perhaps the subtle scent of sex still lingered or our innocent act was too studied, but the suspicion in Dusty's eyes led me to believe he had a pretty good idea what had been going on just a few minutes earlier.

A heartbeat later, his expression seemed more hurt than belligerent. His leg might've been bothering him, but somehow I didn't get that impression. Maybe I hadn't been paying enough attention to Dusty, but I certainly would from now on.

I jumped in with an introduction before he had a chance to say a word. "Hey, there, Dusty. This is Troy Whitmore. He's going to be helping out until your leg gets better. Troy, this is Dusty Jackson."

The way the color drained from Dusty's face convinced me that even the tiny dab of work he'd been doing had been too much for him. Swallowing hard, he stared at me, his big blue eyes displaying more pain than when he'd first been injured. "You're not planning to fire me, are you?"

My jaw dropped. "Of course not. Whatever gave you that idea?"

I felt a swift pang of regret as it dawned on me that his job was Dusty's only concern—not whether Troy was banging the boss. I was absolutely the last thing on his mind. I guess all the attention from Troy had me expecting it from every handsome cowboy who crossed my path.

"Nobody's going to fire you, Dusty. A friend of mine was helping Troy find a job, and this was the best we could come up with." I smiled in what I hoped was a reassuring manner. "Honestly, you don't have anything to worry about, sweetheart. Just take it easy and give your leg a chance to heal."

Sweetheart? What the hell had gotten into me? Troy really must've had me on a roll, because I'd never called any of the men *sweetheart* before in my life. My only hope was that neither of them would notice.

Unfortunately, I'm pretty sure they both heard me loud and clear. A slow smile spread across Dusty's face while Troy's eyes narrowed with suspicion. He couldn't have known how I normally talked to Dusty, but he did know Dusty was the one man on the entire ranch I wouldn't kick out of bed. Praying I wasn't setting myself up for a spectacular failure, I was all for crawling off into a deep, dark hole somewhere until Dusty, God bless him, simply grinned and limped over to shake hands with Troy.

Seeing them there together, smiling somewhat warily at one another was a picture I wanted to hold in my mind for a long, long time. If Troy was the epitome of the tall, dark, and handsome cowboy, Dusty was his slightly shorter, blond counterpart.

Dusty was freakin' adorable. The thought of him getting hurt—possibly even killed—had affected me in ways I wouldn't have admitted to anyone. I cared about him. A lot. I couldn't help it.

With a mop of dark blond curls framing his puppy-dog eyes, straight nose, and crooked smile, he was every cowgirl's dream. Dusty didn't shave very often—once a week on Saturday nights seemed to be his limit—so he usually had that soft stubble shadowing his jaw most women, myself included, find so appealing.

Either way, the vision of the two of them together was

breathtaking. They should have been a country music duo, although after getting a look at them, most women wouldn't give a damn whether they could sing—and there were undoubtedly some men who wouldn't be too critical. Envious, maybe, but not critical.

Perhaps it was only Troy's influence, but I was seeing Dusty from a different perspective. I already knew what Troy looked like without his jeans, but Dusty? Taking that thought a step further, I tried to imagine him lying naked on his bunk and nearly had a stroke. As it was, I staggered a bit and bumped the back of my leg against the bed frame, sitting down rather heavily on the mattress.

In the race to come to my aid, Troy nearly tripped over Dusty's cast trying to get to me first, but I think it ended up as a tie. All I remember is they each had hold of one of my hands to help me up. It was perhaps the first time I'd ever so much as touched Dusty, and between that and the scent of the two of them together, they had me swaying on my feet again. I hadn't realized I was quite so susceptible, but it was the only explanation I could come up with. Admitting I might be coming down with the flu would be much too easy. This was simply overwhelming sexual attraction that quite literally knocked me off my feet.

Calvin stuck his head in through the doorway to the mess hall. "Hey, Dusty? Mind giving me a hand? I sure could use a potato peeler."

Dusty grimaced, but his displeasure wasn't evident in his reply. "Be right there." As soon as Calvin's head disappeared from the doorway, he added, "I'll be glad when I can get back on a horse. I don't much care for helping Calvin with the cooking."

"You should tell him about all the vitamins in potato skins," I suggested, thankful that Calvin's entrance had restored the strength in my legs. "Might convince him to cook them whole."

"Aw, he'd just find something else for me to do," Dusty grumbled. "Like I said, I'll be glad to be able to ride again."

I couldn't help it. Dad wasn't there, nor was Rufus. Troy was the only one who might rat on me, and I didn't believe he would. Releasing Dusty's hand, I reached up to give him a consoling pat on the cheek. "Everyone else will be glad too, Dusty. Hang in there."

The stubble on his cheek was almost long enough to be soft to the touch, and as the pat became more of a caress, Dusty took my hand again, giving it a gentle squeeze. I honestly believed if Troy hadn't been there, he would have kissed it. His gentle eyes and crooked smile nearly melted me into a puddle at his feet.

"Thanks, Angela," he whispered. "I'll try."

I'd forgotten how deep and seductive his voice could be—though to be honest, I couldn't recall whether I'd ever noticed it before that moment. If we'd been more accustomed to doing such things, I probably would've hugged him.

Troy cleared his throat. "It was nice to meet you, Dusty. Have fun peeling potatoes." He gave my shoulder a squeeze. "Angie, would you show me where to put my saddle?"

My response was slow because I was too busy making goo-goo eyes at Dusty, who held my gaze a moment longer before turning toward the mess hall. I was still standing there, speechless, when the door closed behind him.

Troy spun me around to face him with the hand that still gripped my shoulder. "It looks to me like you don't need a boy toy," he drawled. "You've already got one."

"No, not really," I said. "I've always thought he was cute, but—"

"He likes you too," Troy declared. "And I think he's got an idea there might be something going on between you and me. He's acting like he just figured out he'd better pee or get off the pot."

Despite the serious nature of the situation, I couldn't help laughing. "What an interesting analogy to choose. But, honestly, it's never been like this. I don't understand it. There must be something in the air today making weird things happen—or the stars are out of alignment or the earth is spinning backward or something. This isn't normal."

"Since I've never met you before today, I'll have to take your word for it. But really, Angie. I don't believe you're as hard up for a man as you think you are."

"Does that mean you won't stay?" How the hell would I explain why he'd quit before even starting the job?

"Oh, I'll take the job," he said. "But I'm not sure you need me for anything else."

If past history was any indication, he was wrong about that. Very wrong. "I don't get it. Dusty's never so much as touched me before. No one does. It's like it's against the law or something. Maybe he—? Oh, shit, I don't have a clue, but I don't want you to get the wrong idea."

"I think it might have been you calling him sweetheart that gave *him* the wrong idea." His tone contained a sharp edge. Not quite accusing, but close. "Do you always talk to him like that?"

"No, never," I insisted. "It must be your influence. Although if that's all it took, maybe I should have said something to him a long time ago."

"So, you *would* rather have him than me, wouldn't you?" he snapped. "Is that what you're saying?"

"No, it's just that I've known him for a long time and I only met you today... Troy, I've never picked up a hitchhiker before, and I've never made love with anyone but my husband. This is so out of character for me. It's impossible to explain. I only know that when I saw you there on the highway, I knew I had to stop—that it was important somehow. I didn't know how or why, I only knew that it was. You've done something to me, something wonderful, and I thank you from the bottom of my heart. Maybe Dusty was simply responding to the change in me. He can't possibly be interested. If he were, gosh, I've known him for five years—two of them since Cody died. Surely he would have said something before today."

"I would have if it'd been me. You got to me with those big, brown eyes right away. Then when you started crying... What was I supposed to do? I knew I was a goner the moment I took you in my arms." He paused, grimacing as he ran a hand through his curls. "I guess boy toys should be more careful about losing their hearts since it's generally not the sort of thing that lasts forever."

"Yes, but we hadn't discussed your future then, so how would you know—" I broke off as the implication hit me. "Wait a minute. You're saying you fell for me when I started crying and you held me?"

"Might've been when I kissed you," he admitted. "I'm not real sure about the actual timing."

"And I suppose being a goner and falling for someone could be two different things too. I probably shouldn't have jumped to that conclusion."

He shrugged. "It wasn't much of a jump really. I'm not too sure about the difference myself, but I do know it wasn't anything like what I've felt with other women. Ever."

"Which could be good or bad." But it *was* encouraging.

Although what if Troy decided to stay forever? What then? Sure, he was cute, but would I love him?

I let out a ragged sigh. "What a day this has been! I don't think I've ever had one quite like it. Let's give it a rest and go put up your saddle, shall we? I need a break."

Troy grinned. "I'm good for more later on if you want me."

I just shook my head and led the way to the tack room. This fuck every twenty miles was undoubtedly going to kill me, and even if it didn't, then the two when we got there probably would.

Maybe I was too old for a boy toy.

Chapter 7

THE TACK ROOM WAS quiet, except for the cat nursing her kittens in a box in the corner. We found an empty rack for Troy's saddle, then went out into the stable where I introduced him to the horses, including my Palomino mare, Goldie, who was due to foal at any time.

"You can ride Dusty's horse for now," I said. "He's a pretty good guy and shouldn't give you any trouble."

"Dusty or the horse?" Troy teased.

"Both, actually. Never had a lick of trouble from either one of them."

"Until now?"

"I guess you could call a broken leg trouble. But Dusty can still feed the horses, pigs, and chickens, and he can drive a truck, so he isn't a total loss. I hadn't planned on hiring anyone to replace him until you came along. I'm not surprised he thought we might fire him. Although if he thought that, he must not have a very high opinion of us. Firing a guy because he got hurt on the job wouldn't be quite cricket, now would it?"

Troy shrugged. "It happens. Most people seem to think ranch hands grow on trees."

"Not the good ones. It takes a certain kind of man to work on a ranch and live in a bunkhouse. Most guys want a family and their own place, which means a lot of our men are the loner type. They seem to get along with each other pretty well, though. I can't remember the last time Rufus had to break up a fight." I paused for a moment, thinking about what Dusty had said. "You know it still bugs me that Dusty would think we might fire him. It's been ages since we let someone go. Some have quit, but fire one of them? No way! They're more like family than employees—at least that's how I see it. It never occurred to me to tell Dusty his job was safe after his accident—mainly because it never crossed my mind we wouldn't be keeping him on. It's not as if he's never going to be able to ride—the doctor said he'd be fine in a couple of months."

"Sounds like he's heard some horror stories about what happens to broken-down cowboys. God knows there are plenty of them. I've been busted up myself a time or two."

"Yeah, I noticed the scars on your shoulder. Torn rotator cuff?"

He nodded. "I'm surprised you saw those, under the circumstances."

"I don't miss much," I said. "Like the fact that your left boot heel is more worn than the right. You drag that foot slightly, don't you?"

"Torn ligaments in the knee and hip," he replied with a grimace. "Courtesy of a Brahma named Carlos, which is why I gave up bull riding. Son of a bitch threw me up in the air like a rag doll. It's a wonder he didn't kill me."

"I never *could* understand why anyone would feel the need to ride a bull! Bronc riding, yes, although nobody breaks horses that way anymore. But bull riding? As far as I can tell, it's nothing but a male ego thing—a contest to see who has the biggest balls. Most of the time, it's the bull."

"Yeah, well, we're all young and stupid at some point," he conceded. "It just takes some of us longer to wise up."

"No shit. Are you good at anything besides calf roping?" I could've added more to that but thought it best to focus on his cowboy skills rather than his boy toy abilities.

He shrugged. "Lots of things. I can fix fences and brand cattle and give them shots and stuff like that. I'm a decent mechanic and a fair carpenter. Just don't ask me to sing around the campfire."

"Not much of a singer, huh?"

"Couldn't carry a tune in a bushel basket," he said with a grin.

So much for the country music duo idea. "No worries there. I can't sing a note. Rufus can, though. You wouldn't think it, but if you close your eyes, you'd think George Strait was sitting by your campfire. Plays guitar pretty well too."

"You talk about him a lot," Troy observed. "But I still can't figure out whether you like him."

He had me there. I wasn't sure whether I liked Rufus myself. "He hired on here about the time I started high school, and I thought he was totally hot. Curly black hair and steely blue eyes—and he's still got the body he showed up here with. I had such a crush on him, but then I met Cody and the rest is history.

"He worked his way up to foreman, and I married Cody and had the kids, so I haven't given him much thought for a long time now. He's also about twenty years older than me, so there's that. But at thirty-five, he was a hunk. Can't say he's much fun, though, even if he does sing well. He's kinda grim. If I were desperate enough, I might consider him as a potential husband, but so far, I haven't been that desperate. I can't recall him ever having a girlfriend, even when he was younger—at least not that I know of—and he rarely leaves the ranch. I tend to giggle a lot, which I *know* he doesn't like, and he would be absolutely appalled to hear about even half of what we've done today. *Very* straitlaced. He doesn't even let the guys put girlie posters up in the bunkhouse."

"I thought it seemed pretty tame in there," Troy remarked. "You usually have to keep innocent eyes out of a bunkhouse."

"I always assumed that was because of me. After Mom died, I was out there a lot to help with the upkeep and the cooking. Nothing changed when I got older, so maybe that was the way Dad and Rufus wanted it. They're two of a kind when it comes to stuff like that."

"Point made," he said, laughing. "I'll be discreet."

I snorted a laugh. "I even had to be discreet with my husband. Cody and I worked out a code so we could talk dirty back and forth. No one ever caught on, and you wouldn't believe the fun we had." The side-splitting laughter, the camaraderie, the joy…all of it gone. I'd done my best to avoid dwelling on the sorrow and focus on the happy memories. Although sometimes the happiest memories were the most painful to recall. The mere mention of that secret should have triggered a pang, but oddly enough, it didn't.

"I can imagine," Troy said. "You'll have to teach it to me."

Teach it to him? I'd never told anyone about the code. I hadn't even shared it with Jenny, and she was my best friend. Then again, perhaps it was the sort of thing only a lover needed to know…

"Let's see now… If Cody scratched his right ear, that meant he was hard as a rock. If I wanted to suck his dick, I chewed on my fingernail—stuff like that."

"Great idea. What was the signal for fuck me?"

"Biting my lip," I replied. "Although sometimes I'd do it without actually intending to and Cody would start scratching his ear like crazy before I noticed what he was doing." I held up my hand, studying my fingers. "You know, my nails have never looked this good. Dad used to fuss at me for biting them so much. He just never knew what he was actually fussing at me about."

"Maybe we could come up with something he wouldn't take exception to, like rubbing your chin."

"That would work, although he might notice the new gesture. He's fairly observant—even though his eyesight isn't what it used to be. He's been failing for the past couple of years, and watching him deteriorate has been tough. Cody's death affected him almost as strongly as it did me and the kids. He used to say he had no qualms about how the ranch would be taken care of when he was gone. He's not so sure about it now."

"He doesn't think you're up to going it alone?"

"Not really," I admitted. "He says women are too softhearted to make good ranchers. I disagree, but I wouldn't mind having someone to discuss things with. My friend Jenny runs a ranch not far from here. Whenever she has a problem, she bounces it off me. I guess I'll do the same when Dad's gone." I'd never dreamed I'd be living out my life without Cody, much less running the ranch by myself. Not that I'd taken him for granted—I'd cherished every moment of our time together. I just hadn't expected it to be so short.

"What about your sons?"

"Neither of them wants to come back to the ranch after college. I'm glad they have other interests, but it would be nice to think they'd be around to help out."

Hearing hoofbeats, I glanced up as the men rode in, so any further comments Troy might have made were put on hold. Only then did I realize how much I was *not* looking forward to explaining Troy to Rufus. Dad had taken to the idea without too much trouble, but Rufus might be tougher to convince—especially since he hadn't been consulted. However, Rufus understood the chain of command. Dad was the boss and I was right under him. He might voice his concerns, but he always respected our authority.

My mention of Jenny reminded me I'd better give her a call since she was the best choice for someone who might have recommended Troy. As thorough as Rufus tended to be with such matters, I wouldn't have been a bit surprised if he'd called her to check Troy's references.

I had to laugh because Jenny would *never* have sent me anyone as cute as Troy. She would have kept him for herself even if she had to sell off some of her herd to pay him. I only hoped Rufus wouldn't reach the same conclusion.

On the other hand, Jenny had a thing for handlebar mustaches.

Although Troy was clean-shaven, she might have overlooked that deficiency in light of his other attributes. I certainly would have, but then mustaches were never a favorite of mine. Cody had grown one once, but it went up my nose whenever I kissed him, so he shaved it off.

As Rufus dismounted, I thought about what I'd told Troy about him. Yes, he still had the body he came here with. Although he was a big man, if there was an ounce of fat on him, I certainly couldn't see it. He had a commanding presence too—like a military officer or a football coach—and not only because of his size. Something in the set of his shoulders and the angle of his jaw made him stand out from the other men. In the years since I'd first met him, his thick, curly hair had gone from black to gray, and his eyes had become more piercingly blue. His face was leaner, and the lines in it had deepened, but it was the same face I had admired as a teenager.

Becoming foreman hadn't altered him in the slightest. He'd been born for the job. It was his perfect niche, perhaps even his destiny. If he'd ever aspired to be anything else, he kept it to himself, seeming content with his life.

I respected Rufus. He was dependable and always had the best interests of the ranch first and foremost in his mind, but he was tough. I'd seen him working with young horses. Although he was understanding up to a point, the horses always seemed to sense they were up against a much stronger will than their own, a persistence that would outlast them, and a clear knowledge he would triumph in the end. It was simply a matter of time.

In the interest of diplomacy, I figured it would be best to introduce Troy to Rufus and then let Rufus handle the rest of the introductions and the orientation to the ranch. I would let Troy decide what to tell the others about himself.

"Hey, Rufus," I said. "This is Troy Whitmore. He was looking for work and Jenny Pennington sent him over since she didn't need any hands. Dad and I thought he could fill in for Dusty for a while. He's a rodeo cowboy and grew up on a ranch, so he should know what it's all about."

Rufus stepped forward and smiled as he extended a hand to Troy. "Rufus Bentley. Welcome to the Circle Bar K." As always, I felt there was something missing from his smile. Warmth, perhaps, or some other quality that would have made it seem more disarming, rather than a dictate of common courtesy.

"Thank you, sir," Troy replied, giving Rufus a firm handshake.

"We were just about to wash up for dinner," Rufus said. "Come along to the mess hall and we'll go over the job with you after we've eaten."

I decided it was best for me to leave since the conversation would probably be much more interesting if I wasn't around. "I'll see you guys later. I'd better go fix dinner or Dad will be down here pestering you guys for something to eat."

"That wouldn't be a problem," Rufus said, cordial as always. "Not for us, anyway."

Good ol' Rufus. Always perfectly correct, perfectly polite, and perfectly neutral. Marriage with him would be like being married to a cardboard statue. Lifelike perhaps, but inherently lifeless.

With a nod, I headed back to the house.

———

The rest of the evening passed uneventfully. Dad didn't mention Troy, and I deemed it best not to introduce the topic. The way I saw it, the less I said about Troy the better. I didn't want to run the risk of waxing poetic about his sexy eyes or his cute butt, subjects I knew Dad wouldn't care to discuss with me or anyone else. I knew Jenny would, though, and I called her right after dinner.

"Does this mean you owe me one?" she asked after I'd told her about Troy.

"Owe you what?" I was playing dumb even though I was pretty sure I knew the answer. Jenny was fond of men in general, which made it even more surprising she'd never found the right one. Perhaps she enjoyed shopping more than buying. "A favor or a cowboy?"

"I'll take either one," she replied. "Although I'd rather have a nice, handsome cowboy. You know…big and tall with a handle-bar mustache?"

"Yeah, I know the type," I replied. "Haven't seen one around lately."

Unless I were to count Bull Russell, our resident know-it-all, done-it-all cowboy. Bull had no hair on his head to speak of, but he did have a rather dramatic mustache. I'd never been able to figure out why a man who was so well versed in everything wound up working on a ranch. I could only assume it was because he truly was all bull, which might also have explained the nickname.

Bull never failed to have a story to tell about any topic that was mentioned. No matter the job, he'd done it, and no matter the person, he knew their cousin. If asked whether he'd completed some task or other, he never replied with a simple yes or no, but with, "Well, I'm gonna do that when…" or "I didn't do that because…" He always seemed to be on the defensive—possibly because his actions were the sort that usually needed defending—and he was the only one of the hands I found irritating. If he'd been in on a bunkhouse gangbang, he probably would have destroyed the mood by regaling us with tales about other—and much better—gangbangs in which he'd participated.

To the best of my knowledge, Jenny had never met him, and I didn't want to be responsible for bringing them together. She would never forgive me once she got to know him—even if he was big and tall and probably had a big, long pecker to match. Then again, she might be able to put up with a guy who never knew when to shut up; I didn't consider myself capable of getting past it. Bull was one cowboy I would definitely kick out of bed, no matter how big his dick was.

"Okay, then," she said with a sigh. "I'll try not to look a gift horse in the mouth. A favor will have to do."

"I'm sure you'll let me know when you need one. All I really need for you to do is to vouch for the fact that Troy came to you looking for a job—sent by someone you trust or something. Anything to prove I didn't pick him up on the highway."

"Angie, you *know* most hands wander in without much to recommend them. Why are you making such a big deal out of it?"

"Because I don't want Dad to think I only picked him up because he was such a hottie," I said. "I get fussed at for enough things as it is. I don't want that to be one of them."

"I can understand that," she said. "But isn't there some other reason?"

"None I'm willing to admit at this point."

"Aha! So you *did* pick him up because he was a hunk." Her words might have been accusatory, but a note in her voice told me she completely agreed with my reasoning.

"Yeah," I admitted. "Plus, I felt sorry for him. I still can't believe no one else picked him up before I got back from town."

"I certainly would have," she declared. "Wait a minute. That was your truck pulled over on the side of the road this afternoon, wasn't it?"

"I take it that was you who drove by and honked?"

"Yes, it was," she replied. "Where were you?"

"In the truck."

"*Where* in the truck? I didn't see anybody."

At least that meant Troy hadn't been exposed for all the world to see—which might have been awkward if anyone else had passed us by. Jenny was the one person I could count on to keep quiet, especially if I asked her to. Not that I planned to elaborate on what we were doing while we were out of sight, but when I didn't answer right away, she jumped to her own conclusion.

"You weren't lying down on the seat with him, were you?"

And just like the Grinch, I thought up a lie, and I thought it up quick. "Nope. I was having contact lens trouble. I pulled over to rinse it off and I dropped the damn thing. Troy and I were trying to find it when you drove by."

To my surprise, she seemed to believe me. "You ought to give up and have your eyes lasered, Angie. Contacts are too much trouble."

"Yeah, right. If there ever comes a time when that procedure doesn't cost an arm and a leg, I might consider it." I probably could have kept her on that subject for a while longer, but Jenny was not to be deterred from the original topic of my handsome stray.

"Hmm, so he's the helpful sort, huh? You don't suppose he might help you out with some *other* things, do you?" She sounded just suggestive enough to provoke me into responding.

I sighed in what I hoped was a convincing fashion. "Really, Jenny. Is sex all you think about?"

"What? Me? I didn't say anything about sex. I could have been talking about helping you wash dishes or mop the floors. I never mentioned sex."

"When *don't* you mention sex?" I drawled. "It's your favorite topic."

"That's because I haven't gotten any lately," she grumbled. "Almost makes me wish I hadn't thrown my ex out."

"As I recall, that was one of your main complaints about him."

"True, but I thought I'd at least get a steady boyfriend once I got rid of him. These one-nighters are wearing me down."

"That's funny. I thought you liked it that way." She'd told me more than once she preferred variety. Perhaps she hadn't been referring to the men themselves as much as the limits of their imaginations.

"Not really," she conceded. "I'd like to have one long enough to be able to tell who was in bed with me without having to turn on the light."

"That *would* be nice, wouldn't it?"

I didn't think I'd like wondering who I was waking up with myself. Not that there was much chance of that. I could probably identify Troy by his scent alone.

But perhaps Jenny's sense of smell wasn't as discriminating as mine.

Chapter 8

THAT ABILITY WAS PUT to the test a few hours later when Troy showed up in my bedroom, unheralded by anything but his cologne and the sound of his stealthy footsteps, both of which had me awake before he ever said a word.

"Angie?" he whispered.

"What's up?" I asked with a yawn.

His chuckle sounded delightfully wicked. "I'm surprised you have to ask that. I would have thought it was perfectly obvious."

"Yes, but it *is* dark in here," I reminded him. "You might have come to tell me Goldie was in labor."

"That's true, but she isn't. I checked on her before I came in."

"Speaking of which, how *did* you get in?" I could only imagine the fit Dad would throw if he ever happened to run into Troy on the way to the bathroom during the night. He'd probably have the big one—and blame me for it if he survived.

"Through the kitchen," he replied. "Believe me, I checked out the best ways in and out of here this afternoon. It's a good thing you don't lock the doors."

"I'd have given you a key if we did," I said. "Wouldn't want to lock my boy toy out. That would be tacky."

"Not to mention counterproductive."

The bed dipped beneath his weight. Moments later, I heard his boots hit the floor, each with its own quiet thud. I hadn't heard anything quite as comforting since Cody died, a sound that meant a warm, sexy man was about to join me in my lonely bed. Simply hearing it sent a quiver of anticipation racing through me.

"I can't stay too long, though. I told the guys I sometimes wake up during the night and have to walk around for a while before I can go back to sleep. I doubt any of them care if I'm not in my bunk, but someone might wake up and see where I went."

"We can't have that, can we? Especially if it's Rufus. The other guys might not mind you visiting me at night, but you can bet your boots Rufus would tell Dad."

The idea of Rufus on a rampage made me giggle. Showing that much emotion was totally out of character for him. How he could put any feeling into the songs he played was a mystery to me. Perhaps music was his only outlet, or at least the only one he allowed himself.

"Would it really cause that much trouble?"

"Not so much for you. You'd only get fired. I'd be the one who'd have to hear about it for the rest of my days."

"You aren't exactly a kid, Angie." He was being kind. No matter how you cut it, a woman of forty-two was middle-aged.

"Doesn't matter. Rufus would consider it his duty to report a daughter's errant behavior to her father. Remember, I was a teenager when Rufus became foreman."

"But that was *years* ago."

"Sometimes I wonder if he doesn't still see me as a kid. Kinda like how I think of my sons as babies, no matter how old they are."

"Maybe, but you have to admit, it's weird."

"Yeah. It is. Just be careful, okay?"

"I will," he promised. "I won't try to come every night. What with this being my first night and all, I figured they would under-stand if I couldn't sleep. Rufus told me to check on the horses while I was up, so I think he likes the idea."

"He's awake during the night sometimes too," I said. "I've gone down to check on the horses and found him in the barn—although that was usually when one of them had a problem or was due to foal."

"I'll check on them again when I go back," he said. "But right now, I believe I'd much rather check *you* out." He slid beneath the sheets and reached for me only to stop short when he encountered my pajamas as he ran a hand over my hip. "What the hell is this? I thought I told you to be ready for me."

"I didn't know if you'd show up or not, so I went to bed the same as always. Besides, I wasn't quite sure what you meant by that being ready thing." I could only imagine my disappointment if I'd gotten all gussied up in some sexy outfit with makeup, high heels, and fishnet stockings and he hadn't bothered to put in an appearance. An infraction like that would almost have been enough to make me fire my boy toy.

"What I meant was for you to be hot, naked, and raring to go," he murmured against my ear. "Or at least in a gown that was easy to take off."

"I don't like gowns, and it's tough to do all that while you're asleep," I reminded him. "I'll bet your tool doesn't stay hard all night long."

"Maybe not, but it's plenty hard now." Pulling up my top, he leaned in to nuzzle my breasts. "Mmm…That's better. I didn't get a chance to do this earlier, but I sure wanted to. That shirt you had on today was making me crazy."

I'd had on a black T-shirt, of all things. Granted, it had a scooped neckline, but it wasn't revealing, nor was it particularly sexy. Having reached the dismal conclusion it wasn't doing me any good, I'd given up on sexy long ago. I'd even considered cutting my hair, but long hair is so much easier to work with—at least mine is. I'd tried it short once, but the constant attention to keep it looking decent made me grow it out again. Like most men, Cody preferred long hair on a woman. If Troy had waxed poetic about my braids, I could understand that. But the shirt? I didn't get it.

"Crazy, huh? What was so special about it?"

"You've probably never noticed this, but you tend to drive with your left hand. Anytime you raised that arm, the neck of your shirt opened up and I could see inside it."

Of course, to see anything, he would've already had to have been looking in my direction. I doubted anyone else would have noticed.

I might have questioned him further, but since he chose that particular moment to focus on my nipples, I didn't bother. Holding my breasts together, he moved quickly back and forth between them, teasing each nipple to full intensity with his hot, wet tongue. Gasping, I arched my back in response to his touch, involuntarily thrusting my chest in his face.

"Mmm, yeah, Angie," he muttered against my nipple. "I love that." Wrapping his arms around me, he ran a hand down my back and over my hip. "Now, will you *please* get out of these pajamas?"

"Pretty pushy for a boy toy, aren't you?" I grumbled. He could have taken them off himself. Might have been more fun that way.

"I can be as pushy as I want since I'm not a *paid* boy toy. But I did say please. And technically, I'm not a boy toy. I'm a boy*friend*, and I want my girlfriend out of her jammies."

I heaved an exasperated sigh. "Okay. Give me a minute."

I got up and stumbled to the bathroom, figuring I might as well pee and brush my teeth again while I was at it. I found it interesting that Troy considered himself to be a boyfriend rather than a boy toy, but because the fine distinction between the two had escaped me at the moment, I'd let it pass.

Upon further reflection, I decided a boy *toy* might not necessarily care anything about the woman he was with, but a boy*friend* would. I kinda liked the idea—whether he'd meant it that way or not. I figured I could delude myself for a while longer if I chose to see it in that light. But did I really *need* to delude myself? I didn't know Troy very well, but if he was pretending, he was doing a damn fine job of it. Either way, when I went back to him, I was hot, naked, and raring to go.

"I didn't mean for you to leave," he said when I returned.

"Oh, hush up. I have to brush my teeth if you wake me up, otherwise I just can't concentrate. Bad smells and tastes put me off. You might as well get used to it."

"I certainly wouldn't want to ruin your concentration," he said, pulling back the covers.

What I saw then was more than enough to destroy anyone's ability to concentrate. Moonlight shone through the stained-glass panel above my window, providing me with just enough light to see him. He was undeniably ready—*more* than ready; he was straining at the bit. I could see the shine on the head of his stiff penis, see the love drops oozing out over the succulent head like—what was it? Oh, yes, hot fudge on ice cream. It was the tastiest-looking treat I'd had in a very long time, and I made a dive for it, taking the hot shaft in my hand as I crawled into bed, going down face-first into his lap.

"I can see that a trip to the bathroom has done wonders for you, so I won't ever mention it again."

I painted my lips with his salty, slippery fluid before sucking him into my mouth.

"Oh, yeah, Angie," he groaned. "I love that."

I hadn't had the opportunity to suck him as much as I'd wanted when we were in the truck. Cock sucking hadn't even been an option in the bunkhouse. But it certainly was now, and I exercised that option to its fullest extent. Troy was sweet and salty at the same time, such an intoxicating treat for the senses, I probably could've kept going for days on end. He had me so hot I could feel my own dewy wetness pooling between my thighs.

Apparently, so could he. Stroking lightly with his fingertips at first, he slid his thumb inside and unerringly found the right spot.

With a groan, I went down farther on his cock, reaching around him to squeeze his butt with both hands.

I was rewarded with a gush of wetness that filled my mouth, and for a moment I thought he might've come, but the flavor alone identified this as an extra-large dose of cock syrup, and it sent me skyrocketing to a whole new level. I savored his slick rod as he bucked against me, fucking me in the mouth with the same rhythm he used to do me with his thumb.

"Suck me, baby. Suck my dick. Don't stop. *Please* don't stop." The pressure of his thumb, the tasty heft of his cock, and the sound of his lust-thickened voice as he repeated those words nearly drove me insane.

Finally, I couldn't take it anymore. Backing off, I said, "Fuck me," over my shoulder. "Fuck me. Hard."

Troy sat up instantly, rolling me over onto my back and pulling my feet up onto his shoulders as he knelt upright between my thighs and slammed into me. If his thumb had been driving me crazy before, his cock finished me off. I went completely limp, offering no resistance whatsoever save for the tight, involuntary grip I had on his penis. What he'd been doing to me with his thumb had me so sensitized I shot immediately into orbit as my slutty cowboy boy toy slid his big dick in and out of me over and over again. Time became nonexistent, and I barely registered its passage until Troy's muffled cry brought me back to reality. I felt him pump a big load into me as he came for the third time that day.

He leaned over for a kiss as I lay drifting in an orgasmic haze. My scattered thoughts seemed to coalesce, and I found myself thinking a trip to Jackson Hole might've been worth the trouble—maybe even the price of the gas.

Every twenty miles, and twice when we get there.

However, upon further reflection, I decided I'd much rather keep him right where he was and damn the consequences. Surely I could get more out of him if I kept him at home rather than giving him a ride to the rodeo. I knew he would leave eventually, but in the meantime, I would enjoy him and try real hard not to get in over my head.

Falling in love with him would be a huge mistake. Nevertheless, it was one I was sure I could easily avoid. Escaping the notice of Rufus and my father would be a more difficult, although certainly not impossible, task. Even if we did get caught, Troy was right. I was forty-two years old. I wasn't a high school girl messing around with one of the ranch hands.

No. I wasn't a kid anymore, and neither was Troy. We were two consenting adults engaged in a sexual fling that benefited us both.

How much trouble could there possibly be?

Chapter 9

TROY LEFT MY BED as soon as his dick was soft and I didn't see him again for nearly four days. He'd said not to expect him every night, but after that much time had passed, I was beginning to get slightly perturbed. On the other hand, perhaps it was Rufus's fault for working him so hard he truly needed the sleep.

I tried to keep to my usual routine and not make it too obvious I was going out to the barn or the bunkhouse, hoping to catch a glimpse of him. As a result, I *didn't* see him. The way things were going, unless absence truly did make the heart grow fonder, there was absolutely no danger of falling in love with Troy.

Dusty, on the other hand, seemed to be hanging around all the time. If I hadn't known better, I'd have said he'd broken his leg on purpose so he would be in the barn whenever I went out to check on Goldie or decided to go for a ride. The idea seemed preposterous—unless Troy had been right about him.

Anytime I was out with the horses, Dusty came over to talk with me. He never said or did anything that might lead me to believe he felt anything more for me than any of the other men on the ranch, but, except for the sex, he was as attentive as my boy toy should have been. He saddled my horse and offered to do other chores I could easily have done myself. I couldn't remember him ever doing that before—even since his accident. Perhaps he was bored and lonely, and since I was the only one around aside from the horses for the greater part of the day, it was either talk to me or go crazy. After a while I began to suspect he was only helping me to avoid going near the kitchen, thus making it harder for him to get drafted as Calvin's assistant.

During that time, I toyed with the idea of trying to communicate with Troy in some manner, but I couldn't come up with any safe, reliable way to do it. Cody and I had our own code for such things, although we were usually in the same room when we used it, and we'd also had plenty of time alone to discuss the details beforehand. We even had a few things that would work over the phone. Since Troy and I hadn't talked about it, I couldn't very well go down to the bunkhouse and crease his blanket in a special way and have him know what it meant.

On the fourth day, however, I went to the bunkhouse anyway.

After checking out Troy's "room," I concluded he must've been satisfied with the way we'd fixed things up for him on that first day because nothing looked the slightest bit different. Opening a cabinet door at random, I succumbed to temptation, taking his bottle of cologne out for a sniff—although I probably could have buried my face in his pillow, which would undoubtedly smell every bit as enticing. I toyed with the idea of taking a short nap, breathing in the scent of Troy while I slept, but as I put the bottle back, Dusty came in. The strange thing was, he didn't seem to be the least bit surprised—or pleased—to find me there. He stopped short for a moment, his shoulders sagging as though weighted down with disappointment. Instead of a smile, all I got for my hello was a perfunctory wave as he limped over to his bunk.

For him to seem unfriendly was out of character—he'd been talking my ear off for days—unless he was in pain. "Is your leg bothering you?"

He sat down heavily in the easy chair next to his bed. "No."

I'd never heard a shorter "no" in my life—especially from Dusty. Since he obviously didn't feel like talking, I figured I ought to beat a hasty retreat—especially since I was technically trespassing.

Then again, I was second in command on the Circle Bar K, and Troy was a new employee. There were things I had a right—even a need—to know. "Is Troy getting along okay? Has he said anything to you?"

"About what?" Dusty's brusque tone hadn't softened in the slightest.

"Oh, you know," I said with what I hoped was a casual shrug. "Whether he's happy working here or if he needs anything."

"Don't worry about him," Dusty snapped. "He's got everything."

My first thought was that he and Troy hadn't been getting along very well. That might've explained his surly attitude—although it didn't explain why he would be annoyed with me. The best I could come up with was that he was resentful of Troy, but that *he's got everything* comment had me stumped.

Compared with the rest of the men, Troy had practically nothing. He didn't even have a chair, only his bunk. Dusty, on the other hand, had a nice chair, a lamp, and all sorts of amenities, but a more bleak expression I had yet to see on a man. He looked like someone had just shot his dog.

"Dusty, what on earth is the matter with you?"

"Nothing," he replied, although it was perfectly obvious *something* was wrong.

Several moments passed in silence. Evidently he didn't intend to say anything further.

"I'll head on then."

I felt like a poacher who'd been caught coming back over the fence—perhaps not on the property at the moment, but with every indication I'd been somewhere I didn't belong. Would he tell Troy I'd been going through his personal possessions? To be honest, I doubted Troy would mind, especially since I'd helped him unpack his things to begin with. There was a slim chance a report of my visit might give Troy the hint I was missing him, although I wasn't counting on it.

I started toward the door saying, as I always did, "You all let me know if you need anything."

Dusty's mirthless laugh was so steeped in irony it stopped me in my tracks. "Need? I'll tell you what I need. I need to come in here and find you with your nose in *my* cologne—not his."

My eyes widened in surprise. I didn't think he'd actually seen what I'd done. I had no idea what to say, nor could I believe what he'd just said.

Dusty nodded as though acknowledging my response—or lack thereof. "I guess there's not much chance of that happening. Is there?" He sounded so odd, so unlike his usual self. I wondered if he'd been drinking, although he didn't appear to be drunk. He seemed…hurt.

"Let me get this straight," I began, no doubt sounding as puzzled as I felt. "You want me to smell your cologne?"

"No," he replied. "I want you to want to."

He was talking in riddles, and I couldn't help wondering if I hadn't been right about the drinking. Either he wasn't making very good sense, or I was being inordinately dense.

As a rule, I didn't miss much. For example, I'd known Dusty sometimes wore cologne—although why a working cowboy would bother with it, except maybe on a Saturday night when he went into town, was a mystery. Most of the time the men smelled of sweat, horses, and leather—or tobacco if they happened to be smokers like Bull and Calvin. But cologne? Who was supposed to be enticed by the smell? The horses or the cattle?

Then again, if sniffing his bottle of smelly stuff would get him out of this foul mood, it was probably worth doing. "Okay. Where is it?"

"It's on me," he replied. "I want you to come close enough to smell it."

I'd thought about being that close to Dusty before, but knowing

Dad and Rufus wouldn't have approved, I'd kept my distance. At the moment, however, Dusty and I were alone. I even had an invitation—to what, exactly, I wasn't sure, but it was an invitation, nonetheless.

I walked over to him and leaned down. "Any particular spot?"

He pointed to the side of his neck. "Here."

I moved in closer, inhaling deeply. "Nice."

I already knew that because I'd caught a whiff or two of it before. Except this time it went straight to my brain, setting off a chain of primal chemical reactions. Heat emanated from his body, compounding the effect and making the urge to kiss him nearly impossible to resist.

He reached up and put his hand on the back of my neck. Turning my face toward his, he looked me straight in the eye. "Kiss me, Angela," he whispered. "Just once. There's nobody here except you and me. No one else will ever know."

Had he read my mind? *Just once*, he'd said. Would one kiss be enough to satisfy him—or me? Or would one kiss lead to another and another and another…

Maybe he pulled me, or perhaps I fell, I don't know for sure, but a moment later our lips touched and melted into each other. His kiss was soft and wet and went on and on until my knees threatened to give way beneath me. I wanted to sit in his lap and kiss him until my lips were too chapped to continue. My fingers found the tousled blond curls on the back of his head as his tongue teased my lips. His breath was hot on my cheek and a deep groan accompanied his first thrust into my mouth. Was the rest of him as nice to kiss as this? Was he as tasty as Troy?

My eyes flew open and I pulled away from him.

Troy didn't want to share. He wouldn't like knowing I'd done this. Too bad that wasn't an explanation I could give to Dusty.

Dad wouldn't like it, either. He'd been telling me to steer clear of the hands ever since I was a child, which had bothered my liberal soul a great deal. From a purely business standpoint it made sense, but it was also a level of discrimination I'd never agreed with.

I used to think his attitude stemmed partly from the typical fatherly opinion that no man could ever be worthy of his little girl. However, as time went on, I saw it for the prejudice it truly was. He needed men to run the ranch, and I'm sure he respected their abilities; nevertheless, he still considered them to be a step beneath him. Perhaps he believed that song about not letting your babies grow up to be cowboys—or marry one. In my father's eyes, I was the rancher's daughter, and the men who worked for us simply weren't good enough for me.

I didn't want Dusty to think I shared my father's opinion. Unfortunately, his stricken expression made it clear that was precisely what he believed. I was between a rock and a hard place, and the best thing I could think of was to be honest with him—about my feelings anyway.

"Dammit, Dusty," I gasped. "Where the hell did that come from? You practically had me crawling into your lap."

His expression shifted from wide-eyed alarm to a puzzled frown, as though he wasn't absolutely certain my hasty retreat meant what he thought it had. Swallowing with apparent difficulty, he ran his tongue over his bottom lip, seeming to savor the flavor I'd left behind. His deep blue eyes caught mine and held them. "I wouldn't have minded that."

"Yeah, right." I attempted a giggle, hoping to lighten the mood. "Until I broke your other leg."

"You wouldn't have hurt me." His tone never changed, assuring me he had no intention of laughing it off. "Why don't you come back here and try it."

I stared at him dumbly. Dusty was too young and too damned cute to want me in his lap. It was as unbelievable as it would have been for Troy to say he loved me and wanted to spend the rest of his life with me. Then again, maybe Dusty had decided he wanted to inherit the ranch someday.

Given the position I was in, perhaps Dad had been right. It was hard to tell if a man wanted me for myself or for the ranch, and right now I was just love-starved enough to believe any lie I heard. I'd never realized how vulnerable I was, although my reaction to Troy should have been my first clue.

There had been no masculine interest in me whatsoever after Cody died. Now that Troy was around to stir things up, perhaps Dusty saw him as competition and decided to make a definite play for me—which would explain the increased attention. Dusty had to know I was lonelier now than I'd ever been in my life, and with his bum leg keeping him close to the house, he pretty much had me all to himself.

Suddenly, I saw him not as the sweet, adorable Dusty I'd known for years, but as a conniving, manipulative man who'd played me like a virtuoso plays a violin. He might've even staged his accident so he could play on my sympathy. And he'd chosen his time to catch me alone in the bunkhouse awfully well. I'd even called him sweetheart. No wonder he thought I might want to sit in his lap. I eyed him with suspicion. "Why would you want me to do that?"

His gaze never wavered from mine. "Because then I could hold you and kiss you the way I've wanted to for a very long time."

My newfound suspicions even found fault with that. "For how long, Dusty? Just since Cody died or before that?"

"I don't know," he replied. "Maybe I've always felt this way about you. Lately I've seen how lonely you are with most of your family gone, and it makes me want to hold you and try to make that loneliness go away. You've always been very kind to me, and it hurts me to see you like that. You deserve better." He shrugged. "This is the best I can do."

His response may have only been calculated to keep my suspicions from growing, but it brought tears to my eyes anyway.

I was vulnerable, all right. I was wide open for that kind of sincerity to get to me. Troy had made me realize how lonely I truly was, and then he'd avoided me for days. And now, here was Dusty, apparently volunteering to pick up the slack.

Was it possible to have two boy toys at one time? Or were boy toys as territorial and possessive as any man? Had he and Troy discussed my situation? With no spy in the bunkhouse, I had no way of knowing what the men talked about, much less what they might have said about me. For all I knew there might have been some sort of conspiracy afoot, although to what purpose I couldn't quite fathom.

Gazing into Dusty's guileless blue eyes, I saw my error. He had no motivations aside from the one he'd just given me, and I chastised myself for even thinking such awful things about him. He was only showing his concern, and here I was suspecting him of trying to steal the ranch right out from under me. "That's very sweet of you, Dusty."

He looked up at me with that same bleak expression he'd worn a few minutes before. "But?"

"I'm not sure what you mean. But what?"

"You think I'm too young for you," he replied in a hollow, wooden voice. "You want someone older, more capable of understanding you."

"I didn't say that, Dusty."

"No, but you were probably thinking it," he said ruefully. "I know you would because it's true. But I do care about you, Angela. All of us do—although maybe not in the same way. The day Cody died, I wanted to take you in my arms and hold you until you stopped crying. I wanted to help you so badly I could hardly stand it. I couldn't bear to see you that way. But I knew I wasn't the one you loved. You loved your husband, and he was dead. That wasn't the right time for me. But it is now. I love you, Angela. I truly do."

Tears streamed down my cheeks. If he'd said something like

that to me only a few days before, I would have fallen into his arms without hesitation.

But now there was Troy.

Why had Dusty waited until today to tell me this? What was it Troy had said—that Dusty must have gotten the idea there was something between Troy and me and that he'd better "pee or get off the pot"? Was that the reason this was happening now? Was Troy the catalyst? Was Dusty finally jealous enough to speak up?

He'd seen me sniffing Troy's cologne, perhaps realizing I was attracted to Troy and had come out to the bunkhouse hoping to get a whiff of him. The jealousy issue was a much better explanation than my half-baked conspiracy theory. The trouble was, I couldn't respond to Dusty the way I might have if Troy hadn't shown up. Telling him about my relationship with Troy, such as it was, might have made it easier on him. After all, saying you're in love with someone else is perhaps the gentlest way of telling a person you can't love them—at least not in the way they deserve to be loved.

I genuinely cared for Dusty, and I wouldn't want to hurt him for the world. I could have said I hadn't gotten over Cody yet, although that wouldn't have sounded very convincing—not when he'd caught me with my nose in Troy's cologne. The web of deceit was becoming even more tangled, and now Dusty was caught up in it too.

Not having any idea what I should say to him, I must've been staring at him with God only knew what expression on my face. Obviously, this wasn't the reaction he'd hoped for in the wake of his declaration. His face fell, reminding me of someone else I'd had to tell that I couldn't love him—a boy I'd known in high school who hadn't known I'd just started dating Cody.

"I had no idea you felt that way," I said. Dusty had always been friendly, but that didn't mean he loved me. "I never *dreamed*…"

He shrugged in a self-deprecating manner. "It's okay. I never believed you could ever love me back. Like I said, you loved Cody, and I'm nothing like him. Aside from that, what with the attitude around here being what it is, you probably never even thought of me as a man. I'm just another cowboy, and my feelings aren't your concern."

This sounded pretty harsh, even coming from a man who'd been rejected. Although I knew Dad's attitude was probably at the heart of the matter, I'd never been unkind or unfeeling toward Dusty, at least not that I was aware of, and his words cut me to the quick.

"I'm sorry, Dusty. I can understand why you might think that. But, believe me, that isn't how I feel about you guys. As far as I'm concerned, you're practically family. Dad may have been warning me to stay away from the ranch hands since I was a kid, but I still have feelings, even though they may not always show."

"Oh, really?" His hurt and anger gave way to sarcasm. "Why don't you tell me what you *do* feel about me, Angela? I think I'd like to know."

Despite the heat of the day, icy chills gripped my chest. The prospect of telling him the truth made me feel even worse. The painful, heartbreaking truth…"You think I believe I'm too good for you?" I nearly choked on the words. "That isn't it at all. You're—"

I had to stop. The shuddering ache in my chest was too much. I crossed my arms and squeezed, trying to hold myself together. "You're so adorable—but not for a woman like me. You're right. I'm too old. You ought to be out partying every Saturday night with a bunch of hot, young cowgirls crawling all over you. I should have to pay through the nose to get someone like you to say you loved me. That should be my only hope of ever hearing those words come out of your mouth. I still don't believe it, even now."

That was the absolute truth. I *didn't* believe it. Not really. "I've already had the love of my life, Dusty. I can't kid myself into thinking I'll ever find another one. I'm not that lucky."

"You might be, if certain people would mind their own business."

Even though Dusty wasn't mentioning any names, I was pretty sure I knew who he was talking about.

"That's what I get for never leaving home," I said with a grimace. "There are too many men around here who think of themselves as my father. Rufus and Calvin have been here since I was a kid, and they probably *still* see me that way. You would think after raising two boys of my own they would've figured out I'd grown up."

Dusty smiled at me for the first time since he'd walked through the door. "Maybe it's the braids. They make you look like a little girl."

Although the tension had eased a tad, I still felt chilled to the bone. Shivering, I looked down at my hands. They were pale beneath my tan, the nail beds showing the bluish tint I associated with midwinter. "If that's the case, I'd better start wearing my hair in a bun."

"Or you could twist it up with one of those clip things." His teasing smile became a seductive grin. "Be a lot easier to take down."

Thank God for that grin. A suggestive attitude from a younger man was much easier to deal with than a sincere declaration of his love. Placing my hands firmly on my hips, I arched a brow. "You've obviously given this some thought."

"I certainly have." His gaze swept me up and down, making me feel like he'd stripped me naked with his eyes. "*Lots* of thought, especially at night when I'm lying here alone wishing I had you for company."

I let out a derisive snort. "If you're thinking about *me* in the middle of the night, you obviously need to get out more."

"I get out plenty," he protested. "I just don't find anything I like better than what's right here at home."

"Then you aren't looking in the right place. Maybe you should steer clear of the strip joints and go someplace where there are women you might find a more lasting relationship with." I'd heard stories from Jenny about what my cowboys did on Saturday nights. They weren't as wild as some, but they did have their moments.

"I might. If you'll go with me." His eyes held a glimmer of challenge, daring me to take a chance...

Ignoring the fact that after two very dry years a man had actually asked me to go out with him, I took a different tack. "I should do that—should round up the lot of you and drop you off at a bar and pick you up the next morning."

The slow wag of his head was so subtle I nearly missed it. "That's not what I meant."

"I know exactly what you meant," I retorted. "I'm trying to change the subject."

"Mind telling me why? Don't you like me?"

Dammit, if he didn't stop looking at me like that, I was going to forget Troy and pounce on him. "I like you a lot, Dusty. But I can't help thinking the only reason you're saying any of this is due to a lack of options rather than an actual choice."

His shrug conveyed his dim view of my opinion. "I'll go if you insist, although I don't think it'll help. Especially now that I've kissed you. You didn't exactly turn me off."

Where the hell were those "father figures" when I needed them? He hadn't exactly turned *me* off, either. I was actually contemplating how I could have an affair with both him and Troy at the same time when Troy and Bull walked into the bunkhouse. No doubt at first glance, we appeared to be innocent. We were both fully clothed, and Dusty was sitting in his chair while I stood a good three feet away from him. Nevertheless, I felt like I'd been caught with my hand in the cookie jar.

Or Dusty's pants...

Bull made a dramatic full stop in the doorway, tossing his hat across the room onto his bunk in disgust. "Well, shit. I see you're in here goofin' off while we're out workin' our asses to the bone. I guess I need to break a goddamn leg too."

"Be my guest," Dusty snapped right back at him. "Or better yet, why don't you break your jaw so we won't have to listen to you?"

I couldn't have agreed with Dusty more, but it would have been unkind of me to say so. Mentally, however, I was shouting, *Way to go, Dusty!*

Troy simply rolled his eyes and smiled. He'd obviously had to listen to Bull all day and was ready for some peace and quiet. I probably should have excused myself and left before the fight escalated to a brawl. However, feeling the need for some comic relief, I stayed put, preparing to be entertained. Dusty had a razor-sharp wit, and Bull was full of it—up to his eyeballs and then some.

Bull eyed Dusty with frank suspicion. "Are you tellin' me to shut up?"

"Naw, I wouldn't say that to you," Dusty drawled. "I'd tell you to shut *the fuck* up if I wanted you to be quiet."

"You shouldn't talk like that in front of a lady, son," Bull said sternly. "Miss Angela prob'ly don't appreciate that kind of talk."

Bull had as filthy a mouth on him as you might expect from a man who'd claimed to have been, at one time or another, a longshoreman, a sailor, and a roughneck on an oil rig. I also knew for a fact he was the one who took the guys to the more risqué places they'd been known to frequent, so I couldn't help giggling at such a comment coming from him. In his mind, apparently, the only word in his colorful vocabulary that was unsuitable for feminine ears was the f-word.

"It's no laughing matter," Bull insisted, somewhat offended by my display of mirth. "Goddammit, he shouldn't say things like that in front of you."

I was doubled over by that point and couldn't have spoken if I'd tried. I was nearly wheezing as it was.

Dusty grinned at me before aiming a knowing glance at Bull. "I think she wants you to shut the fuck up."

By this time, Troy was laughing his ass off. Bull stomped off, muttering something about "Goddamned, motherf-ing assholes…"

He could imply it, but he wouldn't say it aloud within my hearing even when he was angry. I had to give him credit for that much, although it made his word choice seem even more hilarious. Laughing hard enough to bring tears to my eyes, I keeled over onto Dusty's bunk.

"Aw, now, Bull," Dusty yelled after him. "You went and made Miss Angela cry." With a meaningful gaze, he added, albeit in a much quieter tone, "But you got her in my bed, so I'll forgive you."

Troy was laughing hard enough he might not have heard that last comment. I almost wished he had, since it might have encouraged him to pee or get off the pot too. I hadn't gotten to play with my boy toy much in the past few days. If he didn't start making himself available pretty soon, he might find himself traded in for a different model.

Granted, Dusty had a broken leg, but I'm sure we could've figured out any number of mutually satisfying activities. On the other hand, sneaking into the house in the middle of the night with a cast on his leg would be difficult. All that thumping around might even awaken my deaf-as-a-post father.

For the time being, the more light-footed Troy would have to do. I couldn't help thinking how strange it was for me to suddenly have two men to choose between. Although I might not have admitted it to Dusty, I'd had my eye on him for ages. Never dreaming the interest could possibly be mutual, I'd kept my mouth shut and my hands to myself.

If only I'd known how he felt just a few days earlier.

Damn.

Chapter 10

IF TROY THOUGHT THERE was anything romantic going on between Dusty and me, he didn't let on, and he certainly didn't appear to be resentful in any way. As a matter of fact, he seemed downright grateful to Dusty for being able to shut Bull up.

"Thank you," he said with a fervent sigh. "I've been trying to get him to be quiet and go away for three whole days."

"Aw, it's not hard once you get the knack of it," Dusty said. "He's pretty easy to get riled. After that, all you have to do is make him feel stupid."

I secretly felt that Bull would retaliate someday by pounding Dusty into the dirt—he was a big man, after all. Dusty, although smaller and quicker as a rule, was now slowed down by his cast, making him a much easier target. Hopefully, Bull's sense of fair play would at least make him wait until Dusty was in better shape before he tried to break his other leg.

"Making him *sound* stupid isn't too hard," Troy agreed. "He does that all by himself. It's the getting him to leave that I want to know how to do. Dunno how y'all stand it."

"You'll get used to him after a while," Dusty said. "He's not a bad sort, really. He just likes to talk big—and dirty."

"And *constantly*," Troy added. "Don't forget that."

"I can usually tune him out, but sometimes it's impossible," Dusty admitted. "When it comes to that, you have to run him off or go crazy trying not to kill him."

"I'll remember that." Troy glanced at me lying on Dusty's bunk and something flickered in his eyes, some emotion too quick for me to catch. When he spoke again, his attitude was carefully neutral. "I haven't seen you for a few days, ma'am. How've you been?"

"Oh, about the same," I replied before rubbing my chin with a knuckle and biting my lip. I didn't know if he would remember enough of the code to respond, but apparently he did, for he smiled and scratched his ear.

"Angela says she's going to take us out on the town," Dusty said. "Do you want to go?"

"Now wait a minute, Dusty," I cautioned. "I said I'd round you all up and drop you off at a bar. You're making it sound like I'm going to treat you to dinner and a show."

"Sounds good to me," Troy commented. "I think I'd like to go out with you."

Dusty glared at Troy. "She's not going out with *you*," he snapped. "She's going out with all of us."

I tried to keep my expression as innocent as I possibly could, but what Dusty said made me think of the gangbang in the bunkhouse thing again—although it would probably be more of a threesome since there weren't any others I'd care to mess with. I might have considered Rufus if such behavior wasn't so completely out of character for him. Joe Knight was another possibility, but since he never said much, I really didn't know him very well.

Joe was kinda homely, but I did like him, and he was about my age. Tall and lanky, he was probably hung to his knees, although I was fairly certain I'd never learn that from firsthand observation. Sure, I'd seen him cut up with the guys, but he always acted rather shy around me. I couldn't imagine why he would have been—I wasn't the least bit intimidating—but some men were like that around women.

I'd often wondered how men behaved when they were only in

the company of other men. Any time I was around to hear them, they knew I was there, which possibly affected their behavior. The only way a woman would know such things would be to watch them through a window or film them with a hidden camera.

Men were such mysteries to me. They had drives and reactions I couldn't even begin to understand, despite having been surrounded by them for the greater part of my life. I'd heard it said that men think and women feel, but I wasn't sure I agreed with that. Men probably felt more than they ever let on, and I, for one, thought about stuff continuously. Perhaps I wasn't typical.

Dusty and Troy both appeared to have feelings, some of which happened to concern me. The thought of going out with both men while they engaged in a no-holds-barred competition for my affections sounded absolutely fabulous—although such an arrangement would undoubtedly be more trouble than it was worth. Having some of the others along to dilute the mix was probably advisable.

"That's right, Dusty. I did say I would take all of you. I just never actually said I'd be going *with* you."

"True, but we'd have a lot more fun if you came along," Dusty said. "That way we would all have at least one woman to dance with."

"The idea was for you to meet *other* women," I reminded him. "You already know *me*."

If his lip-curling grin was any indication, Dusty wanted to get to know me better—a *lot* better. "Yes, I do. But I can't dance. I need you to keep me company while the other guys are out dancing with all those hot young cowgirls."

He was using my own words against me, doing his damnedest to get this "outing" to go in a different direction than I'd ever intended. "Uh-huh. Sure. Everyone would think you were stuck hanging around with your mother. Not many hot chicks would wander over to sign your cast if they thought that, and they sure as hell wouldn't try to kiss you."

"Hey, now, there's an idea," Troy exclaimed. "We could tell the girls they have to kiss you before they can sign your cast."

Having recently kissed Dusty myself, I was pretty sure he would be good bait for women whether that rule was mandatory or not. "That's one way to draw a crowd," I agreed. "As cute as Dusty is, they'd be standing in line."

Dusty actually blushed. "Aw, girls never want to kiss me. I haven't had a girlfriend since high school."

"Which is why you need to get out and hunt for one," I said. "All this hanging around the bunkhouse isn't getting you anywhere. What are you, twenty-five? Thirty?"

"Thirty-one," he replied.

Older than I thought. Hmm…

I tried not to get too excited over there being eleven years between us instead of fifteen or twenty. With a brisk nod, I continued. "All the more reason for you to get out there and mingle. You're wasting the best years of your life holed up here on this ranch. What were you planning to do? Wait until your blond curls turn gray and fall out to go looking for love? Believe me, now is the best time to do it."

"Rufus wouldn't like it," Dusty reminded me. "You know how he is about stuff like that."

"Yes, but it's none of his business what you do with your time off. He can't very well keep you from dating someone."

"Maybe not, but he has ways of making you follow his rules. Anytime I've done something he doesn't like, I wind up assigned to the jobs I like least. I'd hate to think what he'd have me doing if he ever caught me in the bunkhouse with a woman."

"Yeah, well, don't feel like the Lone Ranger," I said. "It's a wonder Dad ever let me go out on a date, let alone marry Cody. I'm sure Rufus would rather you guys were all monks like him—which, of course, you're not."

Troy shot me a suggestive, sidelong glance. "And *you* are no nun."

While Troy had every right to believe that, Dusty wasn't aware of the situation and apparently took it as a slur against my reputation.

"What the devil do you mean by that?" he demanded. "You're making it sound like she's some sort of tramp. You barely even know her."

I really needed to have a talk with my boy toy. If Troy kept on making comments like that, he was going to get us both in trouble—and not only with Dad and Rufus. Considering what Dusty had said to me earlier, he wasn't going to take Troy and me being an item lying down.

I put up a placating hand. "Now, Dusty. I'm sure Troy didn't mean it that way, but he's right. I'm *not* a nun. Maybe I *should* go out and try to find myself a new man."

Both men stared at me as though I'd sprouted wings, but neither of them could say a word because they both had secrets that involved me—secrets I was positive they intended to keep from each other. Their openmouthed expressions were so comical, I had to laugh.

Troy started to sputter a protest, but Dusty found his tongue a little quicker. "No way," he exclaimed. "If you did that, we'd spend the whole time busting guys' heads for coming on to you."

I rolled my eyes. "I doubt it, Dusty. Besides, I thought you *wanted* me to go with you. And you wouldn't have to bust any heads because, truth be told, you two are the only ones—" Fortunately, I caught myself before finishing that sentence—especially since Rufus, Joe, and Calvin chose that moment to enter the bunkhouse.

Of the three men standing in the doorway, Rufus alone stood out among them. He'd been a hunk twenty years ago, and he still had that certain something about him that drew the eye. Too bad he was so lacking in personality.

Not lacking in expression, however. His brow was knit in a thunderous frown, and his eyes blazed with anger. Since I wasn't normally the recipient of his ire, this surprised me. Then I remembered I was not only alone in the bunkhouse with two of the men, I was also lying on Dusty's bunk.

I fought the urge to jump to my feet and offer an explanation, but, dammit, I was a grown woman and co-owner of the ranch. I could do as I damn well pleased. If Rufus didn't like it, well then, he could just quit. It wasn't as though he could send me to bed without supper, although reporting my transgressions to Dad would mean I'd have to hear about it for days on end. I was already wondering whether that small rebellion would be worth the price I'd have to pay when I remembered Rufus probably *could* make things harder on Troy and Dusty.

Searching for allies, I glanced first at Calvin, whose jaw had actually dropped, and then at Joe, who, for once in his life, was openly grinning at me instead of staring at the floor, as was his usual habit. That grin made him *so* much more attractive. Ordinarily he was so homely he was cute, but now, with a delighted smile on his face, he was almost handsome. I would definitely have to remember to include him in the bunkhouse gangbang—that is, if one ever actually took place.

Suddenly, where there had been no possibilities before, now there were three…

Rufus was the first to speak. His carefully worded, "Good afternoon, Miss Angela," had a profound effect on every man in the room. Smiles disappeared only to be replaced with solemn, respectful demeanors.

I, on the other hand, was determined not to let him spoil my fun. Smiling, I waved a hand in greeting. "Hi, Rufus. You know, we really need to replace these mattresses. It's a wonder the men don't all have back trouble from sleeping on them."

"Is that what you're doing here?" Rufus asked. "Testing the mattresses?"

His cautious questions made me giggle in a manner I knew he

disliked. "You'll have to blame Bull for that. He made me laugh so hard I fell over on the bed. As for why I was here in the first place, I thought maybe Dusty could use some company."

After a quick glance in Dusty's direction caught his deer-in-the-headlights expression, I deemed it best to retract that statement. I didn't want Rufus to be mad at anyone but me.

I giggled again, doing my best to sound annoying. "I'm kidding, Rufus. I was out here checking the supplies when they came in."

The foreman's frown diminished, but the glint in his eyes didn't fade completely. "And what did Bull say that was so funny?"

"I think you had to be there," I replied. "It loses something in the retelling."

"I see."

I knew I hadn't completely allayed his suspicions, but harping on it would make my story even less convincing. Rubbing a nonexistent backache, I got to my feet with a groan, leaving him to draw his own conclusions. Either way, a change of subject was definitely in order. "So, did you get all the fencing done?"

"Not quite," Rufus replied. "Two more days should see the job finished."

I nodded. "Sounds good. I'll tell Dad. See you guys later." With another wave, I headed for the door. I fought the urge to swat Joe on the buns as I went by, settling instead for a pat on his shoulder. "Keep smiling, Joe. It looks good on you."

I left the bunkhouse without a backward glance. Rufus could think what he liked, but now that I was finally seeing the ranch hands in a different light, he would simply have to get over it. He wasn't my boss, nor was he my father, and I was sick and tired of being alone. The guys were lonely too. Even if I had to sneak them out of the bunkhouse to do it, they were going to have some fun— and so was I.

If Troy didn't show up in my bedroom that night, I was going to fire his ass as my boy toy or boyfriend or whatever he was. Dusty had flat-out told me he loved me, and life was much too short to be kept waiting forever.

Chapter 11

As it turned out, I didn't have to wait forever. Troy slipped in at about one o'clock with some interesting news.

"Whoo-ee," he exclaimed softly. "You should have heard the Miss-Angela-is-strictly-off-limits lecture we got this evening. You might not think you're a nun, baby, but Ruthless Rufus makes you sound like a candidate for sainthood."

"You've got to be kidding," I protested. "Trust me, I'm nothing but a worthless little airhead to him. He's always very polite, of course, but he's never taken me seriously, especially since Cody died. To make anything I say carry any weight at all, I have to make it sound like a direct quote from my father."

Troy snuggled in beside me, his welcome presence suffusing me with warm contentment. "Maybe so, but he's got you up on a pedestal, good and proper. I, on the other hand, think women on pedestals are highly overrated. I prefer my women closer to the ground—makes them easier for someone like me to reach." To lend credence to that statement, he draped an arm and a leg over me and pulled me against the full length of his body. His hard cock poked me in the stomach. "As far as I'm concerned, you're the hottest bundle of woman I've ever had my arms around."

"Nice of you to say so," I drawled. "Especially when I haven't seen you for days on end."

He gave me a quick squeeze. "Sorry about that, but I was in no condition to visit you. I'd forgotten what it was like to spend the whole fucking day in the saddle."

"Not very conducive to fucking, is it?"

"Not at all," he agreed. "But I think the blisters on my balls have finally callused over." Burrowing a hand beneath my head, he pulled me closer, brushing a kiss on my cheek. "So, Angie, since you wouldn't tell Rufus the truth, would you mind telling *me* what you were doing in the bunkhouse with Dusty?"

"Believe it or not, I went out there hoping to find you. Dusty came in and caught me sniffing your cologne."

"That explains why he seems so irritated with me. He likes you, Angela. You know that, don't you?"

"I do now," I admitted. "He told me as much this afternoon."

"I'm pretty sure Rufus knows it too. He directed the lion's share of the lecture right at him. He didn't mention any names, but I'd be willing to bet Dusty won't be visiting you anytime soon, not unless he wants Rufus on his ass day and night."

"Since Dusty's never *visited* me before, I don't think he'll start now." I paused as another thought occurred to me. "I'm curious, though. Did Rufus say anything to Joe?"

Troy chuckled against my neck, releasing tendrils of desire that triggered a delightful tingle in my nipples.

"Not really," he replied. "But you should've heard Joe after Rufus left and we all went to bed. I figured you'd only said that to put Rufus off the scent, but you sure made Joe happy. He couldn't stop talking about it. Do you realize you've never so much as touched him before? He probably won't wash that shoulder for a month."

As rarely as I'd put a hand on any of the others, it was safe to assume I hadn't done it to anyone as shy as Joe. I'd never heard him string more than five or six words together at a time, and he was nearly always staring down at the ground when he said them. The fact that he couldn't stop talking about *anything* seemed a tad out of character.

"I wanted to pat him on the butt," I admitted. "Must be your influence. You've turned me into a real flirt."

"You probably oughta flirt some with me too—and be sure you do it in front of Rufus so Joe and Dusty don't take all the heat. You weren't kidding when you told me we'd have to be sneaky about this. How in the hell do you think you're going to get us all out of the bunkhouse for a night on the town? I wouldn't put it past Rufus to bar the door."

"I'd like to see him try," I growled.

"He just might," Troy said. "We could go without any fuss, but if Rufus knew you were going with us…"

"Sounds like *I'll* be the one who has to sneak out," I said. "I've never been able to understand his attitude—or Dad's. They're two of a kind when it comes to proper female behavior, but at least I don't work for him. It's a wonder the men haven't all up and quit because of his puritanical attitudes."

Troy slipped his hands beneath my pajama top and rubbed my back in a sensuous manner, proving his own attitudes were anything but puritanical. "He seems to have them all brainwashed into thinking a woman like you wouldn't be interested in the likes of them. I wish you could've heard the lecture. It was enough to make a man give up and ship out on a freighter for the rest of his life—or get a job mopping floors in a whorehouse."

"No wonder they act so weird around me! They've always made me feel like I'm bestowing some great favor anytime I glance in their direction. Most of them won't look me in the eye, especially if Rufus is around."

That also explained what Dusty had said when he asked me to kiss him—that we were alone and no one else would ever know about it. Obviously, he'd meant Rufus. Oh yes, the pedestal I'd been put on explained a lot.

"He *is* something of a tyrant," Troy said.

"Yeah, well, I hate to break it to him, but the men probably wouldn't give me a second thought if Rufus had kept his mouth shut and left them alone."

"I doubt that. You're worth second, third, and fourth thoughts." He punctuated his sentence with a deep, searing kiss that put a curl in my toes. "I've missed you, baby."

Clearly there was no need for me to fire his ass as my boy toy—yet. Aside from the fact that his ass was much too awesome to ignore, he did have a reasonable excuse. I'd been saddle sore a few times myself.

As I reached around him to get my hands on his adorable tush, I was reminded of at least one other butt that was drool-worthy. Dusty had a pretty nice one. I knew that because I'd been surreptitiously checking it out anytime the opportunity presented itself for quite a while now. I'd even been known to take a peek at it when Cody was alive. As the saying went, I might have been on a diet, but I could still look at the menu.

I couldn't help wondering who I would pick as the winner of a "Best Buns" contest between my cowboys. Rufus might have won that contest a few years back, but since I was pissed at him, I'd have to disqualify him on the grounds that his butt should be smacked rather than admired. I'd never given any of the others much thought before, which was odd considering my fondness for that particular facet of the male anatomy. I promised myself to pay more attention to them in the future. But at that moment, I had my hands on Troy's sweet ass, and I fully intended to give it my undivided attention.

Recalling the fantasy that had him on his hands and knees with his butt in my face had me reaching for the switch on my bedside lamp.

"What's the matter?" Troy asked, squinting at the sudden brightness.

"Nothing," I replied. "I just want to be able to see you."

"A candle is easier on the eyes and much more romantic."

"Sounds good—that is, if I can find one." Cody and I had used candles from time to time, so I knew I had one somewhere, but it took some digging in the nightstand to find it and a box of matches. I lit the wick and switched off the lamp.

"Would you do something for me?" I asked as I lay back down.

"Sure, babe," he murmured. "I'll do anything you like."

"Turn over on your stomach."

"No problem."

The candlelight flickered as it illuminated the contours of his body, highlighting the curves and deepening the shadows as he moved. Contrary to popular belief, men's bodies aren't all planes and angles. Soft curvatures flowed over Troy's back, beginning with the rolled edges of his shoulder blades and on down into the crevice along his spine. Those same curves rose up to form two mounds that fit my hands as though they had been designed specifically for my grasp.

My fingertips tingled as I traced the hollow of his flanks while I knelt between his parted thighs. I took my time, devouring him with each of my senses, delighting in his soft moans when I touched him in ways that pleased him. Urging him up onto his knees, I moved him back against me before rocking him forward once again. The view from that perspective was somewhat voyeuristic, almost as though I were watching him from behind as he made love to someone else. Whatever the cause, it doubled my desire for him.

I pushed him sideways, enabling light to reach the space beneath him. A sparkling ribbon of moisture trailed from the head of his penis, the mere sight of which made me gasp. Some women will tell you such a spectacle does nothing to entice them; I am not one of those women. My body shuddered with anticipation as I took his hard cock in my hand, feeling its weight and girth. Leaning down, I licked the space just above his scrotum, tracing the line where the two halves of him met to form what resembled a scar.

With gentle strokes, I smoothed the warm syrup along his heated skin until he was wet enough to allow my fist to move up and down his shaft in a frictionless glide. I kissed him, sucking the smooth folds of skin into my mouth along with the most sensitive and vulnerable parts of his delectable body. Teasing his testicles with my tongue, I was rewarded as he groaned into his pillow. I wrapped my free arm around his hip for support and settled in to continue for as long as it took to make him come.

Even though I wasn't getting any attention myself, after a few minutes I was so wet it didn't matter, and I came twice while I was doing him. I knew he would be hard again in twenty minutes, and I would get my turn, so I kept on, relentlessly massaging his cock and savoring his balls until a loud gasp warned me he was almost there. Releasing his scrotum, I rolled him onto his back. Still gripping his slick, engorged penis, I aimed it at my mouth just as he began to spurt. I didn't miss a drop as I went down on him.

Troy seemed almost frantic, reaching for me, begging me not to move because he couldn't take any more. His cock pulsed again and again in the most prolonged male orgasm I'd ever witnessed. Finally, when I thought he could stand it, I sucked his dick dry and moved up to lie beside him.

His eyes were closed, his breathing heavy. Snuggling closer, I lay my hand on his chest. Troy reached up, touching my hand briefly before his arm flopped back down.

"I'll be with you in a minute, baby," he said. "I'm gonna need a little time to recover from *that*."

I let him be and simply lay there, enjoying his warmth and listening to him breathe. How nice it would be to have him with me all the time. So very, very nice…

Bending my knee, I eased my leg over his, increasing my awareness of the slickness between my thighs. I hadn't been that wet in ages, but I knew it wasn't only due to the anticipation of what he might do to me. That arousal was the result of the pleasure of knowing he'd enjoyed what I'd done to him. Knowing I had taken him to a level where he truly couldn't take any more was exhilarating, and it made me long to do it again and again and again. That thought alone sent heat rushing to my core, triggering yet another powerful climax.

Moments later, a miraculously revived Troy began kissing me and pushed me onto my back. Trailing languid kisses from my lips to my breasts, he moved ever downward over my tingling body until he buried his face in my pussy. Once there, he did the most delightful things with his tongue, flicking my clitoris until I thought I'd go mad, then delving deeply for several undulating strokes before starting again. He seemed to be as comfortable as I had been and appeared to have every intention of eating my pussy until I came in his mouth. Still, I couldn't stop thinking about that cream-covered dick of his. I knew I'd never be satisfied until I tasted more of it.

Troy must have read my mind because he got up and turned around. "Hey, Angie," he whispered. "How about sucking my dick while I lick you?"

I caught a brief glimpse of his hard, glistening cock before he slid it past my lips and settled down on me, drawing my clit into his mouth. We sucked each other for possibly three ecstatic minutes until he came with a groan, spurting his seed down my throat. As if his cock in my mouth and his mouth on me weren't enough, he pushed his thumb inside, sweeping circles around my slick inner walls. With a multitude of overwhelming sensations bombarding me at once, I climaxed almost immediately. My orgasmic scream was stifled by the thick cock in my mouth. Otherwise I'm sure even Dad would have heard me.

With a great deal of reluctance, I let go of him and he reversed his position to lie beside me. Taking me in his arms, he kissed me in a lazy, relaxed fashion that reminded me of a slow Southern drawl. I have no idea how long he kept it up, but I was drifting in and out of sleep when he murmured, "Once more and I've got to go."

I'm sure I must've muttered something suitable in reply because he rose up on his knees and found his way inside me yet again, this time using his awesome cock instead of his tongue or his thumb. By then I was so thoroughly fucked I couldn't even raise my head.

Apparently Troy had more energy left than I did. Scooping up my legs, he placed my feet on his shoulders before picking up a steady rhythm that seemed to go on for days. I should've been long past caring whether I ever had another orgasm again, but his cock slowly brought me to life. Soon he had me moaning in ecstasy as my core gripped his cock. His third climax of the night was longer in coming than the first two, but it gave me no less satisfaction.

When he finally left me, I was on the verge of sleep, fully intending to dream up some excuse to double his salary at my earliest opportunity.

Chapter 12

I AWOKE THE NEXT morning feeling better than I had in years—fresh, invigorated, and satisfied. The weather was absolutely beautiful with a sky so clear and blue it hurt my eyes to look at it. The heat wave we'd been experiencing seemed to have passed, the temperature having drifted down to a more normal range. I drove into town to do some shopping, noting that the price of gas had fallen as well.

Unfortunately, anytime I have such a perfect day, storm clouds are nearly always lurking beyond the horizon. I've noticed I often feel the best just before I come down with some bug or other. Perhaps my body knows it's been invaded and the marshaling of the troops gives me an overall boost of adrenaline, but whatever the reason, I can feel my blood pumping and my heart singing.

Granted, amazing sex can evoke a similar response, but I'd had other highly satisfying encounters in my life. This was different, although I couldn't have said why. All I knew was that as I strolled down the grocery aisles, I felt taller, stronger, and more beautiful than ever before. I might have been living inside a different body, one that fit me better and reacted more promptly to my directions— the body I should have had all along. My mood never faltered, even after I paid a small fortune for a few sacks of perfectly ordinary groceries. On the way home, I rolled the windows down and cranked up the radio, singing nonstop at the top of my lungs until I drove up to the house.

Dad was fussing about something when I got there. However,

his griping didn't bother me a bit. I flat out didn't care. A disaster of some kind might've spoiled my mood, but with none in the offing, my head remained firmly in the clouds. Feeling the way I did, I didn't want to have dinner alone with Dad. I wanted company, camaraderie, and conversation. I'll admit to having sounded slightly abrupt when I told him he could either fend for himself when dinnertime rolled around or he could go to the mess hall and have dinner with the guys.

Which was exactly what I did.

I surprised Calvin with a few goodies for the kitchen and stayed to help him prepare the meal. Then I sat down to share it with them. I didn't care if Rufus disapproved. I wasn't going to let him ruin my day. I even hugged Dusty when he came in to help me peel the potatoes, my insistence that they were better with the skins left on having fallen on deaf ears.

I knew the men had been given a lecture about staying away from me, but I'd had no such lecture—at least not lately. I flirted a tiny bit with every single one of them. I even told Rufus I liked his haircut. Saying something kind to Bull was tough, although I did mention that Jenny would adore his mustache, which seemed to please him. When I sat down beside Joe, his blush could've set the table on fire. Later on, I wound up pressing my arm against his side while reaching for the saltshaker. If Troy was correct in assuming Joe wouldn't wash the shoulder I'd patted him on, he was really going to stink up the bunkhouse now.

As I could've predicted, Rufus kept any thoughts he might have had on the sudden change in my behavior to himself. That was my chief complaint about Rufus. He was too hard to read. With the possible exception of the episode in the bunkhouse, his face seldom revealed what was going on inside his head. I didn't want to be the cause of another of his tirades, but I must say, the men seemed happier and more relaxed. I didn't do anything outrageous. I simply behaved the way any woman would while in the company of male friends.

After dinner, Troy and I washed the dishes. Not surprisingly, the cocky fellow had his own ideas about why I was in such a good mood.

"Someone's awfully happy today," he said in a teasing undertone. "Why *is* that, I wonder? You must have had some really nice dreams last night."

"You know, I *did* have a dream," I said. "It was about this hot, tasty cowboy…"

"Hot, tasty cow*girl*, you mean."

"Not in *my* dream. Trust me on this one. In my dream, it was a boy, and he was so handsome and sweet and sexy and wonderful and lovable…" I bit my lip for emphasis. "I could go on, but I wouldn't want him to get a swelled head."

"You're too late," he said, scratching his ear. "That ship has sailed."

"Aw, what a shame. I was looking forward to, um, polishing the brass, blowing out the pipes, that sort of thing."

"Maybe tomorrow," he suggested. "Better not do that too often. You wouldn't want to wear holes in the pipes now, would you?"

"I'd like to try."

We probably would've kept on in that vein for as long as it took to wash the dishes if Joe hadn't come in at that point, telling Troy that Calvin wanted to talk with him. Tossing his dish towel to Joe, Troy sauntered off.

When Joe came over to the sink, I handed him a dripping saucepan, which he promptly dropped.

"Good thing we aren't using Grandma's china." Making a man get all butterfingered and tongue-tied was a novel experience for me, and I must admit I enjoyed it immensely—although I did my best not to laugh.

"Sorry." Blushing, he stooped to retrieve the pan. "I'm not usually so clumsy."

"What's your excuse for being clumsy now?"

He hung his head. "I lied. Calvin didn't want to talk to Troy. *I* wanted to talk to *you*."

This was surprising. "Really? What about?"

"About something Rufus said."

He was silent for a long moment. Apparently, I was going to have to drag it out of him. "What did Rufus say?"

When Joe took a deep breath, I was pretty sure he was about to regale me with the details of the lecture Rufus had given them the night before.

As it turned out, that wasn't it.

"He said Dusty was a troublemaker and he was going to get rid of him."

I frowned. "Troublemaker? In what way?"

Joe shrugged. "I guess because he's different from the rest of us. Rufus thinks he's stirring up things to cause trouble."

"He told you that?"

"No, I heard him tell Calvin," he replied. "I don't think they knew I was listening."

"I don't get it," I said. "Dusty's worked here for years and I've never heard a single complaint about him. And what do you mean he's different?"

"I don't think he's a troublemaker myself. But he *is* different. He's a lot smarter than we are—better with horses, better at a lot of things, not to mention better-looking. I like him, and I'd trust him more than a lot of people you could name."

"So would I." Which was a bit of an understatement. "Did Rufus say what kind of trouble Dusty was supposed to be stirring up?"

"Not exactly. He just said he didn't want that kind of trouble around here."

"Wish he'd been more specific. That could mean anything." I couldn't remember the last time we'd had a problem with any of the men. Perhaps it was because Rufus tended to weed out the bad ones, but I'd never heard him say he was going to "get rid" of someone.

"He said Dusty had made too much trouble already, and he wasn't going to put up with it anymore."

"I still don't get it. Since when has Dusty ever caused a problem?"

Joe shrugged again. "I don't know, maybe it's because he broke his leg."

"I find that hard to believe," I said. "I don't suppose you heard anything else, did you?"

"No. I'd have felt weird telling Mr. Kincaid, but you, well… I just thought you should know." He finished his sentence in a bit of a rush, turning a charming shade of pink when I smiled at him.

"Thank you for telling me, Joe. Now I just have to figure out what I'm going to do about it."

"I'll let you know if I hear anything else." He stood there for a moment, as though he had more to say or was expecting something from me. An instant later, he went and gathered up more dishes.

He was quiet after that. I chattered on about something, I have no recollection of what exactly, but I did notice he got more fidgety with each passing moment.

Finally, I couldn't stand it anymore. "What's up with you now, Joe?"

"Nothing," he replied, his face a wooden mask and his voice perfectly neutral.

"I doubt that," I retorted. "You're acting grumpier than a wounded bear. Come on. Tell me. Or is it just that you don't want to do dishes anymore?"

"No," he replied. "I don't know, I…" He shook his head and shrugged in such a pitiful manner I wanted to hug him.

So I did—which was why when Rufus walked in a moment later, Joe and I were in each other's arms.

Damn.

It was a safe bet that before long, I'd be hearing about yet another lecture—unless Rufus chose to deliver it right there on the spot. I must've been listening to the devil on my left shoulder rather than the angel on my right, because the next thing I did was to take Joe's face in my hands and plant a big, juicy kiss right smack-dab on his astonished lips.

"I hope you get to feeling better, Joe." I patted his cheek. Taking a step back, I aimed a dish towel at Rufus, which he caught on the fly. "Here. You can finish the dishes. I've got better things to do."

Hooking Joe by the arm, I left the kitchen with him in tow, not waiting for a response from Rufus. I hadn't a clue what I was going to do with Joe next. I only wanted to get him away from there before all hell broke loose. Then I remembered I was supposed to be flirting with Troy to take the heat off Joe and Dusty. Thus far, I hadn't done a very good job. Of course, if Rufus really wanted to get rid of Dusty, I could have supplied him with all sorts of excuses, starting with that kiss in the bunkhouse.

On the other hand, Joe's job was probably safe, so maybe it was better to flirt with him instead of Troy after all. I wasn't ready to give up my boy toy just yet, and I certainly didn't want to give Rufus any ideas. In fact, I was trying to figure out a way to keep Troy on after Dusty's leg healed without admitting I only wanted him for my own personal use. Although I didn't see a problem with that, no doubt everyone else would.

Having left the kitchen, I thought it best to leave the mess hall altogether. Joe seemed to think leaving the country was a good idea.

"Boy, am I in trouble now," he exclaimed. "Rufus thought Dusty was a troublemaker. Now he'll be after me."

"I doubt that. Besides, Rufus can't fire any of you without consulting Dad and me, and I wouldn't let them do it."

"I don't think you realize what working here means, Angela," he said in a serious tone. "We got a pretty stern talking-to last night—Dusty in particular—and I don't know if you understand why. Did you know one of the rules for working here is that you are strictly off-limits? It's not written down anywhere, but we all know getting caught even looking at you is grounds for a lecture. If anyone ever said something like, 'the boss is really hot,' Rufus would run him out on a rail, whether you approved or not."

Apparently this had been going on for a lot longer than I thought. Although having heard the most recent story from Troy, I shouldn't have been surprised. "Oh hell. I suppose kissing you will get you tarred and feathered?"

"Probably not, but this is a first. As far back as I can remember, you've never kissed any of us, and while I wouldn't have missed it for the world, I'll bet it causes trouble. I wouldn't be the first cowboy to get fired because of you, and there've been a couple who've gotten the shit beat out of 'em."

"By who?" I demanded, although I was fairly certain I knew the answer.

"Rufus," he replied. "I haven't been here as long as he has, of course, but from what I've heard, he's been doing it ever since you were a kid."

"Why am I only hearing about this now? Why has no one ever said anything to me before?"

He shrugged. "I guess we didn't figure it was worth risking our jobs over. It wasn't until Dusty got hurt that I started thinking there might be more to it."

As little as Joe had ever said to me, I never would've guessed he had a thought in his head outside of what it took for him to do his job. I'd known him for perhaps three years, but now that I thought about it, I really didn't know him at all. Nor could I see what Dusty's accident had to do with anything.

Unless it *wasn't* an accident.

My mouth went dry as I considered what might have happened

to Dusty if his saddle had broken anywhere but in the corral. He could have been out on his own somewhere, looking for strays in a treacherous ravine, just as Cody had been. It had taken two days of frantic searching to find Cody. Two horrible, nerve-racking, terrifying days…

"C'mon, Joe," I said. "Let's go water the horses or feed the chickens or something. I'm not going to say anything more until I know we won't be overheard."

I kept my mouth shut, but my thoughts were racing wildly. There was another difference between Dusty and the other men. He was the only one I'd ever truly looked back at since Cody died. Rufus must have known I liked Dusty and would protest if he were to be fired or beaten to a pulp. But I couldn't have done much about it if he'd had an accident and been injured to the point he would be unfit for ranch work, or if he'd been killed…

Rufus's plan, if it *was* planned, had backfired on him. A broken leg had resulted in me having more contact with Dusty instead of less. Then there was Troy. I wondered if Rufus knew about our arrangement. So far, it didn't appear that he did, and I planned to keep it that way. If the guys I liked ended up having "accidents," then Troy might be in danger at some point.

And now, thanks to me, Joe might also be in danger.

I was beginning to feel like a damned jinx.

Chapter 13

Darkness had already begun to fall by the time Joe and I left the mess hall, and the first chill of autumn gave me goose bumps as we headed toward the stable. At least I *hoped* it was the weather, although the chilling thoughts running through my mind might have been responsible.

I flipped on the lights as we went in through the open doorway to the barn. I didn't want anyone accusing Joe of sneaking off with me—if it ever came to that. Unless someone had followed us, we would be alone there. Everyone else was still in the mess hall, sitting around shooting the breeze after dinner.

I led the way to Goldie's stall. From that central location, we would be able to see or hear anyone approaching from either direction. Goldie stuck her head over the door and nuzzled me gently.

I leaned back against the stall door. "Okay, Joe. You've really got me worried now. Tell me what you're thinking."

His quick nod and grim smile suggested the story wasn't going to be pretty. "Like I said before, Dusty's not stupid. He knows enough to check his saddle every so often and make sure there's nothing worn out on it. I examined that saddle after it broke—we *all* did— and it looked like the billet had just worn through from rubbing on the ring where it attaches to the saddle. But the more I thought about it—and Dusty said this too—he'd replaced those billets not long ago. I remember watching him do it.

"Now, the leather could've had a defect in it that might cause it to break like that, but I doubt it. I've never had one break on me before, and I've ridden with some that were a lot older than the billets Dusty replaced. I got to thinking about how it might've been tampered with, and I think if you used one of those little round files—like what you'd use to sharpen a chain saw—you could rub the leather really thin from underneath where it's folded over. Looking at it from the outside, you'd never notice it. If you took it apart, you would see it, but since those billets were fairly new, Dusty would never have thought he needed to do that. Anyway, it bothered me then, and after what Rufus said about getting rid of him…well, you see why I had to say something to you."

"Yes, and I'm glad you did. But why would Rufus do such a thing? Why would he single Dusty out?" I already had my own suspicions. If Joe's reasoning was the same as mine…

"Maybe he thinks you like Dusty."

Bingo.

"I can't remember ever doing or saying anything that would give him that impression. At least, I don't think I have. I mean, did you know?"

Joe shrugged. "No, but if I had to pick the one man out of all of us you *might* be partial to, it sure as hell wouldn't be Bull."

"I can't argue with that, but it's still a pretty flimsy reason to stage an accident—or fire a man."

"Just because I didn't notice your preference doesn't mean Rufus didn't," Joe pointed out. "He's pretty well tuned in to that sort of thing."

"Apparently." Rufus couldn't possibly have known I'd had the occasional fantasy about Dusty. Maybe I kept my gaze on him just a little too long or smiled at him with a bit more tenderness. Whatever I'd done, Rufus must've seen it. "Will the world end because I'm fond of Dusty? What's so damned special about me, anyway?"

A funny smile quirked the corner of his mouth. "Aside from the fact that you're absolutely adorable, there *is* the ranch to be considered.

You, of all people, should know what this place is worth—and unless I miss my guess, you'll be inheriting it fairly soon."

I grimaced. "You've noticed that too. I know Dad isn't doing very well, and the fact that he tends to ignore anything his doctor tells him doesn't help much. He's too stubborn for his own good. But are you saying you think Rufus wants the ranch?" I shook my head in disbelief. "If that's the case, he's sure going about it the wrong way. He's a good-looking man, Joe. I had a major crush on him when I was in high school. If he wants the ranch so damn bad, he should be making a play for me himself instead of running off the competition."

Joe shrugged. "Maybe he didn't think he'd stand a chance with someone like Dusty around. Neither would I, especially since Dusty does like you. A lot."

Apparently everyone knew about Dusty's feelings.

Except me.

I tried not to think about that. "And without Dusty, my only other choices were you, Bull, Calvin, and Rufus. I can't stand Bull, Calvin is too much like a father to me, and you're so quiet I've never spoken more than a few words with you—"

"Aside from the fact that I'm ugly as homemade sin."

"Oh, you are not," I snapped. "You're downright charming when you smile, but instead of smiling, you're always walking around with your head hanging down and never saying a word."

As if on cue, Joe's gaze immediately dropped from my face to the floor. "Yeah, well, that's enough about me." A moment passed before he lifted his chin, his eyes seeking mine once more. "What it boils down to is that without Dusty here to compete with him, Rufus just might stand a fighting chance."

I stomped a foot in frustration. "Then why didn't he find an excuse to fire Dusty years ago? What was he doing? Making me wait until I was so love-starved I'd come prowling around the bunkhouse looking for him?"

"Maybe." He shrugged. "Are you? Love-starved, I mean."

"What the hell do you think?" I was slightly exasperated with him until I remembered that what Cody and I had done with our spare time wasn't common knowledge. "I realize you couldn't have known the details, but Cody and I were very happy together. I *miss* that. I miss it so much that I—"

"Found a stray cowboy and brought him home?"

I blew out a breath. "Was it that obvious?"

He nodded. "Given that Troy's even better-looking than Dusty, it's no wonder Rufus is getting worried. He'll be trying to find a way to get rid of *him* next."

"Unless this whole thing is a concoction of our own suspicious minds," I cautioned. "Although I have to admit, it *does* seem kinda fishy."

"Yeah. Too bad we don't have any proof."

"No shit. You guys need to be very careful and watch out for each other."

"I don't think Rufus could get rid of all three of us." His lips curled into a delightfully devilish smile. "Maybe we should keep him guessing."

I grinned up at him, shaking my head. "And here I always thought you were shy."

"You know how it is. You kiss an ugly guy and tell him he has a charming smile and…" He shrugged, still smiling at me.

I patted his arm. "It's nice to know I have that effect on a few of you, anyway. I was beginning to think I'd sprouted warts or something. I felt like a freakin' leper. But you're right. We probably *should* keep him guessing."

A cluster fuck in the bunkhouse might make enough noise to attract attention…

Sometimes the ideas popping into my own head amazed me. Fortunately, Joe wasn't privy to those thoughts or he'd have been blushing like a beet.

"Does that mean you might kiss me again?" Whereas he'd seemed hesitant before, now he seemed…hopeful.

"Maybe, but only when someone else might see us."

"Damn." He swore so loudly, Goldie threw her head up in alarm and nearly hit me in the face. "I was kinda hoping for right now."

"It wouldn't help if we didn't have a witness, Joe." I pushed Goldie's head aside. Too bad *she* couldn't tell Rufus I'd been alone in the barn with Joe, because then he might have gotten his wish. As it was, I didn't see the point. Kissing Joe wasn't something I'd ever considered doing before, and that kiss in the kitchen had only been intended to needle Rufus. Under ordinary circumstances, I probably never would have done it—or even *thought* of it.

"You wouldn't get any complaints from me," he said. "And if we practiced, it might be more convincing."

I might've reacted with an eye roll and a giggle, but I couldn't argue with him because he did have a point.

He took a step closer. "Aw, c'mon, Angela. What could it hurt?"

I giggled again. Here was Joe, of all people, making me feel like a silly schoolgirl—and at my age too. "Where the hell is Rufus when I need him?"

"Washing dishes, I hope." Darting a glance at each end of the stable, he took another step toward me.

"Maybe I should go back and give him a hand. He must've been good for something all these years if he's been keeping you wolves in line."

"I guess so." Joe's smile disappeared and he stared at the ground again, mumbling, "If you could call a guy like me a wolf."

"No, you're not a wolf. But you could've made up all that stuff you just told me. That way I'd think you were one of the good guys, and you'd be in the perfect position to take advantage of me."

"I've never taken advantage of a woman in my life." Spearing his fingers through his hair, he kept his gaze fixed firmly on the dirt, apparently still finding it easier to look at anything besides me. "At least I don't *think* I ever have."

This was more like the Joe I knew. Never saying much and rarely glancing in my direction. Then, almost as if he'd heard that thought, his eyes slowly sought mine. His smile was wistful rather than wicked or charming. "Let me put it this way, Angela. When it comes to matters of the heart, I've always been the one to get the shaft."

If he kept on with this morose train of thought, I would have to kiss him just to cheer him up. I tried for a teasing tone. "Uh-huh. Now you're playing on my sympathy."

"Not really. It's the truth."

Obviously, he was in no mood to be teased. My choices were either kiss him or get the hell out of there. "I've already got more irons in the fire than I need. I don't think I could manage another one."

"It wouldn't be like that, Angela," he promised. "I wouldn't expect anything more than a hug or a kiss once in a while." He sighed. "It sure would beat the hell out of what I've been getting up to now."

"But one day you might get greedy, Joe. What would happen then?"

"When have you ever known me to be greedy?"

I was forced to admit I hadn't. Joe wasn't like that. I'd never seen him eat very much or get in anyone else's way. Anytime the men were lined up for anything, he was always somewhere toward the back of the pack and accepted whatever was left without complaint. No, he didn't want much. Not from me, anyway. My chest tightened painfully. He would have me in tears if he kept it up much longer.

In the next instant, Goldie apparently decided to add her two cents' worth to the conversation and gave me a nudge from behind that sent me staggering into Joe's waiting arms. I held onto him for support for a second or two, but Joe didn't act like he wanted to let go—at least, not yet.

After thanking Goldie for her assistance, he proceeded to give me a good, long hug. "You gave me a hug and a kiss a while ago. All I'm asking is that you let me return the favor."

I hadn't seen this much action with this many different men since, well…ever, and I guess it went to my head.

It was only a kiss—such a simple thing, really. I didn't think it would matter, didn't think anyone would care, and I certainly wouldn't lose my heart, so, in the end, I glanced up at him and nodded.

That was my first mistake.

Joe took a long time to lean down to kiss me, touching my lips tentatively when he finally reached them. No, Joe wasn't greedy, nor was he one to rush things. He took his time, seeming to savor every moment I gave him. His gentle hold slowly became a caress, encompassing every part of my body within his reach. His lips took all that my own had to offer, and I couldn't help responding, moving a shade closer and holding him a teensy bit tighter.

That was my *second* mistake…

Joe might not have been greedy, but he obviously thought I was asking for more. Deepening the kiss, he swept his tongue slowly over my lips before slipping past them. I could've clenched my teeth to keep him out, but, quite honestly, it never occurred to me to do that. Maybe I wanted it as much as he did, or was at least curious, but either way, before long, the kiss wasn't friendly and comforting anymore. It was intensely sexual, bordering on erotic. The rest of my body responded with enthusiasm, making me wonder what sort of effect this kiss had on him.

Unfortunately, acting on that curiosity was mistake number *three*…

Pressing against him in an effort to discover whether he was as hard as I was wet, I must have ground my hips just enough to encourage him to explore places I should've insisted he leave alone.

I say *should* have, because I didn't.

Those parts were reminding me that some of them had a will of their own—as well as the power to make me follow their lead if

I didn't keep a close watch on them. My right hand was the first to assert itself, sliding down from the unexceptionable location of the middle of his back—first to his hip and then on around to cup his left cheek—and not the one on his face, either.

"What the hell are you doing?"

Dammit.

Of all the people in the world who might have followed us to the stable, it had to have been Troy…

Chapter 14

I PULLED AWAY FROM Joe just in time to catch Troy's expression of hurt and outrage before he turned and stomped back toward the open doorway.

"Wait, Troy!" I ran after him. "Wait!"

"What for?" he shouted over his shoulder. "What am I supposed to do? Stand around and watch while you fuck him?"

I caught up with Troy right outside the barn. "I wasn't going to do that. I—It's hard to explain. Troy, please don't be angry, it's just that, um…you kinda had to be there. I'm sorry."

"I keep forgetting I don't really know you at all." His voice was clipped, angry. "This could be normal for you, and how the hell would I know? Rufus may have been right. Maybe he felt he had to keep the cowboys away from you so you wouldn't be tempted since apparently it doesn't take a helluva lot to do it. I guess I should have realized that from the start. You're a little too easy for me, Angie. Maybe I should move on."

Now, *I* was pissed. "I haven't heard you complaining about me being too easy up to now. As I recall, it was you who asked me if I wanted a—how was it you put that? A slightly used boy toy?"

"Yeah, well, you took advantage of me," he retorted. "I was thirsty and hungry and exhausted and had just gotten dumped on the highway by my girlfriend. Then you came along and gave me everything I needed in the space of an hour."

"And why do you think that was?" My tone was softer now.

He'd been hurt every bit as badly as I had been, and his wounds were still raw. I needed to remember that. "Because I was used to doing it? No, Troy, it was because it *was* unusual. I was so lonely. Trust me, I needed you just as much as you needed me."

"You didn't need me," he insisted. "You've got Joe and Dusty. You don't need *me* at all."

"Yes I do. Joe just—"

"—happened to come in and tell me some trumped-up story about Calvin wanting to talk to me so he could get you alone. And now I find you out here kissing him."

Obviously, I was going to have to tell him everything. "Troy, take it easy and let me explain. Joe wanted to talk to me about something Rufus said. I brought him out here so we wouldn't be overheard. I'm not in love with Joe, but he's every bit as lonely and miserable as the rest of us. I was only trying to—"

"Cheer me up," Joe spoke up from behind me. "It wasn't what it looked like, Troy." Joe's sidelong glance assured me he understood my motives completely. "I had an idea there was something going on between the two of you. I guess I was right about that."

"If you thought that, then why did you kiss her?" Troy demanded.

Joe scuffed the toe of his boot in the gravel, staring down at the ground again. "You know how it is when a woman you care about says something nice to you," he mumbled. "It gave me…ideas."

"Oh yeah?" Troy's voice had lost some of its heat. He seemed slightly mollified by our explanation, although not entirely. "Would you mind telling me whose idea it was for Angie to put her hand on your ass?"

"Mine," I conceded, waving my errant fingers at him. "All mine. You know how I am about that. My right hand is the one to blame. It has a mind of its own sometimes."

My confession drew a glimmer of a smile. "Yeah, I know about that." He glanced at Joe. "Angie likes ass."

"No kidding?" If the light had been better, I'd have said Joe's eyes were twinkling.

Troy nodded. "You should have seen what she did to me last—"

"Hold on there, Troy," I cautioned. "Let's not be telling him everything. He might go running to Dad or Rufus, and then I'd be in even more hot water."

"Aw, I wouldn't do that," Joe insisted. "But I wouldn't mind hearing more about what you did to him. My own fantasies are getting kinda worn."

"Use your imagination, Joe," I suggested.

"Your *wildest* imagination," Troy amended. "That way you might be able to think of something half as good as the reality."

"Oh, don't tell me that," Joe groaned. "I feel deprived enough as it is."

"Okay. That settles it," I said. "We are *all* going out on Saturday night, and we're going to find you a girlfriend. I'll pimp for you if I must, but one way or the other, I'm getting you laid."

"Promises, promises," Joe mocked. "Bull's always saying shit like that, but it never happens."

I shot him a scowl. "Oh, come on, Joe! You wouldn't want the kind of woman Bull hangs around with, would you? I'm gonna find you a nice girl who'll love you to pieces. I already know a few things I can pass on as incentive."

"Like what?"

"Oh, you know…great kisser, nice ass, hung to your—"

Joe silenced me with a hand over my mouth. "Hush, now. You couldn't possibly know any more than that. Troy's ready to mop up the floor with me as it is."

"She's right, though," Troy admitted, albeit with obvious reluctance. "I've seen you coming out of the shower, Joe. You're hung like a stud horse."

I gazed up at Joe with newfound respect. "Damn. I *knew* I

should've installed a peephole in the bunkhouse. Just think what I've been missing."

Not surprisingly, Joe seemed rather pleased, smiling sheepishly as he shuffled his feet. "I dunno about that, but I can tell you this much, Angela. If you had a peephole, and we knew you were watching, there wouldn't have been a soft dick in the place. We wouldn't have told on you, either."

Honest to God, I hadn't had this much fun in years. "Aw, you mean your dick would get hard just because I looked at it? I never knew I had such an effect on you guys. Let me see." I reached for his zipper.

"None of that, now." Grabbing me from behind, Troy pulled me out of range. "I think we've created a monster, Joe. What do you think we should do with her?"

"I know what I'd *like* to do with her," Joe said, chuckling. "But I don't think you'd approve."

"Ooh," I said with fiendish glee. "Cluster fuck me in the bunkhouse?"

"Cluster fuck?" Joe's eyes were as big and round as a pair of teacups. "Where on earth did you ever hear *that*?"

"My husband," I replied. "You guys never knew about Cody and me, did you? On a typical day, we did the deed at least twice—and more often than that if we had the chance. I never bothered to check you guys out—never really *needed* to—partly because I didn't have the time. Cody kept me pretty busy."

Joe let out a low whistle. "I had no idea. I always knew you and Cody seemed happy, but I never knew you were *that* happy."

"Well, now you know," I said. "Is it any wonder I've been such a wreck since he died? I miss him every day, and not only because of the sex." My throat constricted on a sob. "I loved him, Joe. I loved *being* in love with him, and I loved *making* love with him." I paused briefly to wipe my eyes before tears ran down my cheeks. "Imagine what it was like for me to have that and then suddenly be plunged into the sterile existence I've had to endure ever since. No one looks at me, or touches me, or in your case, hardly ever even speaks to me."

"I'm surprised you didn't throw a rope on Dusty and tie him to his bunk and have your way with him," Joe agreed. "Hell, I'm surprised you didn't get desperate enough to do it to me."

"Now, Joe," I chided. "You're not to say things like that about yourself anymore. I won't allow it. A woman wouldn't have to be desperate to want you. She'd just have to be—"

"Blind?"

"I wasn't going to say that," I insisted. "I was going to say… I don't know what, exactly, but it wouldn't take desperation. She'd have to get to know you well enough to appreciate your, um, hidden attributes."

"Meaning you'd have to show her your dick," Troy said, as though any clarifications were needed. "Trust me, Angie, if you'd ever seen it, you would *never* have picked me up, that's for sure."

"That good, huh?"

"I'm not overly fond of them myself," Troy said candidly. "But I know a first-class dick when I see it, and he's got one."

"What about Dusty's?" I was fascinated by the peculiar nature of this conversation, discovering things I never dreamed I'd ever have the chance to learn. "Is it as big as yours?"

"Never seen it when it was hard," Troy replied. "But Joe there, he's hard most of the time."

I gazed at Joe with increased admiration, but I was also a tad concerned. "How do you ever manage to ride a horse? That has to be uncomfortable."

Joe rolled his eyes. "Aw, he's making that up. It's not hard *all* the time, and to the best of my recollection, he's only seen it once."

"So, Joe, have *you* ever seen Dusty's tool?" Knowing I might never have this opportunity again, I intended to pump them both for all the information I could get.

Bowing his head, Joe scratched the back of his neck as though trying to remember. "Can't say I ever have," he finally said. "He doesn't sleep naked, so I've never seen it when he gets up in the morning, for example. Now, Bull, on the other hand... I've seen his plenty of times."

"And?"

Joe's grin was wider than ever. "Mine's bigger."

I giggled. "I was hoping you'd say that. Now, let me get this straight. Bull's is smaller than yours, yours is bigger than Troy's, and we don't have any idea about Dusty. Is that right?"

"Hold on there now," Troy said. "You're making it sound like Bull and I are the same size."

"Well, aren't you?"

Troy shook his head. "I'm pretty sure I've got him beat too."

"Great," I said. "Now, we just have to find out about Dusty."

"Find out what about me?" Dusty hobbled down the bunkhouse steps. "What are you guys talking about out here in the dark anyway?"

I considered it fortunate he hadn't heard any more than he had, because if *he* could hear our discussion, Rufus might have overheard us too.

"Come over here for a minute, Dusty," I called. "There's something I want to ask you."

Joe let out a loud guffaw. "Be careful now, Dusty," he said between chuckles. "You might not like the question."

I'd never seen Joe laugh like that before, and I was very happy to have witnessed it at last. Sex wasn't the only thing I'd missed since Cody's death.

Fun.

Laughter.

Joy.

My life had been devoid of those things in recent years. At the time, I didn't even have my sons to joke around with. Only the occasional phone call since they'd gone back to college. I was so happy to finally have some fun with my cowboys; I never wanted it to end.

"Go on now," Troy urged. "Ask him. I want to see his face."

Neither Troy nor Joe knew anything about the kiss I'd shared with Dusty in the bunkhouse. Nor did they know that if things had gone a bit differently, I might have already known the answer to that question. The trouble was, Dusty hadn't been in on the discussion the way the rest of us had, and he'd probably think we were nuts. I didn't quite know how to phrase it.

"What's up?" Dusty asked, eyeing me expectantly.

"I'm conducting a survey," I began, trying to ignore the chuckles from Joe and Troy at Dusty's choice of words. "We're comparing, um, equipment size."

"Aw, now, don't be namby-pamby about it, Angie," Troy said. "Ask him to show you his dick."

Dusty gulped as though he'd swallowed his own tongue. For a second there, I thought I might have to Heimlich him to get him to start breathing again.

"Be quiet, Troy," I admonished. "No one else had to show me theirs. I'm conducting a survey, not making an actual comparison."

"It'd be more fun if you did," Joe said under his breath. "A *lot* more fun."

"True," I agreed. "But I think I'll stick to the original plan. Now, Dusty, comparatively speaking, where does yours fit in the bunkhouse lineup? You know, bigger than this one, smaller than that one—that sort of thing."

He gaped at me for a long moment before he spoke. "I don't know that I've seen all of them."

"That's okay," I said, doing my damnedest to keep a straight face. "Just tell me how you'd fit in with the ones you've seen. I think between the three of you, you've probably seen them all."

He shook his head, smiling. "I can't believe this is what y'all were out here talking about. I guess that's what I get for butting in on a private conversation."

"Actually, you came at about the right time," I said. "Go ahead and tell me, then we can talk about something else."

Dusty took a deep breath and plunged ahead. "Bigger than Bull. Not as big as Joe. Never seen Calvin, Rufus, or Troy."

"Well, isn't that nice?" I said, not bothering to hide my delight. "Everyone is bigger than Bull. I always knew there was a reason I didn't like him."

"I always figured it was because he was an asshole," Dusty remarked.

"Yes, but there had to be something else to clinch the matter. I believe this is it. Maybe we should call him Pencil Prick instead of Bull."

"There's still the question of which of the two of us is bigger," Troy said, indicating himself and Dusty.

"You two might want to sort that out for yourselves and get back to me later," I said. "Unless, of course, you want me to, um, judge the contest."

Troy and Dusty exchanged a glance.

"Sure, why not?" Troy said with a shrug.

"Holy shit," Joe exclaimed. "I can't believe you'd agree to that. 'Specially after you got all pissed when you saw me kissing her."

Dusty's eyes nearly popped out of his head. "You kissed Joe? Again? You've got to be kidding me."

"Okay, okay," I grumbled. "So I've kissed all three of you. Are you going to ask me to decide who the best kisser is?"

Troy put up a hand. "Now hold on a minute. You kissed Dusty too?"

I was getting in deeper and deeper shit with each passing moment. Honesty truly was the best policy. "Remember that day you caught me in the bunkhouse with him? He asked me to kiss him, so I did."

Troy's hand dropped so fast he might've been swatting flies. "Fuck."

"Dammit, Troy, will you make up your mind?" I snapped. "You're willing to compare penises with him, but not kisses?"

"It's different when all you're gonna do is *look* at our dicks," Troy said with a scowl. "I never said I wanted you to try us all on for size."

"Good, because I wasn't planning to," I said. "Although…"

"Oh, here we go," Troy grumbled. "Cluster fuck time."

"Really?" Joe's eyes lit up like a kid's on Christmas morning. "Sounds like fun."

I rolled my eyes. "No, not *really*. Besides, if I did that, none of you would ever trust me again. I have to draw the line somewhere." Not that I wouldn't think about it.

Probably my best fantasy ever.

"I'm glad you feel that way," Troy said. "Because I'm about to give up my claim."

Dusty pounced on that one right away. "What claim?"

"Oh, that's right," I said. "You don't know. Troy has been my secret pal ever since he got here." I hoped Dusty understood now why I hadn't encouraged him any more than I had. I liked Dusty a lot, and I certainly didn't want to hurt his feelings.

"Better not let Rufus get wind of it," Dusty advised. "Or he'll be in bigger trouble than I am."

"Speaking of trouble," I began, "did you know he was planning to get rid of you?"

"I figured that would be next," Dusty admitted. "But, hell, he'd have a much better case against the other two. I mean, he actually *saw* you kiss Joe."

"So he's talking about that already, is he?" *Why am I not surprised?*

"You better believe he is," Dusty replied. "And when it comes to getting angry, he is the weirdest man you've ever seen. He goes sort of blank—doesn't scream or yell or anything, but you know something will happen eventually. He doesn't get mad. He gets even."

"Joe and I have been discussing that," I said. "I think there's a bigger problem here than we realized. I think the best solution is to not let him single any of you out, which is why we're *all* going out on Saturday night. I've got a little dust to blow in ol' Rufus's eyes."

And that was exactly what I promised myself I would do. I would dance and flirt with every last one of them. I'd even flirt with Pencil Prick if he decided to come along—although it would probably kill me to do it.

"Good idea," Joe said. "Dibs on the first dance."

"Guess I'd better get a dance card for you guys to fill out, huh?" I winked at him. "After all, I wouldn't want to cause any trouble." Chuckling, I waved a hand and started toward the house. "Well, good night, boys. See you at breakfast."

I'd only taken one step when Joe tapped me on the shoulder. "Aren't you forgetting something?"

"I don't think so," I replied, frowning.

"The survey?" Troy prompted.

"You don't seriously want me to—"

"Oh, yes we do," Dusty declared. "I want to know which one of us you would choose."

Given the way he'd worded that last statement, I suspected Dusty of throwing down the proverbial gauntlet. Not who would win, but who I would *choose...*

"Okay," I conceded. "But let's go someplace else. I need better light."

Chapter 15

THE TACK ROOM WAS the obvious choice of venue for a biggest dick contest. With no windows and decent lighting, it also had a door that could actually be closed and locked.

Look but don't touch.

I must've repeated those words in my mind a hundred times during the short walk to the tack room. Troy would go ballistic if I touched Joe's dick or Dusty's balls, and I wasn't sure I could actually do any touching without adding in a bit of fondling. At least, not where Dusty was concerned.

My heart hammered even faster than my icy hands trembled. One touch of my chilly fingers would probably make any of them deflate.

Maybe.

I reminded myself that I was already familiar with everything Troy had to offer, and he was no slouch in any department.

Especially that fabulous ass…

"Okay, guys. Line up over here," I said, indicating an open space beneath the bare overhead lightbulb.

Not knowing which of them had the larger tool, Troy and Dusty eyed each other with doubt. Joe, on the other hand, obviously knew that for once, he had the other guys beat all to hell and back, and his smug smile proved it.

"Let's start with bulges." Strolling along the lineup, I noted that while Troy and Dusty each had a nice-sized lump behind their zippers, Joe seemed to have very little. Frowning, I studied them closely. "Hmm… I think I'll have to give this one to Troy—better definition and a slightly larger wet spot."

That wasn't too surprising. I already knew he could pump out the juice—one of his more endearing traits, in my opinion.

Troy aimed a smirk at his competitors. "That's one point for me."

"Should I be writing this down?" I asked.

Dusty chuckled. "Don't worry. We'll remember."

Clearing my throat, I rubbed my hands together, hoping to warm them up a bit. Unfortunately, it probably appeared as though I was getting ready to grab something.

Look but don't touch.

I dropped my hands to my sides. "Now then. Let's unbuckle the belts and undo the zippers. I think you should do it one at a time so I can get the full effect. Extra points for attitude. Dusty, why don't you start us off?"

How I kept from laughing myself silly as the guys each gave their own impression of a male stripper was beyond me. Then again, maybe I was too damned turned on to giggle.

I was practically drooling as Dusty leaned back slightly and gave it his all. The deliberate unbuckling of his belt. The dramatic flip of the button. The painfully slow lowering of the zipper. The quick push that dropped his jeans to his knees. Hell, even his cast, which hit him at mid-thigh, was sexy.

"Nice," I managed to say. "Next?"

Troy began his routine by grinding his hips to some slightly off-key sound effects.

"You really can't carry a tune in a bucket, can you?" I observed.

"Maybe not, but I *do* have a nice, juicy dick."

I certainly couldn't argue with that assessment. "True. Some deficiencies can be forgiven in light of other assets."

Troy's moves were more spectacular than Dusty's—lots of

suggestive gyrations followed by a pelvic thrust I could almost feel—although no less stimulating.

I nodded my approval. "Good job. Joe?"

With no fanfare whatsoever, Joe dropped his pants.

My jaw went with them.

I realized then why there had been no bulge. His cock hadn't been attempting to escape through his fly. Rather, it formed a thick, straight ridge from his crotch to his navel. The head peeked out from beneath the waistband of his briefs.

Actually, *peeked* is the wrong word because at least two inches of that humongous dick were clearly visible. Upon closer inspection, I noted that it actually extended beyond his navel.

"Holy shit." I'd seen bigger tools on a stallion, but I couldn't imagine how any human male could have outdone him and still be able to walk.

"Scary, isn't it?" Troy whispered.

Pressing my fingers to my lips, I bent down for a closer inspection. "Damn." I drew away slightly. "Lose the undies."

Freed of restraint, Joe's penis fell forward like the door on a dishwasher, bouncing a few times before coming to rest in a perfectly perpendicular position. I was glad I'd taken a step back; otherwise, it would've clubbed me in the nose. I stared at it, blinking my eyes, convinced I couldn't possibly be seeing it correctly.

"Don't bother, Angie," Troy said. "Your eyes aren't playing tricks on you. It really is that big."

"Jesus," I said with a breathy exhale. "I had no idea…"

"Deceptive, isn't it?" Dusty pushed his own briefs down, revealing a respectable and very nicely shaped seven or eight inches.

Troy followed suit, revealing a stiff member almost exactly the same length as Dusty's. "See? Not even close."

Three cocks. Three lickable, suckable, fuckable cocks.

They were even drooling. Unfortunately, I couldn't touch any of them, much less fuck them. At least not at the moment. I might get a taste of Troy later on, although to be perfectly honest, I couldn't imagine actually fucking Joe. Tab A was clearly too big for Slot B.

Grabbing a nearby stool, I sat down with a thud and drew in a ragged breath. "Okay. No contest there. Let's see some balls."

On cue, all three men lifted their dicks and thrust their hips forward. Joe's scrotum hung low and full with testicles that nearly matched his penis in size. Giving my head a quick shake, I moved down the row to Troy. I knew from experience he had some nice nuts on him, but when my gaze slid to Dusty, my mouth went dry.

"Perfect." Perfect size for sucking, perfect oval shape, and nicely covered with golden curls. "The clear winner."

"Now for the best ass," Troy said with a smirk.

Shuffling their feet, the men turned around in unison. Joe had a nice pair of buns, even if they were kinda skinny. Dusty's were firm and adorably furry. Troy's ass, on the other hand, was world-class: hollow-flanked, well-rounded, and clearly defined with a pair of dimples at the top of the crack.

"No contest."

Chuckling, Troy aimed a wink over his shoulder. "And we all know what Angie likes."

Later that night, I got my hands on that fabulous ass—but not before spending an inordinate amount of time mulling over the day's events.

After everything that had happened earlier in the evening, I didn't expect Troy to put in an appearance at all—and not only because he might still be miffed with me for kissing Joe. Rufus was bound to have been extra vigilant—unless he only thought he needed to keep a closer watch on Joe and Dusty. As new as Troy was to the ranch, I doubted Rufus would've suspected him of sneaking into my room, especially since he'd apparently swallowed Troy's tall tale about needing to go for strolls in the middle of the night. Although I might have been a lonely widow, I'd never been what anyone would call promiscuous. Therefore, welcoming a virtual stranger into my bed wasn't typical behavior for me. Rufus had no reason to suspect I was anything more to Troy than his new employer.

Still, the fact that Rufus had anything to do with who I welcomed into my bed had me royally pissed. Damn that man! I could've been…

What?

Having an affair with Dusty?

No. Probably not.

Well, maybe. But would I have considered it before Troy came along? Would I even have had the guts to say anything to him? Or was the catalyst theory correct?

Dusty had said he loved me. He'd seemed sincere, although I still wasn't sure I believed it. Then again, how often did a man come right out and say those words? As tough as it was to say them when they were true, I couldn't imagine why he would lie.

He wouldn't. Not unless he was the troublemaker Rufus had accused him of being—and I didn't believe that for a second. I still thought Dusty needed more options. I couldn't shake the idea that he would be settling for me if we ever got together, and I couldn't figure out why he would do that. Joe was right about him being different. Dusty had a lot to recommend him, not the least of which being his sense of humor.

On any given day, his comments had me laughing my ass off, and he'd been chuckling along with the rest of the guys during the contest. With all that giggling going on, I was surprised any of them could keep an erection. However, none of them appeared to have any trouble whatsoever in that respect. I still couldn't quite wrap my head around that. Three men with cocks as rock-hard and ready to go as I would ever see in my life, and I hadn't even touched them.

But what if I had? Would The Great Tack Room Gangbang have gone down in Circle Bar K history? Would I have feasted on a banquet of cock and balls and ass before getting the fucking of my life? There were enough dicks to fill every place I had to put one. That the contest had remained amusing rather than escalating to an all-out ménage said a lot for my guys. It demonstrated their respect for me, but more than anything, their hands-off behavior proved none of them were willing to share. They had been interested to see which one I would pick, not whether I was willing to fuck all of them at once.

In the wake of two very dry years, the fact that I had a choice at all was unbelievable. The trouble was, any one of them could've made me happy. The necessity of excluding the other two was what made it so hard. In a different place and time, I could see myself loving each of them, which might have been why I'd kept my options open by giving everyone their own honorary title.

There were definite differences between them. Joe was a nice guy, but to be honest, even after giving birth to two children, I doubted he would fit. There was, after all, such a thing as *too* big. From a purely sexual compatibility standpoint, Troy was the only proven entity, although I had no doubts Dusty could give him a run for his money—with or without a cast on his leg.

Then there was the fidelity issue. I had Dusty and Joe pegged as one-woman men, whereas Troy struck me as being more of a player, whether he thought I was too easy or not. That trait alone would rule him out. I had no desire to give my heart to him only to have it tossed aside.

Age was also a factor. Joe was closest in age to me, and Dusty and Troy were only a year apart. They were both too young. Rufus was too old—and I was going absolutely nuts thinking about it.

Then again, perhaps my own options were as limited as Dusty's. I could've gone honky-tonkin' with Jenny anytime I wanted and found someone completely new.

Was Dusty the reason I hadn't bothered? Had I been *waiting* for him to make a move or just *wishing* he would?

The gist of it all was that Dusty was the best choice—the one I'd had my eye on for ages, yet had never seen as a possibility. But how could I feel that way about him and keep on fucking Troy?

I realized then what the difference was. Troy knew he was temporary. *I* knew he was temporary. Dusty was long-term, long-haul, 'til death do us part. Maybe I wasn't ready for that. Maybe that was why I hadn't acted on my feelings toward him and why I was still hesitating...

When Troy stripped off his clothes and slipped in beside me, I could've said no, could've told him to leave. Too bad he was irresistible.

Perhaps I had fidelity issues of my own.

"I'm surprised to see you," I whispered.

He chuckled. "Did you really think after showing you my dick tonight I wasn't going to come in here and nail you with it?"

"Hmm... Hadn't thought about it that way, but you're right. I'm kinda primed for it myself, and your adorable ass could stand some attention."

"How so?"

"I didn't see a mark on it. I think I'd like to put one there."

"Hmm... Hickey or actual teeth marks?"

"Both, I believe. It's time someone put the Circle Bar K brand on you."

"Want me roped and tied and branded, huh? I guess there are worse things."

"Roped and tied?" I echoed. "Does that mean you're into bondage?"

"Never tried it," he said after a moment's hesitation. "Not sure I'd like it, though. I like being able to move."

I'd noticed that. Troy was nothing if not…mobile. "No ropes then. Just the brand."

"Works for me." Spearing his fingers through the hair at my temples, he kissed me so thoroughly I wasn't sure I'd have enough strength left to brand anything, let alone leave a mark on his delectable ass. I melted into the mattress as his hands slid down to my waist. His skin was hot against my own, and his cock poked at my hip. When I reached down to wrap my fingers around it, he pushed my hand away.

"I think I'd like to eat some pussy first," he said. "Hot, wet, *delicious* pussy…"

As though he'd struck a match to it, my core ignited. Heat roiled up from my center, making my nipples pucker and tingle with anticipation. His kisses drifted lower until his tongue brushed my nipples and lingered there.

"Feel good?"

"Mmm…" was my only reply.

He went right on sucking, licking, tasting. Feathery touches sent impulses racing along a pathway tying my nipples to my core. I thought it strange I'd never realized such a direct connection existed. Perhaps I'd only forgotten it.

My stomach muscles cramped as he teased my navel with his tongue, making me burst into giggles. "That tickles."

"I know," he said. "It makes you laugh, and I like hearing you laugh." I could feel the vibrations of his voice against my skin. Or maybe it was his breath. Either way, I was glad when he moved lower. Kisses there didn't make me laugh. They made me writhe and moan and fly off into oblivion.

My arms had been stretched out on the sheets. Now I grasped his head, fisting my hands in hair just long enough for me to do it.

"Oh, yeah, Angie. Love that. Make me eat you," he whispered. "Push my head down between your legs."

I was already doing that, but I pushed harder anyway. "Eat me," I whispered. "Suck my clit." I'd never said anything like that in my life. It was him, granting me permission, giving me the encouragement I needed to be bold.

"Feels so damn good…" The first touch was a thrust of his tongue into my wet folds rather than a kiss. "You taste so delicious, Angie. Spread your legs a little more."

I did as he asked, and his head bobbed up and down as he fucked me with his tongue. My clit throbbed. Corny or not, no other word could even begin to describe the intense response to the flick of his tongue on that one tiny spot…

"Damn, that's incredible."

"Shh… Don't talk. Don't want to be distracted. I'm…busy…" He sounded different, his words muffled against my labia. "Love this."

He kept on until I thought I'd go mad. I was nearly there when he drew back and pressed my legs together. "Turn on your side and arch your back."

I couldn't imagine why until he licked me again. That position thrust my clit forward, allowing him free access to my wet, sensitive flesh. His fingertips teased my nipples at the same time, but with a different pattern, a different rhythm. Arching my back even more, I thrust my hips forward as he sucked my clit into his mouth. My nipples hardened as he rolled them between his fingertips, triggering indescribably exquisite sensations. My mind went blank as his lips circled the tight bud, his breath hot on my skin.

So hot, so unbelievably hot…

There it was at last. The signal, the ignition, the point of no return. My eyes squeezed shut as my mind stepped back from the reality to observe it, waiting for it, allowing it to grow until—

My ecstatic cry should've awakened everyone within a ten-mile radius. Despite his smug chuckle, Troy kept right on teasing me, the rough texture of his tongue coaxing, prodding, demanding more. I gave it to him with every gasp and moan and thrust…

With a satisfied grunt, he rolled me onto my back. Nudging my thighs apart with his knees, he crawled up over me and slid inside.

"Oh yeah," he growled, his voice trailing off as he began to move. "So tight…so hot…so wet…"

I knew him now. Knew the feel of him deep inside me, knew the rhythms he liked, knew his flavor, his scent.

Familiar, yet still something of a mystery.

Rocking into me, he set a pace I was certain he could maintain for a long, long time. I felt his thrusts, heard the creak of the bedsprings and the soft slap of skin on skin. The joining of two separate beings.

Yeah. This is nice. I could get used to this. Perhaps I already had.

Too bad it couldn't last.

His explanation of why he'd come to me that night didn't quite ring true. He couldn't have known what I'd been thinking about during those wakeful hours. Somehow, he must've read the writing on the wall and realized my true emotions lay in a completely different direction. He could give me pleasure and accept it from me in return. However, this tryst contained an emotion I hadn't felt before. A pang of regret. A wave in farewell. One last fling before parting.

His warmth surrounded me and yet failed to reach the center of my being. Something had happened. Something out of my reach, beyond my control.

He was the same man. He felt the same, smelled the same, and even tasted the same. When he climaxed at last, his cock filled me with the same creamy semen as it had before. He even made the same sounds.

Oh yes. I knew him quite well.

But he wasn't mine.

He wasn't the one who occupied my thoughts and starred in my dreams. Dusty was that man. Troy was a crutch, a substitute for what I truly wanted and needed. His good-night kiss was sweet and the taste of him lingered long after he was gone, and yet somehow I knew beyond that last mind-blowing orgasm lay an abyss. I had just experienced something that could never be repeated. I can't say how I knew it, but this was the last time.

He wouldn't come back again.

Chapter 16

NEEDLESS TO SAY, I didn't sleep very well after that. By morning, whether I had stayed awake waiting for him to show up or been fucked all night long simply didn't matter. That fabulous frame of mind I'd enjoyed the day before was gone, replaced with inner turmoil and indecision. I plodded mechanically through the morning chores and then went out to check on Goldie.

Her udder looked like it was about to pop. In fact, it was already dripping milk—*white* milk, rather than clear liquid—and as anyone who's ever waited anxiously for a mare to foal can attest, that's about the best sign of impending labor there is.

The mare seemed calm enough, so it was safe to assume she would wait until the middle of the night to foal. If she'd been agitated, I wouldn't have left the barn, and I probably would have camped out in the tack room all day.

Not that horses aren't capable of foaling all alone—in fact, they prefer it. Still, it's one of those events horse breeders like to be on hand for in case there's a problem. Besides, this foal was more important to me than most. I'd bred Goldie to one of the top stallions around, and added to the fact that she'd been a champion barrel racer back in my racing days, their offspring would be quite valuable.

I hadn't talked with any of the men yet. Even Dusty seemed to be making himself scarce, so I had no idea whether Rufus had delivered another lecture the evening before. Troy hadn't said anything about it, so perhaps he hadn't. Maybe Rufus had finally realized the utter futility of his meddling. I certainly hoped so. Now that I knew about those lectures, it embarrassed me to think a ranch foreman would feel the need to chastise the hands for getting rowdy with the boss. Not only was it embarrassing, it was downright ridiculous. Surely, he would get over it eventually—especially if I made it clear that protecting my virtue was not his responsibility.

If I'd known what was going on behind my back sooner, I think I would have said something to him then, but the nagging suspicion that Dusty's saddle had been deliberately tampered with made me hesitant. If Rufus was capable of something that heinous, I didn't want to stir up any more trouble by confronting him.

Would a confrontation reveal anything? Rufus was such a hard man to read. Dusty was right about him going blank when any other man would've been cussing a blue streak. Figuring out what might be going on in his head was tough, and it was a given he wouldn't confess.

I'd also considered the possibility that Rufus wasn't responsible for Dusty's "accident." The only other suspect I could come up with was Bull. Dusty made no secret of his dislike for Bull, and he picked on him constantly. Perhaps that was what Rufus meant when he'd referred to Dusty as a troublemaker. I had a hard time justifying that, though. Dusty might have a broken leg now, but on the whole, he was a decent, hardworking, intelligent man. Why Rufus would favor Bull over him was difficult for me to understand. Bull also had a bit of a temper. I wouldn't have put it past him to try to even the score, although I'd have guessed his retaliation would be more along the lines of a practical joke. Humiliating, perhaps, but nothing that would cause actual harm.

After assuring myself Goldie wasn't going to foal any time soon, I decided to go for a ride. A good gallop across the open range had always been the best way to purge the cobwebs from my brain, and my head certainly needed clearing. I took my big paint gelding out of his stall and saddled him up, still curious as to why Dusty wasn't around to help. Perhaps knowing Troy was more to me than simply one of the guys had made him back off a tad. I only knew I had no intention of nosing around trying to find him. If he wanted to see me, he knew where I was. If I wasn't in the office, I was either in the barn or my work room—which is where I probably should've been. I had orders for three stained-glass doors, and Jenny wasn't the only one getting impatient.

My artwork had been the main thing that kept me sane after Cody died—especially on the days I was stuck indoors. Sometimes, when loneliness threatened to overwhelm me, I worked late into the evening. I knew I had to keep busy, so I'd put a couple of ads in various newspapers and had received several orders as a result. Subsequent orders had come about through word of mouth, and they'd kept me steadily busy for the past year or more. Prior to that, I'd contented myself with doing windows for the house, although the kids had teased me about making the place seem more like a church than a ranch house.

I didn't care. Although living in an all-male household had prevented me from decorating with frilly curtains or lace, stained glass added beauty rather than femininity to an otherwise austere setting and was much better tolerated. From a thematic standpoint, most of the windows were scenes of ranch life, so they fit the overall scheme better than lace would have anyway. I was quite content to design windows using horses, cows, and mountains, in addition to the occasional cowboy or Native American. The local wildflowers were also popular, and I was working on a desert flower scene at the time. The promised date had already passed, but I went for that ride anyway.

Apache hadn't been out for several days, and he was as anxious for a good run as I was, making a whip and spurs completely unnecessary. Knowing the craggy rocks at the top of the slope would slow him down without any help from me, I aimed him up the hill behind the house and let him fly. Upon reaching the summit, we turned and continued along the ridge at a much more sober pace. I thought about heading up to the fence line where the men were working to see how the job was progressing. Figuring it was as good a destination as any, I cantered off in that direction.

I slowed my horse to a walk now and then, taking the time to enjoy yet another perfectly beautiful early fall day. The leaves were beginning to turn and the sky was a crisp, clear blue. I could hear birds calling to one another, but aside from that, the silence was nearly complete—which was why I was able to hear someone yelling for help.

The closer I got, the more familiar the voice sounded.

Dusty.

From my position high up on the ridge, I would never have spotted the truck if I hadn't been able to hear him. The truck had plowed into a thicket at the foot of the hill and was almost completely obscured by branches. The fact that the truck was green didn't help matters, either.

As Apache and I slid down the steep slope to the thicket, I decided right then and there the next truck we bought was going to be red. After that, I was going to put homing beacons on my cowboys. This "accident" crap was starting to get old.

Grateful once again for having a horse that was trained to ground tie, I dismounted quickly and started pulling branches away from the driver's-side door. One of the larger limbs had gone partly through the open window, jamming the door shut. Dusty's blond curls were barely visible through the tangled foliage.

"Oh my God! Dusty, are you okay?"

"I guess I've been in tighter spots," he said with a weak chuckle. "But I can't remember when that might have been."

"Stop trying to be funny," I snapped. "Are you hurt?"

"Not really," he said. "Although I *am* sort of…stuck."

"Stuck? Why didn't you back the truck out of there? How the

hell did you end up in there, anyway?" I was just scared enough to be angry with him for getting into such a fix to begin with.

"I can't back it up because the front end is hung up on a tree stump or something." Wincing, he shifted his weight in the seat. "I sort of lost control of the truck."

"And why was that?" I pulled more branches out of the way, but I couldn't budge the one that had the door jammed.

"Well, you see, there was this rattlesnake, and I got kinda…nervous."

"Holy shit," I exclaimed. "Is it still in there with you?"

"Uh, yes, it is," he replied. "Which is another reason why I can't move."

"Where is it?" Just then, I heard it, rattling ominously from inside the truck cab. Apache heard it too. Although he backed off a few steps, thankfully he didn't go any farther.

"I've got it pinned under my cast," Dusty said. "I'm afraid if I move, it'll get my other leg. It's already struck at my boot five or six times. It's really pissed, if you know what I mean."

"Yes, I do," I replied. "Why didn't you just shoot the damn thing?" I knew for a fact that truck never went out without a rifle in the rack, and there was always a pistol in the glove compartment.

"Tried that. It's kinda hard to get a gun out of a rack when you're trying to keep your foot on a rattlesnake. I, um, dropped it down behind the seat. Can't reach the glove compartment, and even if I could, there's another branch jammed in through that window."

Peering past him, I saw that the passenger door was also wedged shut by the trunk of a large tree. I couldn't have gotten the door open to get the pistol, nor could I get to the rifle behind the seat with Dusty sitting in it. "Well, shit. I don't suppose you've got a chain saw handy, have you?"

"In the back of the truck," he replied. "The chain is really dull, though. I was bringing it back to the shed to sharpen it."

"If it works at all, it'll be better than nothing." I had to pull even more branches out of the truck bed to find it. The gas tank was full; however, I'd never been much good at starting anything with a two-stroke engine. As a result, I was panting and nearly spent before the engine finally roared to life.

The dull chain seemed to take forever to cut through a relatively small piece of wood, but at last I managed to cut through it and pulled it out of the way before cautiously opening the door.

My first reaction was to scream when I saw how big the snake was—one of the largest rattlers I'd ever seen up close—and I'd seen plenty over the years.

"Boy, Dusty, when you decide to get trapped with a snake, you really pick a monster, don't you?"

"Only the best will do," he replied with a halfhearted grin. "Do you think you could grab its tail and throw it if I raise my foot?"

"I doubt I could throw it far enough to keep it from biting me, or fast enough to keep it from biting you," I replied. "I don't think we can count on it to slither out of the truck without sinking those fangs into something if you let it loose. We're going to have to kill it to get you out of there."

"And just how do you propose we do that?" he asked. "Cut its head off with the chain saw?"

Considering how long it had taken me to cut through that tree limb, I had my doubts. "I suppose I could try—although I don't think I could do that without hurting you."

"I was kidding, Angela," he growled. "I've got a good hold on it for now, but it's hard to tell how long I can keep it up. It's pretty strong."

"I'll bet it is." From what I could see of it, the snake was huge. Its body was almost as thick as a motorcycle tire and it had a head bigger than a man's fist. "Let me check the back of the truck again. I might find something I can use. Hang on."

"I'll be right here," he said grimly.

I climbed back into the truck bed, hoping to find a hatchet or some other sharp object. Unfortunately, beyond a mattock, which I would have no room to swing, there wasn't much. Only an empty gas can, several metal fence posts, and a tangled roll of rusty wire.

"Hey, what about the fence posts?" Dusty asked. "Do you think you could pin the snake down with one of them long enough for me to get out?"

"I could try," I replied. "You'd have to move pretty fast, though. If that snake gets to twisting around, I don't know if I could hold it for long."

"I'll be the fastest man with a cast on his leg you ever saw," he assured me. "Now we just have to figure out the best way to do it."

I examined the fence posts with a somewhat skeptical eye. That snake was much thicker than the posts, and I wasn't sure I could exert enough force to keep it from wiggling out from under the end of one of them. A smaller snake would have been no problem, but this was one great-great-granddaddy of a rattler. However, no better ideas came to mind, so I pitched one of the posts off the truck and climbed down after it.

Aiming the blunt end of the post toward the floorboard, I worked it gingerly around Dusty's leg. Unfortunately, I couldn't pin the snake down because every time I moved, it struck and I missed. In addition to being quite heavy, the post was difficult to maneuver, and I was already pretty tired from fighting with the chain saw.

"It's no use, Dusty," I panted, looking up at his sweat-streaked face. "I don't think this is going to work. The post is too long for me to get the right angle."

"Well, dammit, what else can we do?"

"I could ride for help, but—" I paused as I gazed past him to the rear window and smiled. "I've got an idea." Climbing up on the running board, I reached past him to unfasten the window. I had to put my hand on his shoulder, and when I leaned over, his face was right up against my chest.

Dusty sighed, wrapping an arm around me for support. "I've always wanted to be in a position where your tits were in my face. Can't say this is how I'd envisioned it, though."

"Better enjoy it while you can, sweetheart, because I'll only be here for a second," I said as I fumbled with the latch. "Just don't bite me."

"Don't worry, I won't. But if I'm gonna die from a rattlesnake bite, I want my last moments on earth to be good ones."

I finally got the latch undone and slid the two sides of the window open, giggling as another thought occurred to me. "Guess I should have taken my shirt off first, huh?"

"That would have been a nice touch." He rubbed his face against my breasts like a cat seeking a caress. "Remind me to suggest that the next time I get trapped with a rattler."

"There'd better not *be* a next time."

I backed out of the door, pausing along the way to give Dusty a big, juicy kiss. "For luck," I said and climbed back into the truck bed. Choosing another post, I inserted it through the open window and aimed between Dusty's knees for the snake. However, as before, I couldn't pin it down. Every time I thought I had it, the scaly hide slid over its rounded backbones. I simply couldn't get a firm enough hold on it to give Dusty time to escape.

Finally, I felt something catch on the end of the post.

"Have you got it?"

"Maybe." I sort of had it pinned, but I wasn't sure I'd be able to hold it when he moved his foot.

"Maybe?" he exclaimed. "I want better than maybe, if you don't mind."

"Right now, maybe is the best I can do. The damn thing keeps striking at the post, and—shit. It got away again." Then I gasped as another thought occurred to me. "Hold on. I've got a better idea."

I pulled the post back out through the window and reversed it, aiming the pointed end at the snake. "Come on baby, bite me," I murmured. "Bite me. Hard."

"I thought you said *not* to bite you." Dusty sounded somewhat bewildered.

I was beginning to wonder if he hadn't hit his head when he wrecked the truck. Then again, in his predicament, I probably wouldn't have been very coherent myself.

"I wasn't talking to you, Dusty. I was talking to the snake." I teased its mouth with the end of the post. "Come on, baby, open wide. This won't hurt a bit." I held my breath as the snake struck, then rammed the spear-shaped end down its throat as hard as I could, pinning it to the floorboard. "Okay, Dusty!" I shouted. "Go!"

The rattler went wild as soon as Dusty moved his foot, and it took a considerable amount of force to hold it down, even with the degree of leverage I had on it. It twisted and writhed, flipping its rattle like a mace as Dusty wiggled out from under the post and fell out the door, landing smack-dab on his cute little keister.

"Get out of the way," I yelled. "I can't hold it much longer."

Dusty scrambled away from the truck and managed to get to his feet with the aid of a low-hanging tree limb. "Let me get the horse, and then you can let that thing loose." He limped over to where a very apprehensive Apache was standing and gathered up the reins. The fact that the gelding hadn't bolted long ago said a lot for his training. I guess we had Rufus to thank for that. The man was one hell of a horse trainer, even if he was kinda weird.

I released my hold on the post and the snake fell out, landing in about the same spot Dusty had. At first I was afraid it might decide to stay and fight, but apparently it'd had enough for one day. After one last hiss in parting, it slithered off into the thicket.

As I stood gaping at the spot where the snake had disappeared, the horror of the situation finally got to me, giving me a bad case of the shakes. Faint and nauseated, I collapsed on the truck cab, breathing hard.

Dusty led the reluctant horse over to the thicket and reached up a hand to help me down. "Come on, Angela. It's gone now. Let's go home. We can come back later for the truck. It's gonna take more than the two of us and a dull chain saw to get it out of there, anyway."

As he stood there, gazing up at me with those big, blue eyes, I burst into tears. "That's twice I've had to watch you almost get killed, Dusty. This has *got* to stop! I can't take any more."

"Hey now. I'm not dead. I'm not even hurt except for the seat of my pants." His voice was gentle as the breeze ruffled his curls. "It's a long way back to the house, so you need to get going. You can drive back up here and get me. I'll be fine."

I blew out a breath. "You're right. No need to get all mushy on you, is there?"

He shook his head. "Not unless you really want to."

Oh, I wanted to, all right. Unfortunately, I knew I shouldn't.

Story of my whole fucking life.

Lately, I'd been giving in to too many impulses that were causing trouble for everyone concerned. I had only myself to blame for most of it. Still, every now and then, I wanted to be able to do whatever I felt like doing without having to think it to death first. Especially in a situation such as this where my first impulse was to grab Dusty and kiss his lips off. Not like the playful kiss for luck I'd given him earlier to break the tension, and not so much because I loved him, but because I was so very, very glad he was alive and unhurt.

I didn't, of course. Dusty gave me a leg up on Apache, and I rode back to the house alone, trying to figure out how the hell a rattlesnake that size had ever managed to get into that truck.

Chapter 17

I MADE IT BACK to the barn without incident. After stabling Apache, I started back to the house just as Dad came across the yard. He was moving so slowly it hurt me to watch him.

"Been out ridin'?"

I nodded. "Dusty had an accident. I need to go back and get him."

"Again? What's he broke this time? His fool head? He wasn't riding with you, was he?"

"Of course not, Dad. He was in the truck. I just happened to find him." I hesitated for a long moment, wondering how much I should tell him. He was my father, and although I knew I could trust him, I also didn't want him going off the deep end and having a stroke or a heart attack. "He wasn't hurt, but the truck is stuck in a thicket. It's going to take some work to get it out of there."

"How the hell did *that* happen?" Even though his words were typical, he sounded so querulous and old—not at all like the man I'd known all my life. "That boy has been more trouble lately."

"Oh, don't you start that too." I knew I'd have to tell him everything or he'd be blaming Dusty for wrecking the truck, although it hadn't appeared to have sustained much damage. Still, what were a few dents on an old truck when compared with Dusty's life? "It wasn't his fault. There was a rattlesnake in the truck and he lost control."

"Ha," he said gruffly. "A likely story. He was probably drunk and hallucinating."

As exhausted as I was, the effort to keep from screaming in

frustration nearly sapped the last of my strength. "When have you ever seen Dusty drunk? Besides, if he was hallucinating, so was I because I saw it too—probably the biggest snake I've ever seen. It's a wonder Dusty wasn't killed."

"Hmm… He's had an awful lot of accidents lately and still managed to stay alive. Maybe God doesn't want him."

"I certainly hope not," I said. "Not yet, anyway." Maybe when he was old and gray and his mind was gone, but not right now.

Dad was silent for several seconds. I could almost see the wheels turning in his head. "Maybe it's you that wants him."

His continued scrutiny made me glance away. This was a conversation I wasn't ready for, nor was I in the mood. "Dad, please…"

"He's kinda young for you, isn't he?"

I took a deep breath and counted to three. "Probably. I'm afraid that doesn't concern me at the moment. I need to go back and get him before something else happens to him. Do you want to come with me?"

"Naw, I don't think so." Suddenly, he seemed even more feeble and tired than he'd been only minutes before. "I was coming to see if you wanted lunch. I cooked up a pot of chili. Guess you can have some when you come back." His gaze swept over me again and he smiled. "You be careful now, young lady."

"Don't worry, I will."

Choosing to overlook the "young lady" remark, I headed for my truck, thinking how odd it sounded following his observation that Dusty was too young for me.

Maybe I hadn't chosen to discuss age differences with him because he was right. Dusty was too young for me—or rather, I was too old for him, especially if he wanted any kids. Although having a tubal after my second baby had sure opened up my sex life with my husband, I doubted Dusty would want a woman whose equipment no longer met factory specs. At some point he would realize life with me would be just, well…life with me. Maybe I was putting too much emphasis on it—some men say they don't really care about having kids—nevertheless, that issue might turn out to be a major stumbling block between me and a relationship with any man, let alone the younger ones.

Not that it mattered. Even though Dusty claimed to love me, I couldn't let it go any further. It wasn't fair to him. The fling with Troy might be over—and I was okay with that—however, an affair with Dusty would be entirely different. I didn't think I could get that close to him without falling in love in the process.

I climbed into my truck and drove out across the cattle bars and on through the field to where Dusty waited for me. Grateful for dry weather and the lack of mud, I drove faster than I probably should have, half afraid what I'd jokingly said to Dad might be true, and that something else might have happened to Dusty before I could get back to him.

I needn't have worried. When I arrived, he was resting in the cab of the truck as though he hadn't a care in the world. Still, judging from the evidence that had begun to pile up, I couldn't quash the notion he might be living on borrowed time.

He smiled and waved when he saw me coming. Why would anyone want to hurt such a sweet, adorable guy?

"That was quick," he said as I climbed down from the truck. "While you were gone, I looked underneath here, and I think with a couple of jacks, we can lift the front end up enough to clear the stumps it's hung up on."

"Sounds good," I said. "You guys ought to be able to handle that. If not, we could get a wrecker out here without too much trouble."

"I don't think we'll need it. If nothing else, we can use the boom on the tractor. That might even work better than jacking it up."

"We'll cross that bridge when we get to it," I said. "Right now, all I want to do is go home and try to think about something else. I bet we *both* have nightmares."

"No kidding. One thing for sure, I'm gonna check under the seat of any vehicle I get into from now on."

"I don't blame you for that. Any idea how it got in there? Is there a hole in the floorboard?"

"I don't think so. The windows were open, though. Maybe it crawled in that way."

"I suppose it could have, but why on earth would a snake do such a thing?"

He shrugged. "I dunno. Weird shit happens all the time, and God knows there are plenty of rattlers around these parts."

"I've been thinking about it ever since I left you here, and I can't come up with any reasonable explanation for a snake to be in a truck other than having been put there deliberately."

"Maybe," Dusty said, frowning. "I don't know anyone with the balls to mess with a snake like that—and why would anyone want to, anyway?"

I was forgetting Dusty hadn't been there when Joe told me about his suspicions about the way his saddle might've been tampered with. More than anyone else, he was the one who needed to know. "You obviously haven't put things together quite the same way I have. I think someone is trying to do away with you. I'm just not sure who."

As I might have predicted, his response was somewhat skeptical. "Do away with me? Why would anyone want to do that? I'm no threat to anyone. I don't have any money to speak of, and if I have any enemies, I sure as hell don't know about them."

"I can think of two people who might not like you, although I'll admit, it sounds pretty ridiculous for them to go to that extreme. I didn't think about it myself until Joe told me he'd overheard Rufus saying he wanted to get rid of you."

"I'm sure he only meant he wanted to fire me," Dusty pointed out. "He wouldn't have to kill me."

I heaved a sigh. "True. What about Bull? You pick on him an awful lot. Do you think he's finally had enough?"

"Aw, Bull's nothing more than a bag of hot air," Dusty insisted. "He'd never hurt a fly, and you know it. You're letting your imagination run away with you."

"I hope you're right," I said with a shudder. "But if you've got a better explanation as to how a relatively new billet on your saddle could suddenly give way and a big, honking rattler would take a notion to go for a ride with you, you be sure to let me know. I'm fresh out of ideas."

"Bad luck?" he suggested.

"Oh, come on, Dusty. No one's luck is *that* bad."

"Maybe not, but I still don't believe any of the guys here would try to bump me off. Even though we may not always see eye to eye, for the most part, we get along pretty well."

He was right about that, too. Except for the occasional needling he gave Bull, all the guys seemed happy to be working for us. I'd never heard any complaints from any of them, even about Rufus. Sure, he could be pretty tough, but I'd never known him to be unfair.

"Okay," I said. "Just remember I'm not the only one with suspicions. If Joe has doubts… I dunno. You might want to watch your back. Rufus is Joe's prime suspect, and he thinks it's because of me."

Dusty didn't take any time at all to come up with the same idea Joe and I had. "Do you think he wants you or the ranch?"

"It's hard to say," I replied. "If anyone were to ask me, I'd have said Rufus thinks I'm nothing more than a silly little woman. He's never given me any reason to believe he feels otherwise. I suppose he might be willing to put up with me if it meant getting his hands on the ranch, but I don't believe that, either. None of this makes any sense."

"Which leads me to believe it's all a bunch of bull," he said. "Rufus isn't a greedy man, Angela. This isn't like him."

He was right about that. It was *completely* out of character for

Rufus to do any of the things I suspected. Too bad I couldn't shake the notion that at least part of it was true.

"Okay, but if you have one more accident, I'm going to send you away for your own protection. I can't have another man getting killed on this ranch, Dusty. Especially you."

I paused, biting my lip as I realized how that sounded. I'd already gone over all the reasons why romance with Dusty was a bad idea. Now here I was making him think he meant more to me than the others.

Time for some damage control.

"Oh hell, I wouldn't want anything to happen to any of you guys. Maybe I'm too paranoid for my own good. You be careful, Dusty. I mean it."

"I will," he promised. "By the way, don't you mean 'especially not Troy'?"

Despite the light, teasing note in his voice, the expectant gleam in his eyes proved he'd caught my slip of the tongue—and cared enough to want to clarify its meaning. Perhaps I was wrong to dismiss the possibility of a closer relationship with him. He might be younger than me, but he wasn't a kid. He was a grown man who undoubtedly knew what he wanted.

Must be nice…

I made a face at him. "No, Dusty, I meant exactly what I said. Come on, let's get out of here."

As we climbed into the truck, I was glad I hadn't retracted that statement because I *did* care more for Dusty than I did for Troy. Whether I loved him or not had nothing to do with it. Granted, Troy was a ton of fun, but I'd only known him a week. Dusty had been part of my life for years. I cared very deeply for him, and though our relationship wasn't intimate, I loved him every bit as much as I would have loved my brother if I'd had one.

Well, no…maybe not *quite* like a brother. There was more to my feelings for him than *that*…

I was rapidly running out of reasons *not* to love him, and lately I seemed to be spending more time with him than anyone else, including the man who was supposed to be my secret lover. Then there was that other factor to be considered, the one that had nagged at me all night long.

He'd told me he loved me.

And that was a pretty hard thing to ignore.

We drove back to the house in relative silence. As quiet as he was, I thought perhaps Dusty was beginning to realize he might actually be in danger. Either that or he was simply exhausted. As stressful as my day had been, I could've done with a nap myself—and I hadn't been the one involved in an accident with a rattlesnake.

I let Dusty out at the barn and drove on up to the main house. I felt better after eating a bowl of my dad's awesome chili, so I took some of it down to Dusty, thinking it might help him feel better too. I figured I ought to check on Goldie while I was at it, after which I was determined to take that nap. Knowing my mare's foaling habits like I did, it was a safe bet I wasn't going to get any more sleep that night than I had the last.

I checked the mess hall first, thinking Dusty might have gone in to grab a bite. He wasn't there. Leaving the bowl on the table, I went off in search of him, only to find him sound asleep on his bed. Tiptoeing so as not to wake him, I went back to the mess hall to retrieve his lunch—although by the time he got around to eating it, it would probably qualify as dinner—and set it on the nightstand beside him. As I turned to go, I was overcome by the desire to simply sit down and watch him while he slept.

Knowing I might never have the opportunity again, I took a seat in the easy chair beside his bunk. I sat there, gazing at him, recalling the times I'd watched my children sleep, their deep slumber relaxing their features just as Dusty's were now. What would I do if anything bad happened to him? I'd practically gone into shock when Cody died, and I never wanted to feel that way again as long as I lived.

I would, of course—unless everyone I cared about somehow managed to outlive me, which, given my father's current state, was highly unlikely. I'd heard it said that no one should ever outlive their children, and I believed that to be true with all my heart. But what about outliving a spouse? Any married person stood a fifty-fifty chance of suffering a tremendous loss. Marrying a younger man might prevent me from having to endure that pain and anguish again. Although I knew it was selfish of me, at least I was being honest with myself.

The fact that Cody had been killed instantly had been my only consolation in the aftermath of his death. He hadn't suffered. I was grateful to have been spared from watching him die a painful, lingering death—from my own perspective, as well as his. If he'd died at a ripe old age, I might have been better prepared for the end when it came—not that it would've been any less painful.

Selfish or not, I still wished he hadn't died at all, and that he had lived long enough to see me go before him. Sure, I survived, and I was doing much better now. However, there had been a time when I didn't think I would get through it. Everything reminded me of him. Every silence that would have been filled with the sound of his voice. Every moment of laughter we would have shared. Every lonely feeling that wouldn't have existed had he lived.

Joe was right in saying it was a miracle I hadn't come out to the bunkhouse seeking solace long before this. The trouble was, until he'd broken his leg, Dusty wouldn't have been there. He would've been out working with the other men, and I would have visited the bunkhouse only to find even more emptiness.

But Dusty was here now. Did he know how precious he looked lying there asleep? Did he have the slightest idea I felt the way I did? Probably not. I'd never said anything to him, and I'd tried very hard not to let my feelings show. Obviously, I hadn't done a very good job if Rufus suspected me of carrying a torch for Dusty, although sometimes longing gazes are more easily seen by a detached observer.

Dusty's smiles… How I'd cherished the few that were openly aimed in my direction. Did he know that? Did he know how often I sought him with my gaze? How long it had lingered? Perhaps Troy had been right in suspecting that I *did* have someone already. I hadn't realized it at the time, and I seriously doubted I would have had the nerve to do anything about it even if I had. I wouldn't have thought I would stand a chance with Dusty.

Unfortunately, if what he'd said was true, he didn't think he stood a chance with me, either. I still found that difficult to believe, even knowing he'd been warned off by Rufus enough to convince him his feelings were pointless. He'd told me things I never dreamed I would ever hear him say, and I'd had to put him off because of Troy.

Troy, whom I'd picked up from the side of the road like a stray dog. Troy, who might stay on after Dusty recovered or he might not. Troy, about whom I knew virtually nothing, nothing beyond where he was from or the date of his birth. I might've been imagining things during his last nocturnal visit. Nevertheless, I was pretty sure he was done with me.

None of that mattered now. Deep down, I'd already made my choice. And he lay sleeping, right there in front of me.

Chapter 18

EXHAUSTION OVERCAME ME AT last, and I drifted off to sleep. A deep, contented slumber from which I awoke to discover Dusty lying on his bunk in silence, regarding me with thoughtful eyes.

My smile was rather sheepish, for I knew I shouldn't have been there. "I brought you some lunch, but you were already asleep."

He smiled at me in a most peculiar manner, prompting me to ask if I'd been snoring.

"No," he replied, still with that same enigmatic smile. "You weren't making a sound." He paused for a moment, visibly steeling himself as if about to say something very difficult to express. "You know when you said something earlier about not needing to get all mushy? I really wish you would have. You saved my life, Angela. You know that, don't you?"

"Yes," I replied. "I suppose I did."

"In some cultures, I would belong to you now."

With no idea how to respond, I waited anxiously for what he would say next.

"I wouldn't mind that," he went on. "Not one little bit."

I glanced away, unwilling—or unable—to meet his gaze any longer. Had he somehow read my thoughts while he lay there dreaming?

"What would you have done if I hadn't sent you home after you got rid of that snake? Should I have done that, or not?"

"That depends on what you wanted me to do." I spoke with caution, unsure as to where this was leading or how far it would go. "I'm guessing I might've gotten pretty mushy."

"I said you could if you wanted to," he reminded me.

I took a deep, fortifying breath before coming to what I considered to be the catch. "But you didn't say *you* wanted it, did you?"

"No," he admitted. "I should have, though. I was being noble or some stupid shit like that. Troy seems like the jealous type. When I kissed you that day, I didn't know you were seeing each other."

"And I couldn't tell you. I'm sorry about that. I didn't want to hurt your feelings, but I didn't see how I could possibly explain it without mentioning Troy, and he was…a secret."

He nodded. "But I know now, so I thought you should probably go on home without, well…you know." Toying with the edge of the quilt, he studied it for a moment before glancing up at me. "That was pretty stupid of me, wasn't it?"

"Possibly," I admitted. "No one would have ever known. Not even Troy."

His voice dropped to a whisper. "Come here, Angie. Get mushy on me now. Please. I *belong* to you. You can do anything you want with me."

"Anything?"

"Anything." Heaving a sigh, he held out a beckoning hand. "Just so long as it's not *nothing*."

I was in his arms in a heartbeat, kissing him like I'd never kissed anyone before. Raining hungry, passionate, loving kisses all over his face, letting them spill down his neck like hot wax. Then I went back to his lips and melted all over again. Twining my arms around his shoulders, I squeezed him as hard as I could. He was mine, and I wanted him so desperately…

"Oh, Angie," he murmured. "Love me, use me—abuse me if you like—but please don't stop. I'll just up and die if you stop."

Unbuttoning his shirt, my kisses moved lower until my chin touched his belt buckle.

He groaned, sounding as though the air had been ripped from his lungs. "Oh God, Angie. Please don't stop there."

Unbuckling his belt, I unzipped his jeans and dragged them down over his hips along with his briefs. His cock snapped up to meet me, and I kissed him shamelessly up and down his engorged shaft.

"It's yours," he gasped. "Take it."

Needing no further encouragement, I went down on him with gusto. I glanced up as Dusty sucked in a breath, the air hissing through his teeth. Blond curls framed his handsome face, and his eyelids had drifted to half-mast. Having drawn in that breath, his mouth now hung open—although whether in ecstasy or surprise, I couldn't have said.

His cock was hot and hard in my mouth, and his slippery essence coated my tongue. I sucked more syrup from his slit, delighting in his moans and sighs as I smoothed it over his skin. My own moisture began to pool at the apex of my thighs, doing nothing to soothe the searing ache growing inside me. Only Dusty could ease that pain. I toed off my boots, yanked off my jeans, and straddled his hips.

Slowly impaling myself with his hot cock, I closed my eyes, savoring the size and heat of him. Every direction I moved brought with it new and exciting sensations. Pleasing, yet stimulating…

Wonderful.

Oh yes. This was what I'd been missing—not Troy, not Cody, but Dusty…my darling Dusty. He was the one. I knew it now, though I was at a loss to explain *how* I knew it. Perhaps it was the way he cradled my hips with his strong hands, or the way he managed to thrust against me quite effectively despite the cast on his leg. I had no idea why, and yet something was different. Something perfectly, magically, undeniably *right*.

My orgasm began the inexorable buildup to detonation, and I squeezed him deep within me, my tight inner muscles provoking his own gasping response as I groaned in mind-shattering ecstasy.

Oh my God, yes…

My mind shouted the words, telling me in no uncertain terms

that this was what I'd been waiting for all my life. Seconds later, Dusty came so hard he nearly bucked me off. I held on, riding his climax, forcing my hips down harder while relishing each and every power-packed jolt he fired into me.

As I looked down at him, taking in his dazed expression, his eyes, his hair, his face—his adorable, lovable face—something seemed to snap into place with a nearly audible click.

Troy had been right. I *didn't* need him. I already had someone to love—perhaps as much, if not more so, than I had loved Cody—and it wasn't my boy toy. It was this man. This man whose life I'd saved, whose smile filled me with delight, whose lips made me sure I would stop breathing if I never tasted them again. I'd been in love with him for ages. I simply hadn't realized it until that moment.

"Do you have any idea how much I love you?" His whispered words duplicated my thoughts exactly. "Any idea at all?"

"No." I might have thought I knew, but I wanted to hear it from him. "Tell me."

His smile was wistful. "I knew you and Cody were very happy. I knew I'd never get the chance to show you how I felt, but I stayed on anyway. All I needed was to see you once in a while, perhaps even exchange a few words with you. I thought I could live with that, but on those days when I didn't get to see you I felt wasted and empty.

"When Cody died, it was even worse. You were free, but with things the way they were, I still couldn't have you. I should've quit this job years ago. Trouble was, every time I thought I could do it, you'd smile at me and I'd forget all about leaving. I never went looking for another woman because I loved you too much for anyone else to keep my interest for more than five minutes." Tears shimmered in his eyes, threatening to run from the corners of his eyes if he so much as blinked. "Do you have any idea what it's like to love someone that much and not be able to have them? Do you?"

Gazing at him through my own tears, I nodded.

"Cody," he said flatly. "You still feel that way about him, don't you?"

I shook my head. "Not anymore." I leaned down and kissed him gently. "Not anymore and not ever again. I have you to love now. You're the one I want. I won't ever need anyone else as long as I have you."

He didn't seem convinced. "What about Troy?"

"Troy was a lot of fun, but I don't love him. Hell, I barely even know him."

"And Joe?" Dusty pulled me down beside him on the bunk. The arrangement was crowded, but cozy.

"You're really leaving no stone unturned here, aren't you?" I chided. "No, I don't love Joe—although I probably could love either of them if I put my mind to it. On the other hand, loving you doesn't take any effort at all. That happened all by itself. I don't know when, exactly, but it did happen."

Dusty seemed relieved, letting out a sigh as he hugged me. "I remember *exactly* when it happened to me. You were out in the barn with that big, black gelding you used to have—you know, the one that would bite any of us who walked by? Anyway, you were brushing his shoulder and he curled his head around and lipped you on the seat of your pants. I was afraid he was biting you until I saw it was more of a kiss than a bite. All you did was pat him on the nose. Later on, you gave him a kiss and a hug, and I thought: Now *there's* a woman so completely lovable even a mean old horse can't resist her. What hope did I have?"

Tears stung my eyes as I recalled those times. Galloping across the range on a horse I trusted with my life. I'd had other horses, none of them quite like that one. "Good ol' Victor. I still miss him. He was the absolute best. It about broke my heart when he died."

"I would have given a lot to have been in Cody's place, even then. To be the one to console you, to put my arms around you. You never knew that, did you?"

"No," I replied. "Although at the time, I probably would've welcomed a hug from any of you guys. My God, I was miserable! I've had lots of horses in my life, but I *loved* that one. The vet had done all he could, and for a while there, I thought he was going to be okay. But then he went down again, and I knew it was over. I sat up with him all night, and anytime I left him, even for a minute, he'd nicker at me when I came back, right up until the moment he died. I probably should've had the vet put him down, but I didn't have it in me. I didn't want to let him go."

I hadn't thought about Victor in a long time. Like every other loss, the memory still hurt. Losing Cody was a million times worse, but Dusty and I had shared those losses. We had a history together. It made a difference.

"I don't want to let *you* go, either," Dusty said after several minutes of quiet reflection. "But you might want to put your jeans on. The guys will be back any time now."

Romantic interlude over, back to reality.

"Yeah, well, if you don't want Bull ragging on you for lying around sleeping all day, you might consider getting up yourself." Getting reluctantly to my feet, I fished around in my jeans for my panties and put them back on.

"I don't know if I can. Some wild woman just had her wicked way with me." He might've sounded innocent, but the glint in his eyes was impossible to miss. "I may never walk again." His jeans were still at half-mast and his shirt lay open, revealing the golden hair on his chest. A nest of blond curls surrounded his cock, which rested on his thigh. I stood there, staring at him, knowing I'd have to go a long way and see a lot of stuff before ever laying eyes on anything more appealing. Steeling myself against the desire to lick him clean, I tossed him a box of tissues before snatching my boots and jeans from the floor.

Dressing as quickly as I could, I shot him a scowl. "You'd better get up. If you lie around long enough, someone might put a rattle-snake in your bed."

"You still think that was deliberate, don't you?"

I stopped dead with one leg in my pants, watching in awe as Dusty dried himself off before wiggling back into his jeans. That simple act might not have the same effect on every woman, but I, for one, couldn't move a muscle—or even breathe—much less answer him until he was finished.

Apparently, he mistook the reason for my silence. "You do, don't you? I don't believe it myself. There's absolutely no reason for anyone to want to kill me—although Troy might have a decent motive."

"Troy?" I'm sure I looked every bit as perplexed as I felt. "Why on earth would he—"

The "well, duh" expression on Dusty's face answered my question.

"Oh yeah. Right. I see your point." I sat down heavily in Dusty's chair. "I'm gonna sound real stupid telling him I'm in love with you when I've been denying it left and right ever since he got here."

Dusty's grin was decidedly smug. "I guess that cute ass won't get him everything, huh?"

I wrinkled my nose at him. "At least his dick wasn't bigger than yours. Otherwise I never would've given him up for you."

He gasped in mock dismay. "Is that all I am to you? A big enough dick?" His lower lip stuck out in an exaggerated pout.

Among other things.

Even pouting, he was still adorable. "Oh no, you're much more than that. As I recall, your ass was pretty nice too—and you *did* win the cutest balls contest."

He chuckled. "What would you call a guy who had my balls, Troy's ass, and Joe's dick?"

"Honey," I replied, reaching for my boots. "Sweetheart, baby doll, darling—"

"Enough of that," he grumbled. "I get the picture. So, what would you call me? You know…the one with cute balls, decent dick, nice ass, and a broken leg?"

I pulled on one boot and then the other, making him wait until I was finished before giving him my answer.

"Mine," I replied, grinning like the proverbial cat that got the cream. "All mine."

Chapter 19

ALL I HAD TO do now was figure out what to tell Troy.

My supposition that he wouldn't be back might simply have been a figment of my imagination. He certainly hadn't said anything, and I considered it extremely rude to put him to the trouble of sneaking into my room in the middle of the night only to be told he'd been replaced.

Tacky, inconsiderate, if not downright mean.

He'd had his suspicions, of course—suspicions I'd done my damnedest to allay. I hated to admit to telling such blatant lies; although at the time, I hadn't realized I wasn't telling the truth. I was actually more mistaken than anything.

Still, Troy wasn't the sort to stay down for long. Case in point, the ease with which I'd resurrected him in the wake of his adventures on the way to Jackson Hole. I had replaced his previous girlfriend with no trouble at all. The trick now would be to find someone to replace *me*. The fact that I was the only woman around for miles made the night out with the guys more important than ever—although the evening probably wouldn't proceed according to my original plan.

I gave Dusty a kiss and left the bunkhouse before anyone else came in for the night. I would've liked to have heard him telling the others about the rattlesnake incident, but I didn't want the conversation hindered by my presence. No doubt Dusty would tell me what was said later on. I only hoped I'd planted enough suspicion in his own mind for him to pay close attention to their reactions.

Dad was napping when I got back to the house. After putting a chicken in the oven, I worked on the bookkeeping until my vision started to blur from staring at spreadsheets. I went back to the kitchen to finish the dinner preparations at around five thirty, and Dad shuffled in about the time it was ready.

I was pleased to note he didn't seem quite as tired as he had earlier. "Have a nice nap?"

"Sure did," he replied. "Did you and the boy get that truck out of the thicket?"

"Didn't even try." I wasn't about to touch the "boy" part of that question—simply wasn't in the mood. Besides, I was fairly certain he'd only said it to harp on his belief that Dusty was too young for me. "It was caught on some stumps. Might have to use the tractor to get it out. I'm sure Dusty will tell the others about it. They can get it tomorrow."

"Shouldn't have to take time out of the fencing work for that." He shook his head. "Still don't buy that rattlesnake story."

I had to count to three before I could make even a remotely civil response. I set a bowl of mashed potatoes on the table next to the platter of baked chicken. "It isn't a story, Dad. It's the truth. Trust me, there was a snake. And the world won't end if the fencing project gets delayed another day."

"Never had troubles like this when Cody was in charge," he muttered as he took a seat. "Things around here have gone straight to hell."

Dad never had liked the idea of me running the ranch, but this slam was even more pointed than usual.

Wait for it...

"You should act your age and quit mooning over those young boys," he declared. "I still say Rufus is the best man for you. He wouldn't run off with some young girl the minute your back was turned."

And he would be a much better boss than you are.

He didn't say that, of course, but I knew he was thinking it. This time, I took a deep, cleansing breath before I answered him. "Dad, tell me again why it's okay for me to marry Rufus, who is nearly twenty years older than I am, but it's not okay for me to marry a younger man." I carefully avoided using Dusty's name, although it probably didn't matter. I'm sure he knew precisely who I was referring to.

"Because it's not natural," he insisted. "That's just not the way it works."

I dumped the green beans into a bowl and set them on the table. "Okay, men usually want younger women, I'll give you that much. But why is it so unnatural for an older woman to be with a younger man?"

"A younger man would want to father children, and you couldn't have them."

Dad might've hit my main concern right on the head, but he'd missed the flip side of the argument.

I sat down and scooted my chair up to the table. "What makes you think an *older* man wouldn't want children? As far as I know, Rufus has never had any kids. He'd probably be tickled to death to have a twentysomething wife and a baby. Geez, Dad. To hear you tell it, I'm not much good for anything. Maybe I should just wander out into the desert and die like an old squaw."

"I didn't mean that and you know it," he grumbled. "Besides, who would take care of your dear old dad if you were gone?"

Apparently, taking care of Dad was my only excuse for not walking off to die in the desert. What in the world would I be good for after *he* died?

"I'm sure Rufus would look after you." I knew I was being catty, even though that was more than likely the truth. Rufus would have been happy to be Dad's caretaker, and he probably would've done a far better job of it than I ever had—mainly because Dad respected Rufus's opinions. "Good ol' Rufus. He seems to be the answer to everything."

"He's a fine man," Dad said firmly. "Better than most, and certainly better than any of those young good-for-nothing cowboys we've got working for us."

My jaw dropped in astonishment. "Good-for-nothing? They're all honest, reliable men, and they work very hard for us. Why on earth would you say a thing like that?"

He placed a placating hand over mine and patted it. "You're right. They're all good workers. They just aren't good enough for you."

We were talking in circles. I wasn't good enough to run the ranch, and none of the men were good enough for me. Except Rufus.

What a choice.

Then again, maybe we *weren't* talking in circles. Dad's answer to everything really was Rufus. To him, Dusty was only a hired hand. I would never convince him Dusty was the right man for me—or the ranch. Rufus had been the foreman forever. He was accustomed to being in charge of the men, and Dad had always trusted him to make sound decisions. Now that I'd heard about guys being fired or beaten up because of me, I couldn't help wondering if Dad had known about any of it. Somehow, this didn't strike me as the right time to ask.

Truth be told, I still wasn't sure I was the right woman for Dusty. But regardless of who I wound up with, there was no need for anyone else to make up my mind for me. Not at this point in my life.

I let the matter drop until we were nearly finished eating. Dad never was one to talk much once he'd tucked in to his dinner anyway, and it gave me the chance to let my temper cool before reopening a rather touchy subject.

"Dad, I understand how you feel about the men in my life," I began, doing my best to keep smiling. "Fathers never think anyone is good enough for their daughters. But remember, *I'm* the one who'll have to live with whichever man I choose, not you. Besides, I made a pretty good choice the first time, didn't I?"

"Yes, you did," he admitted, albeit a bit grudgingly. "Although I had my doubts about him in the beginning."

"It's okay to have doubts. Just as long as you don't condemn that person outright." I paused, taking a breath that nearly burst my lungs. "And you're right about one thing. I do have a very strong liking for Dusty. And he…well…he likes me too."

He shook his head. "I still say Rufus would be better."

"But I don't *love* Rufus. He's probably the most unromantic man I've ever met. Granted, he's attractive, but he's about as much fun as a root canal."

"Fun isn't the only consideration," Dad said. "There's respect and companionship and—"

I nearly choked on the sip of tea I'd just taken. "Respect? Rufus has no respect for me whatsoever, and he makes no effort to hide his disgust whenever I giggle—to him it's like fingernails on a chalk-board. I wouldn't be married to him for six months before he made all the laughter in me die, just as surely as the sun rises in the east and sets in the west. Rufus would stifle me in ways you couldn't begin to imagine."

Oddly enough, he didn't dispute that point. Perhaps he thought I needed stifling. "And Dusty? What would he do for you?"

"He would love me, Dad. *Love* me. Do you have any idea how important that is? Rufus would *never* love me. He seems almost incapable of it."

"Maybe not, but that Dusty would break your heart," he warned.

"And Rufus would make me feel like I didn't have one," I countered. "I'd much rather take a chance on Dusty. Rufus would destroy what love I have left in me, and I don't want that. Not now, not ever." Pushing away from the table, I got to my feet. "Now, if you'll excuse me, I need to get things straightened up here so I can go check on Goldie. I'd bet money she foals tonight, and I intend to be there for the event."

I gathered up the dishes and carried them to the sink, rinsing them off before putting them in the dishwasher with a bit more vigor than the task required.

No, I wouldn't be able to stand a week of being married to Rufus, especially in light of my suspicions. He might marry me and then decide he needed to get rid of me too. Not that there was any chance of that happening. I couldn't imagine any set of circumstances that would induce me to marry him.

What troubled me the most was what might happen to Dusty. If my deductions were correct, there had already been two attempts on his life. That second attempt probably would've killed him if I hadn't run across him when I did. The thought of finding him dead from a rattlesnake bite made my blood run cold. I wasn't about to sit around waiting to see if the third time was the charm. I wanted to stash him in a hotel somewhere so Rufus, or whoever was out to get him, would never find him.

"Now, Angela, all I want is for you to have someone to help you run the ranch when I'm gone. Cody would have done a fine job of it, but with him gone, Rufus would be my first choice. He knows how to manage things and would be a big help to you."

Clearly, he'd missed the part about love being the most import-ant factor. "I believe I'd rather run things on my own." I nearly had to bite my tongue to keep from blurting out my suspicions. But that's just what they were. Suspicions. I had no proof whatsoever. "He's a good foreman, I'll grant you that, but I'd hate to be the one to promote him into a position of incompetence by making him a partner." Not that I would keep him on once I was the sole owner of the ranch—at least, not unless someone else turned out to be the culprit.

"What makes you think he'd be incompetent at owning a ranch?"

"I don't know, Dad," I said with a weary sigh. "Just a gut feeling. Besides, if I married Rufus, who would be foreman?"

"Calvin, I guess," he replied. "He's been here the longest."

"Going strictly by seniority, huh?" I gave this a moment of consideration. "Calvin's never been in charge of anything but the kitchen. I don't know if he'd be up to the foreman's job or not."

As I went back to work on the dishes, another thought occurred to me. "How come you don't think I should marry Calvin? He's older, reliable, and all that. Why not him? Oh no, let *me* answer that," I said, not giving him a chance to reply. "He's never had any kids, so he'd want a young, fertile woman."

"Don't get smart with me, young lady," he said, his smile belying his scolding tone. "Actually, Calvin did have a wife and kids at one time, but you know how it is with cowboys."

"Oh yeah." I sang the last line of the chorus to "Mamas, Don't Let Your Babies Grow Up to Be Cowboys."

"Damn, I love that song," he said with a wistful sigh. "It says it all."

"If you believe that sort of thing," I said. "Although I guess I did too, or my sons would've grown up to be cowboys."

"Too bad about that," he said. "We wouldn't be having this problem if they'd liked ranching."

"You never know. One of them might change his mind someday, and then we won't have to worry about it anymore."

"You mean *you* won't have to worry about it anymore," he corrected. "I don't think I'll make it until then."

"You just might." I did my best to appear more cheerful and confident than I actually felt. His rapid deterioration had me worried. "After all, stranger things have happened."

"Not *that* strange, and not lately."

That's what you think. I know of some pretty strange goings on…

"I'm going to bed," he announced. "Good luck with the mare."

"Good night," I said. "Sleep well."

With a nod, he pushed himself slowly up from his chair. I turned back to the sink, not wanting to witness the evidence of his growing infirmity. It was much too painful to watch. Before long, he would need a walker to get around. I didn't think I would like that.

But then, neither would he.

Chapter 20

By the time I got to the barn at about eight thirty, the sky was already fully dark, and as I'd expected, Goldie was pacing in her stall. Despite her restlessness, she joined the other horses in nickering at me when I arrived. When I slipped into her stall for a quick check, I discovered that while her water hadn't broken yet, the muscles in her hindquarters and around her tail were so relaxed the foal would probably fall out with one push. Tonight was definitely the night. I plugged my baby monitor into the outlet by her door, flipped off the lights, and went to the tack room to wait.

I kept one of the beds from the bunkhouse in there for just such occasions, and I'd checked it earlier that day to make sure there weren't any mice nesting in it. My intention was to leave the lights off and lie down, hoping Goldie wouldn't realize I was there and be disturbed by my presence. No doubt a carryover from their days as prey animals, horses can delay labor for a good while if they're nervous. Having a baby when wolves were prowling around wasn't a good idea for any species, nor did mares like having any humans in attendance.

Tiptoeing into the tack room, I closed the door quietly and switched on the portable receiver. I listened for a moment, then after satisfying myself I could still hear her moving about in the stall, I went to lie down on the bed.

Unfortunately, someone was there ahead of me. I knew that because I sat on him.

With a squeal worthy of finding another granddaddy rattler, I sprang up and stumbled toward the door, fumbling for the light switch.

"Hold on," he whispered. "I've got a lantern."

With the scrape of a match and a flare of the flame, the wick began to glow. I waited until the light was sufficient to confirm my suspicion that it was Dusty lying there in the bed before I said another word. As touchy as things were around the ranch these days, it didn't pay to jump to conclusions. I certainly didn't want to make the mistake of snuggling up with Bull or Rufus thinking it might be Dusty—or even Troy.

Talk about your embarrassing situations...

I hadn't had a chance to talk to Troy as yet, and even if he *had* been waiting for me in that bed, I would've had a tough time telling him we were through. He hadn't done a damn thing to deserve being dumped, and to be honest, I felt kinda guilty about that, especially after all the fun we'd had together. I couldn't very well give him one last fuck for the road, but if he'd been the one waiting for me, I could've at least gotten the confession over with. Singling him out for a private chat would be awkward at best. Needless to say, I wasn't looking forward to it.

Fortunately, Dusty wasn't privy to any of those thoughts.

"There now." After setting the lantern on a nightstand he'd created by upending an old tack trunk, he rolled onto his back. "Isn't this romantic?"

He had certainly been busy. A bouquet of late-season wildflowers arranged in an empty Corona bottle sat next to the lantern, and he'd put clean sheets on the bed along with several extra pillows. Not exactly the Ritz, but for an impromptu tryst, he hadn't done too badly.

His broken leg was propped up on a pillow with a sheet draped over it. With the possible exception of a splash of cologne, that cast was all he had on.

I stood there, spellbound, as his cock pulsed, emitting a glistening trickle of syrup, thereby putting the icing on the cake of my wildest dreams. He might have been the September centerfold for *Erotic Orthopedic Monthly*—if such a publication existed. The only thing missing was the staple in his navel.

"Yes, it is," I replied after a quick clearing of my throat. "Very romantic." I probably should've left it at that, and I would have if my practical nature hadn't gotten the better of me. "But you know most people keep their clothes on while they're waiting for a mare to foal."

"True," he admitted. "Actually, I was hoping you'd get here sooner so we'd have more time. Guess we'll just have to make the best of it." He paused as a sly smile lifted the corner of his mouth. "Of course, if we make lots of noise, Goldie will know we're here and it'll take her longer."

I knew I needed to keep my voice down, but I couldn't help giggling. "Yes, but I've been waiting a whole year for this foal. Are you telling me you're gonna make me wait even longer?"

He shot me a wink. "It'll be worth the wait. I guarantee it." Grasping his cock in one hand, he traced a fingertip over the swollen head. "Why don't you sit down and take it easy for a while? You've had a busy day."

"So have you," I reminded him. "Shouldn't you be sacked out in your bunk for the night?"

"Later," he replied. "I took a nap this afternoon, remember?"

"Yes, I remember. You look absolutely adorable when you're asleep." And even better when he was awake…

"So do you. I'd like to see you asleep in your own bed sometime—after I've made love with you and you're all curled up and naked under a blanket, sighing and smiling in your sleep."

Actually, I thought I'd like very much to see *him* that way. Perhaps we could take turns…

"Why don't you get undressed and come to bed? Goldie's had

plenty of experience delivering foals. Even if we miss it, I'm sure she'll be fine."

"I know. But it's fun to be there when it happens."

"It's fun to be here too," he pointed out. "Or it would be if you'd do what I asked you to. Come on, Angela, my sweet guardian angel. I'm yours, remember? Come play with me. I've been saving my love for you for such a long time. It'll take years and years for me to give it all to you, and I don't want to waste a moment."

Dusty had always had a quick tongue and a ready wit, but I'd never known he could be quite so persuasive. Before I knew it, I'd peeled off my clothes to stand naked before him, watching as his eyes savored my body, caressing my tingling skin from six feet away.

His cock pulsed again and another gush of fluid followed the first, making me long to sip the sweetness from him.

"I've never seen anything so beautiful in all my life," he whispered. "My angel, my lovely angel, my adorable Angela. I love you so much, so very much."

The hopeless romantic in me responded instantly, although I couldn't imagine any woman, hopeless romantic or not, resisting Dusty at that point. A whole stable full of newborn foals couldn't have lured me away from him.

Goldie and her baby were momentarily forgotten as I went to him, melting into his arms and seeking his lips for a long, deep kiss. He tasted sweet. Not minty or tingly like toothpaste, but soft and warm like honey or butterscotch. His kiss went far beyond mere excitement. It intoxicated me, driving out all resistance and rational thought, leaving me helplessly entwined in his embrace, vulnerable to his every whim.

His strong hands caressed me much as his eyes had done, leaving a glow of warmth in their wake, making me feel as though my body, my skin, my whole *self* was the most precious thing he'd ever held in his hands. I felt dazed and drunk with sensations as he sought out the highly sensitized areas clamoring for his attention. His lips drifted from mine to venture ever lower, ever closer to where his face had been that afternoon. I wondered what it would have been like to have climbed topless into the cab of that truck, without a rattlesnake there to complicate things, and let Dusty bury his face between my breasts, feeling his warm breath on my damp nipples as he licked them.

Seconds later, I discovered what I had missed as the soft stubble of his beard brushed my delicate skin, teasing my nipples to aching arousal before he took them, first one and then the other, into his mouth. Both of us moaned as he languorously teased the rigid peaks with his tongue. Once again, I felt that while my enjoyment may have been his sole object, his own pleasure seemed to be far greater than mine.

Hungry to experience that same sensation for myself, I kissed his curls, seeking out his body with my palms. Pressing hard against his skin, I longed to take him inside me, somehow absorbing his essence from where my hands made contact. I roamed his entire body, pushing him away from me in an effort to expose his most sensitive parts as I sought to show him how much I wanted him to be a part of me, to complete me. Cupping his penis in my hand, I let the drops of fluid flow onto my fingers like honey from hot bread.

He expanded in my grasp, thrusting against my palm, coating it with his hot, slick syrup. I held him, caressed him, and squeezed him, delighting in his every sigh and every groan. Each push against my hand stretched the limits of my restraint. He made me feel as though he wanted me so badly he would take any part of me he could get, and that need propelled me to new levels of desire.

Releasing the breast he was devouring, he fell back helplessly against the pillows.

"Oh, Angel," he sighed. "Oh *yes*…put your hands on me." He went on, his words punctuated with gasps. "I can't take it. I need… Oh, *please*…"

His voice trailed off as he pushed me down on him. I say pushed, but it was more like a nudge—a request rather than a demand, though it didn't matter to me. I would have done it anyway—could hardly wait, in fact. He slid past my lips with a groan, and I took his delightful balls in my hand and gently caressed them—teasing, scratching, and tickling them until he had my mouth so full of his honey I had to back off to swallow—an act that detonated my first orgasm of the evening. I was glad I'd withdrawn a bit or I might have done some damage. During the few moments it took me to recover, Dusty made a move.

"I need to fuck you."

Those words burst from him like floodwater from a crumbling dam. I don't know how he did it, but suddenly my head and shoulders were hanging off the edge of the bed. One leg was draped over his hip and the other was curled between his legs with my calf pressed against his butt. In that position, his cock slid straight into me. He rammed me so hard he had to hold onto my legs to keep from fucking me right off the bed. The thought of what he would be able to do with a fully functional left leg boggled my mind completely, leading to orgasm number two, which Goldie had to have heard, although I wouldn't have precisely called it a *scream*.

Dusty never let up for a second but continued on as before, rutting in my body as though he would die or go mad if he stopped, gasping my name and clutching at any part of me he could reach. I heard a loud, pounding noise and thought one of the horses was trying to kick out of its stall, but soon realized it was the heel of Dusty's cast hitting the wall beside the bed. I had just decided Goldie must have heard that too, when I went spiraling off into space with orgasm number *three*...

My mind got a bit fuzzy after that—in fact, I damn near passed out—but Dusty's sharply uttered, "Angel!" brought me to my senses as he came. I lay there in a daze, feeling his paroxysms and listening to his panting breaths until he slowly returned to normal and quieted down some. Then I heard something else—and so, apparently, did he.

"Did we knock over the flowers?"

Frowning, I glanced up, noting that the Corona bottle was still standing. Then I realized what we'd heard.

"Holy shit! Goldie's water broke! Pull me up!"

Dusty clasped my outstretched hand and hauled me back up onto the bed, dislodging himself so abruptly the empty feeling came as a bit of a shock. I shuddered as his hot sauce flowed out, spilling onto the sheets in such an erotic fashion I almost said to hell with the horse and stayed right where I was. I gave that idea about one second's thought before leaping to my feet. I could have Dusty anytime I wanted, but this foal was only going to be born once.

Staggering slightly as I regained my equilibrium, I snatched up my jeans and pulled them on, doing my best to ignore the semen running down my leg. I ran barefoot through the barn—a mistake I vowed never to repeat—dragging my shirt on over my head as I went. Flipping on the light to Goldie's stall, I was just in time to see her give the first push.

The two hind legs hadn't emerged as yet, so I couldn't tell if the foal was male or female, but what I *could* see sent my excitement level soaring.

Unfastening the latch, I took a moment to calm myself as I stepped into the stall. Kneeling down in the straw, I took the foal's seemingly lifeless head in my hands. Sliding my fingers down the sides of its nose, I cleared the nostrils of mucus, then held its face between my palms as Goldie gave another push. I watched with tearful joy as the foal's nostrils fluttered, and he blinked as though waking up from a long nap.

"Hot damn, it's a boy!" Not only was he palomino, he had a

blaze and four white stockings to boot. "Jenny's gonna be pea green with envy."

Goldie rolled up onto her belly and curled her head around to see her newborn son, calling to him with a soft nicker.

"You did good, Goldie. What a beautiful baby!" I glanced up as Dusty leaned over the stall door. "Ain't he cute?"

Dusty looked pretty damn cute, himself. His curls were ruffled and his shirt was unbuttoned.

Positively delightful…

"I think we'll name him…hmm… How about—oh, I know! Dustin's Delight—or maybe Delightful Dusty, or Adorable Dusty or—"

"Better stick with Dustin's Delight," he said with a chuckle. "Most people don't know that's actually my name."

"Yeah, well, I know it." I gave the foal a kiss on his precious little nose. "I write it on your paycheck all the time."

"True."

I sighed. "Doncha just love the way a foal's whiskers are all soft and curly and their ears look too big and they're all legs, and—"

"So this is where everyone is tonight," Troy said, coming up from behind Dusty to peer into the stall. "What have we here? A new addition?"

"Oh, Troy," I exclaimed. "Just look at him! Isn't he gorgeous? He was definitely worth the wait."

"Yep, that's just about the prettiest foal I've ever seen." Troy gave Dusty a sidelong glance that must've gone all the way to his toes. Then he arched a brow at me. "That being said, would either of you care to explain what happened to Dusty's pants?"

I couldn't see a thing from where I sat, but if Dusty's pants were missing, there was probably still some sticky stuff in his hair—and I don't mean the hair on his head. I could only assume Troy had seen that, too.

Groaning, I squeezed my eyes shut. "Dammit, Dusty! Why the hell didn't you get dressed?"

"Have you ever tried to get your pants on in a hurry with a cast on your leg? It's a real bitch. Besides, Troy's seen me without my pants before."

I thought Dusty was being rather cavalier about the matter, and I shot him a meaningful glare, hoping to shut him up.

"That's true," Troy admitted. "But the last time I saw you naked, you didn't look quite so…whipped, if you know what I mean."

He was obviously referring to the Biggest Dick contest. All three of them had been hard as rocks at the time.

"Your dick would be soft too, if it'd done what mine just did," Dusty snapped. He sounded a tad defensive. The best I could tell, he was missing the point entirely.

"Dammit, Dusty," I growled, startling the foal. "Will you please shut up?"

I could see the fight now. Dusty swinging away at Troy with nothing on but a shirt and a cast. Troy kicking Dusty in his cute little nuts. Me watching them beat the shit out of each other while wearing a pair of jeans that were soaked with semen and amniotic fluid.

That's what I get for being so damned fickle.

I shuddered to think what Cody would have done in such a situation. Somehow, I don't think he would've been content to kick Dusty in the balls. He probably would've ripped them off—or at least tried to.

"No, let him talk," Troy insisted. "He's just digging himself in deeper." He looked down at Dusty's groin again. "From the look of things, though, I'd say he's already been in some seriously deep"—pausing for effect, he rolled his eyes toward me with an accusatory stare—"pussy."

"Okay," I said, throwing up a hand. "I give up. You caught

me. The truth is, you were right. I didn't need a boy toy. I already had a man I was hopelessly in love with—I just didn't realize it at the time."

Troy eyed me with suspicion. "You're sure you're in love this time? Really sure?"

I nodded. "Absolutely."

He exhaled sharply. "I guess it wouldn't do any good to beat the shit out of him then, would it?"

I shook my head. "Nope. If you beat him up, I'd only hate you for it."

Dusty ducked his head, but not before I caught a glimpse of the smile he was trying to hide.

"What?" I demanded as Dusty's smile turned into all-out laughter. "What's so damn funny?"

"Sorry," he said between chuckles. "I can't keep a straight face anymore. He knows, Angel. I told him already."

"Shoulda beat the shit out of him then," Troy muttered. "But he'd just told us all some cockamamie story about going for a ride with a rattlesnake. I think he fell asleep at the wheel and ran into those trees and then made up that story to cover his ass. But since he'd already had such a lousy day, I felt sorry for him and decided not to throw any punches."

I could think of at least part of Dusty's day that hadn't been quite so lousy, but I chose not to mention it. "Well, thank you for that much. You could've been really nasty about it." I'd never dreamed it would be that easy.

"Yeah, well… I'm not your husband, Angie. I wasn't even openly your boyfriend. Besides, I only showed up here a short while ago. The stuff that's going on between the two of you started long before that. Let's just say I know when to throw in the towel." His expression was wistful at first, then changed to something quite fiendish. "So who's better? Me or Dusty?"

"You should probably include Cody too," Dusty suggested diplomatically.

"Yeah," Troy agreed. "Dusty, Cody, or me, Angie? Who was the best?"

I could be every bit as fiendish as Troy when the spirit moved me. And at the time, I felt a little retaliation was in order for the way they'd teased me. "That's a tough one." I nuzzled my new baby boy. "What do you think, Delight? Should I tell them the truth or make something up just to make them feel better?"

"Oh, come on," Dusty urged. "Don't be coy about it. I'm the best, right?"

"Nope," I replied with a sad shake of my head. "It's not either of you—or even Cody." I shrugged helplessly, letting out a heavy, reluctant sigh. "You see, Joe has this thing he does with that big dick of his…"

Troy slammed his hands on the top of the stall door. "Dammit! I knew it! I knew she fucked him. She took one look at that huge cock and couldn't keep her hands off it."

Sharing a conspiratorial smile with the foal, I said meekly, "Couldn't keep my lips off it, you mean."

Dusty let out a growl. "I'll kill him."

"Wouldn't do any good," I said sadly. "The deed is done. You've both been out-fucked by Big Ugly Joe—who isn't a bit ugly when he's fucking, by the way. He's awesome—not that you two don't have your good points."

"Such as?" For some peculiar reason Troy seemed a bit perturbed with me.

Imagine that…

"Now, now. No need for sarcasm," I said. "You each won a category in the contest. You'll have to be satisfied with that, because right now, I have another man to deal with." Goldie had chosen that moment to get to her feet, and I still had work to do, although in my haste to attend the birth I'd forgotten to bring a few things with me. "Dusty, would you get my foaling kit, please? It's that wicker basket on the shelf in the tack room."

"Sure," he replied. "Be right back."

Troy went with him. They must not have realized I could hear their conversation, but as quiet as it was in the barn that night, I was able to catch most of it, starting with Troy asking Dusty if I'd sucked his balls yet. I didn't hear Dusty's reply, but I knew I hadn't done it to him any more than I'd fucked Joe, so I could pretty much guess what he'd said, especially when Troy followed it up with, "I'm here to tell you, you haven't *lived* until Angie's sucked your balls while she jacks you off. It's totally fuckin' *wicked*."

"Yeah," I told Goldie with a giggle. "Cody liked that too—but Joe's balls were too big—"

"I heard that!" Troy shouted.

"—so I could only suck one at a time."

I had to cover Delight's tiny virgin ears after that.

"Whoa, momma," I whispered to him. "And I thought Bull had a foul mouth."

Chapter 21

THE NEXT FEW DAYS were pretty busy for me. I now had two boys named Dusty to play with, and I'm not sure which of them was the most fun. Unfortunately, the underlying anxiety that something might happen to the two-legged Dusty had me on edge when I should have been happier than I'd been in ages. I still hadn't worked up the nerve to say anything to Rufus about my relationship with Dusty—and probably never would—but I think Dad knew it without being told. He was bound to have gotten the picture pretty clearly the last time we'd talked—at least I hoped he had. I really didn't feel like spelling it out for him.

Rufus was another matter altogether. I'd never been able to talk with him about anything personal. Aside from the awkwardness factor, my private life didn't concern him—although he'd apparently made it his business to keep the cowboys out of it.

I told the guys to be ready for a Saturday night on the town but didn't say a word to Rufus. If they wanted him to know, they could tell him. I couldn't help feeling ridiculous tiptoeing around a man who was as much my employee as he was my father's, but I'd been in awe of Rufus for most of my life. Coming right out and telling him I was in love with one of the men he'd tried so hard to keep away from me wouldn't be easy.

I still didn't completely understand the reason for my reticence. When I was younger, yes, but now? It seemed unnecessary, although perhaps it had simply become a habit. Suspecting he was behind

Dusty's mishaps was the most likely reason, but Rufus might not have been to blame at all. Bull could easily have been the culprit and was getting back at Dusty for all the ribbing he'd given him over the years.

Still, it seemed odd for him to choose this particular time to take his revenge—just when I'd finally begun to realize Dusty was the man for me. I couldn't accuse Bull or Rufus of trying to harm Dusty. I had no proof, I had only suspicion, and I couldn't go around dropping hints without some good, solid evidence—especially since those accidents might have truly been accidents.

For one thing, I'd never known any of the men to mess with snakes enough to be able to safely stow one in a pickup truck. And while Joe's suggestion of how the saddle might have been tampered with was feasible, there was no proof of that, either—and there never would be unless someone confessed to having done it. There might have been motive—albeit rather flimsy—and opportunity, but there was still no proof.

—–ᵕᵕ—–

Jenny drove over on Thursday afternoon to see Delight. She owned the stud—a stunning creature I would have given my eyeteeth to own—which made her something of a grandmother to the foal. Jenny swore she would never part with that horse for any price, but I may have gotten the best end of the deal. Delight had a lot of potential, aside from being a palomino. Unless he turned out to be a holy terror as a stallion, I would never give some veterinarian the opportunity to cut his balls off and throw them in a tree, which is what my vet normally did when he castrated a horse.

I was rather shocked the first time I saw him do it, and though I did retrieve one of them to give it a proper burial, I couldn't reach the other one, so I suppose the birds ate it. Still, it struck me as being a rather nasty thing to do to someone. I would have thought a man would have more respect for the testicles of another male, since, generally speaking, they go to such lengths to protect their own. I mean, you never hear one man saying to another, "I'm gonna cut your balls off and throw them in a tree," even as a threat.

Jenny was quite envious of the new addition to the family and made no secret of the fact that she wouldn't mind having one like him.

"He's a keeper," she declared.

"You bet he is," I said. "He's not going *anywhere*."

After a quick glance over her shoulder, she aimed a conspiratorial smile at me. "Speaking of men you'd like to keep, where's the cowboy I'm supposed to have sent you?"

"Out working somewhere," I replied. "Which reminds me… there's something else I wanted to talk to you about. I'm taking the guys out on Saturday. Most of them don't have cars of their own, so they usually end up at strip joints with Bull. God knows Rufus would never take them anywhere. Anyway, I wanted to take them someplace nice where they could meet women they might be able to have more lasting relationships with, if you catch my drift. What's the name of the place you and your friends go to?"

"Cactus Bill's," she replied. "It's not too wild, unlike some other honky-tonks I could name. We go there most Saturday nights."

I smiled at her pronunciation of the word "nights," which served as a continuing reminder of her Texan heritage.

"Sounds perfect. Think you could be there this Saturday? My cowboys need someone to dance with besides me."

"Wouldn't miss it," she said.

"Apparently Rufus has been trying to discourage the men from so much as glancing in my direction ever since I was a teenager. I can't help but think he's gone about it the wrong way. He should've been encouraging them to go out partying instead of sitting around the bunkhouse with me being the only woman in sight. He would have had no worries at all, because I know there are lots of prettier women out there—yourself included."

She denied being more attractive than me but seemed pleased to hear it, nonetheless. She was also younger, which was another point in her favor. Although Jenny and I were about the same size, my hair was straight and dark while hers was a soft, light brown that fell in spiral curls down her back. She had an open, expressive countenance with one of the more kissable-looking pairs of lips I'd ever seen and a charming smile. To meet her, you might at first think she was rather quiet and shy, but upon further acquaintance, she would often surprise you with the frankness of her speech, particularly about her sexual desires. Unfortunately, while she liked men as a group, she hadn't managed to find the right individual as yet. The stories about her ex-husband were legendary, containing every reason why a woman should never marry.

"I'll be sure to dance with all of them," she said. "Any guys with handlebar mustaches?"

I rolled my eyes. "I've never understood why that is so important to you, Jenny! You married two men with mustaches and divorced them both. You need to use better criteria than that for choosing a husband."

"Oh, I know," she protested, laughing. "But mustaches are so sexy. I lose my head."

"Try keeping your head for a change and look at the men themselves, rather than their facial hair. You might have better luck if you go by, oh, I don't know…" I paused, tapping my chin. "Personality maybe? Or character?"

Not surprisingly, Jenny responded with a grimace. We'd had that same discussion a time or two before. I hoped I could come up with a good reason to leave Bull and his mustache at home, but I wasn't sure I could count on it. With any luck, Bull would think Cactus Bill's was too tame.

—◦◦◦—

"I believe I'll come along too," Bull said when I drove around to pick up Dusty, Troy, and Joe.

Calvin had declined, and I didn't mention it to Rufus for obvious reasons. I hadn't wanted to ask Bull, but I had to be fair.

"I think I'd like meeting some nice, sweet pussy for a change," he added.

Trust Bull to have a different slant on the idea. Joe gulped, nearly swallowing his tongue. Troy snickered, and Dusty rolled his eyes in the clearest I-told-you-so look I'd been on the receiving end of in quite some time. I counted to three, holding back a retort with an undoubtedly visible effort.

"Well, I would!" he insisted. "I mean, I like hookers, but you have to pay them."

"You have to pay other women too," Troy said wisely. "Only they don't ask for it up front." With a sidelong glance at me, he added, "You have to, um, work for it."

I suppose I deserved that, but as I recalled, he'd gotten my money's worth too. I made a mental note to take him to task for that remark, even if I had to wait until later on to do it.

As usual, Dusty couldn't keep quiet when a "Bull-bashing" opportunity arose. "What's the matter, Bull? Haven't you got enough money to pay a hooker?"

"I got plenty of cash," Bull retorted, rising quickly to the bait. "I just don't want to waste it paying top dollar for pussy when I can get the same thing for the price of a drink. I need new tires for my car."

Giggling helplessly, I motioned for him to get in. "Dammit, Bull. Will you please shut up and get in the truck?"

"I don't see what's so goddamned funny," he grumbled as he squeezed into the backseat with Troy and Joe. Dusty needed to sit up front to have room for his cast, which made things in the back a bit cramped. Joe was sitting behind him with his knees practically up under his chin. "It's the truth. I like getting laid as much as the next man, but hookers are expensive."

"Well then, I'm glad we asked you," Dusty said. "Now you can go to the bar and dance with some cheap women and then ask them if they'll fuck you for free."

"Goddammit, Dusty," Bull shouted angrily. "I've told you before not to say that word in front of Miss Angela. You watch your mouth."

"Aw, do us all a favor and shut up, Bull," Dusty said. "Angel's heard the word 'fuck' before. In fact she's been known to say it herself." He shot me an evil grin. "Ain't that right, Joe?"

I could see Joe's befuddled face quite clearly in the rearview mirror. "What're you asking *me* for?"

"I just thought you might remember something." A saintly smile replaced Dusty's wicked grin. "Something Angel might have said in—oh, I dunno—the heat of the moment, perhaps?"

"Shut up, Dusty," I growled, gunning the engine before starting down the driveway. "Don't say another word."

"I'd like to know too," Troy said. I glanced in the mirror just as he gave Joe a nudge. "Didn't she ever say something like, 'Oh, Joe! You're so fucking awesome'?"

Joe's eyes widened in horror. "She's never said anything like that to me in her life. What makes you think she would?"

Dusty shrugged. "Oh, just something she told us once." His dastardly grin returned. "Something about the way you look when you're—"

Dusty didn't finish that sentence because I punched him in the ribs as hard as I could. "I thought I told you to shut up, Dusty. I mean it now. Be quiet."

"Beating up on the help, now, are you?" Troy teased. "You can get in all kinds of trouble for that. He could file a lawsuit against you."

"Oh yeah?" I stomped on the brake. "Listen, if this is what I get for taking you guys out for the evening, maybe I ought to turn around right now." Troy didn't have on his seat belt and, as a result, ended up facedown over the console between the front seats. "I thought I told you to wear a seat belt, birdbrain." I could tell he wasn't hurt. He was laughing much too hard for that.

"Aw, come on, Angie," he said. "We're just teasing you."

I grabbed a handful of his curly black hair and pulled his head up. "I've got a good mind to throw you out on the highway. You can be an annoying little devil sometimes."

"Yeah, but I'm cute," he reminded me, the evidence of that statement mere inches from my face.

"Yes, you are," I agreed. "Too cute for your own good. If you were homely, you might learn to be nicer."

"I'm nice," he insisted. "Though I must not be as cute as Joe or you'd say I looked awesome when I was—"

I still had a grip on the back of his head, so I shut him up by the most expedient method. I kissed him—hard—driving my tongue as far into his mouth as it would go. I waited until he began to respond with some degree of enthusiasm before pulling away, muttering, "Now, will you please shut the fuck up about Joe?"

"Yes, ma'am," he replied. "Whatever you say."

"Okay then, boys," I announced. "Sit down, be quiet, and everyone put their seat belts on, or we're not going anywhere."

"Tough little angel, aren't you?" Dusty commented, grinning as he rubbed his sore ribs.

"I've lived on a ranch surrounded by men for most of my life," I replied. "I've learned to adapt—although you guys are making me wish I'd brought Rufus along to keep you in line."

"Thank you so much for *not* bringing him," Troy said. "He's already pissed enough as it is. You should have seen the look on his face when he got a load of that truck stuck in the thicket. Believe me, this would only make it worse."

"Yes, but it'd sure be nice to get in trouble for something we were actually guilty of for a change," Joe said. He must've forgotten about me kissing him in front of Rufus, although he hadn't been the instigator. Then again, that kiss wasn't what had Troy and Dusty on my case, and I knew it. I drove on, holding my breath, waiting for one of them to pounce.

Dusty drew in a breath as though about to take the bait, but Bull cut him off. "I'm never in any trouble," he declared. "Rufus has never hollered at me for anything."

I found that hard to believe. Granted, I'd never actually seen Bull get a lecture of any kind, so he might have been telling the truth, but I'd also never known him to give me the kind of looks Dusty gave me from time to time. The best I could tell, it was usually my fault when one of the men set Rufus off—that is, if what Joe had told me was true.

I'd seen several cowboys come and go over the years. Joe seemed to think many had lost their jobs because of me, and I had no reason to suspect him of lying. Perhaps that was why Rufus seemed so bent on eliminating Dusty. Bull had never shown any interest in me, and I wouldn't have encouraged him if he had. Left up to me, I'd have found some excuse to fire him a long time ago, simply because I didn't like him. It would have been grossly unfair of me to do that, but no more unfair than Rufus firing cowboys for giving me the eye. If Rufus didn't want the men flirting with me, he had a lot more to complain about with Dusty than he ever would with Bull. Therefore, if he wanted to stop their bickering, Bull, rather than Dusty, would have been his first choice as the one to keep.

"Yes, Bull, I'm sure you've always been the perfect cowboy. Keep up the good work." I wished my mirror had been aimed at him so I could have seen his reaction, but I needn't have bothered. As always, Bull had something to say.

"That's right," he said. "Rufus told me I'm the best goddamn hand on the ranch. He knows a good man when he sees one, even if some assholes around here don't."

A scathing glance in Dusty's direction had undoubtedly accompanied that statement because I caught a glimpse of Joe's smile before he turned toward the window.

Dusty was biting his lip, obviously doing his best to hold back his retort. I reached over and patted his arm. "I've always thought Dusty was the best, but perhaps I'm a bit prejudiced."

That, of course, set off a whole wave of protests from everyone else, so I kept on driving, letting them yammer on about it until we got to Cactus Bill's.

Chapter 22

As HONKY-TONKS GO, CACTUS Bill's was much like any other, complete with a scuffed dance floor, a really loud band, a bar running the entire length of the building, smoke-filled air, and alcohol in bottles, glasses, and the occasional mason jar.

At least they *had* glasses. Once, in another place, the waitress had answered my question about the lack of bottled Corona with, "Oh, we don't allow glass in here, honey." I didn't bother to ask why. The reason was far too obvious.

That was the one and only time Cody and I had ever patronized that particular bar, even though they had a nice dance floor. Cactus Bill's had a much better reputation, with the result that the women outnumbered the men two to one. Needless to say, every cowgirl's head swiveled in our direction when I strolled in with my string of cowboys.

Then again, Dusty's next words to Bull might've had something to do with that reaction.

"There you go, Bull," he said, clapping a hand on Bull's shoulder. "A veritable feast of nice, sweet, *cheap* pussy."

What made it even funnier was that Bull didn't see anything wrong with that pronouncement—no doubt because Dusty had omitted the f-word.

It took me a while, but I finally found Jenny sitting at one of the larger tables with her sister Rachel and a willowy blond I'd never seen before. If she'd brought anyone else with her, they must have been on the dance floor at the time, so I deposited Dusty in a chair and took the seat next to him, intending to stay there for the entire evening. Troy, however, seemed to have other plans for me, because after the introduction, he ignored Jenny, Rachel, and her friend, whose name turned out to be Caroline, and seized me by the hand, spiriting me off to the dance floor.

As I might have expected, he was a much better dancer than I was, and all I really wanted to do was to stand back and watch him. The vision of Troy out on the dance floor in boots, jeans, a fancy Western shirt, and a black Stetson was a sight no cowgirl worth her spurs would want to miss. I could barely keep up with him during the first dance, but the second dance was to a much slower and quieter song, and I took the opportunity to fuss at him for the "having to work for it" comment he'd made earlier.

"Well, I did," he protested. "I've had to rope and brand calves, fix fences, and all sorts of hard work."

"Yes, but I *paid* you for that," I reminded him. "You might not have cashed your paycheck yet, but I did write you one. I remember doing it very distinctly. Technically, the sex was a bonus, so I'd keep quiet if I were you or I might dock your pay next time."

"Why, Angela," he teased. "That sounds like sexual harassment."

"Maybe. But I didn't exactly have to twist your arm to get you to participate. *You're* the one who showed up in my room. I don't recall having to beg or threaten you, much less go drag you out of the bunkhouse."

He grinned. "You're right. If anything, it was a perk. One that I'm going to miss, I might add."

"You didn't think it would last forever, did you?"

"Well, no," he admitted. "But I thought it might last at least a month."

"I guess you can blame Dusty for that."

"I certainly do," he said. "*And* Joe."

"Why Joe?"

A mischievous sparkle lit his eyes. "You did say he was the best."

I loved Dusty, true enough, but I sure was going to miss being on the receiving end of that particular look. Too bad I couldn't keep them both. Generally speaking, men were much too territorial for that, although I've always considered sharing to be a good thing. Mind you, I'd never been faced with such a dilemma before. Cody had been my one and only for years, and with him close to hand I hadn't done much boy watching—hadn't even felt the need—until lately. The trouble was, I seemed to like most of what I saw—including Joe—who very well might have been the best for all I knew.

"You're right, I did say that, but that wouldn't have necessarily eliminated you."

As the dance continued, I couldn't help wishing Dusty had been the one in my arms rather than Troy. He was handsome and a terrific dancer, but…

"It wasn't a question of who had the best equipment or technique, Troy. It was a matter of who I loved the most. I've had a soft spot in my heart for Dusty for a long time. I've only just met you. Joe's been around for a few years, but he never said much, so I had no idea what he was really like. It's hard to say you love someone when you don't really know them. Oh, you might *think* you do, but in the end, most of what you love is either in the way a person looks or what you imagine they might be like inside. You might *fall* in love at first sight, but to really *be* in love takes time."

His smile disappeared, replaced by a far more serious expression than I'd ever associated with Troy. "That's fine for you, Angie, but what about me? Did you ever consider that I might be in love with you?"

I studied his face for a long moment, trying to decide whether he was teasing me. I didn't think he was. "I pretty much caught you on the rebound—and you seem to rebound pretty quickly. Besides, you haven't known me any longer than I've known you. Do you usually fall in love that easily?"

He didn't respond right away. "Maybe. I have a tendency to go wherever my dick points. And right now, it's still aimed squarely at you."

"That's because I've been your only target. There are three available women at our table, alone. Surely one of them can get a rise out of you. All you have to do is give them the chance. I've always thought Jenny was one of the prettiest women around these parts, but her taste in men is pretty lousy. I don't know Caroline at all, but she's very pretty too, and Rachel... Well, what can I say about Rachel? Men have overlooked her for most of her life, but she's got a heart of gold just like her sister. She's probably got enough love stored up to overwhelm any man with sense enough to tap into it. She strikes me as the female equivalent of Joe—a really good woman who's been waiting around for someone to realize her worth."

Troy seemed unimpressed by this, which made me long to smack him. I'd known several women I could've wrapped my arms around and loved to pieces if I'd been a man. Too bad they weren't the sort men typically found attractive. Men must see women differently, because when a man goes looking for a lover, the woman he chooses isn't necessarily the type who would also be a good friend.

Perhaps that was why friends seldom become lovers. A woman once told me that while she loved her husband, she didn't really like him. I couldn't see that as making for a very lasting and joyous relationship. Needless to say, hers wasn't.

Cody used to complain that women tended to choose the pricks over the nicer guys. Of course, pricks were nearly always handsome devils who made women cream their jeans rather than warm the cockles of their hearts.

I was incredibly lucky to have Dusty, who affected me both ways. I liked Troy, and he was a lot of fun, but I didn't love him. Given the choice between him and Joe—one strikingly handsome and the other with a face only a mother could love—I probably would've taken Joe. Perhaps age had altered my perspective, because in my youth, Troy would have won that decision, hands down.

Apparently, Jenny thought he was pretty hot too.

"Where on earth did you find *him?*" she whispered in my ear when I finally pleaded exhaustion and returned to the table.

"Shh... Not so loud. That's Troy, the one you supposedly sent me, remember? But I've sort of changed my mind about him."

Her silent "Oh" and the lift of her brow told me she understood that Troy was now available.

Apparently, I was wrong about that because less than a heartbeat later, she shifted her attention to Bull, flirting like a cheerleader in the men's locker room.

The handlebar mustache strikes again.

I wanted to strangle her.

Judging from the empties sitting in front of him, Bull had already downed two bottles of Coors in the time it took for Troy to dance me to death. Bull drunk would undoubtedly be even more obnoxious than Bull sober, and if that were the case, this was going to be a very long night. I had half a mind to haul Dusty off to another table so we wouldn't have to listen to all the crap. Dusty was sure to start ragging on him, which would probably wind up as an all-out brawl. I was beginning to wish I'd never come up with this idea.

In the meantime, Troy had traded me in for Caroline and was off dancing with her while I sat between Joe and Dusty drinking a Coke, hoping no one would notice there wasn't any rum in it. Rachel, a taller and slightly older version of her sister, sat at the far end of the table. Notoriously shy with men, Rachel had never married and rarely dated. She was nowhere near as open and lively as her sister, but I'd known her for years and liked her very much. What I'd told Troy was no more than the truth because she really did have a heart of gold. A good sense of humor too, if you hung around long enough to realize it.

Dusty draped his arm over the back of my chair, leaning close enough to whisper in my ear. "Sorry I can't dance, Angel. I'd really like to get you out there so I could have a good excuse to get my arms around you. That way you could feel how hard my dick is."

"My goodness, how romantic," I said with a giggle. "You sure know how to make a girl feel loved."

He grinned. "I hope so, 'cause I really do love you."

"Hmm… Let's see how you feel after a few beers. If you still love me when you're good and drunk, we'll know it's true love."

"I always thought it was the other way around."

"Yes, but that's only true if you fall in love with someone when you're already drunk. It's different when you fall in love sober. Then again, the real test is whether *I* still love you when you've been drinking. For all I know, you might turn out to be as big a prick as Bull."

"Damn." Dusty stared at his half-empty bottle of Coors like it was full of rattlesnake venom. "If that's the case, I'll never touch another drop." Giving the bottle a tiny shove, he added, "I think I'd rather die than be anything like Bull."

Apparently having overheard the tail end of our conversation, if not our confessions of love, Joe laughed and took a swig from his own beer. "What did you do for entertainment before you had Bull to pick on? Pull the wings off flies?"

"Aw, I wouldn't pick on something as innocent as that," Dusty protested. "I only pick on things like Bull and…" He paused, apparently searching his memory for any creature unfortunate enough to be included in the same category as Bull. "Rattlesnakes."

"Hold on now," Joe said. "The way I heard it, Angela was the one who saved you from that snake."

"Yes, but I had my foot on it," Dusty said. "Trust me, it was feeling picked on." With a shudder, he reached for his beer.

"I thought you weren't going to drink anymore," I teased.

"Sorry," he said after a long pull from the bottle. "The thought of having to deal with that snake and Bull at the same time is driving me to drink."

Troy and Caroline returned and grabbed a quick drink before heading back out to the dance floor. She must've had more stamina than I did. I might be able to keep up with Troy in bed, but on the dance floor, he was a bit much for me. I was kind of annoyed that he hadn't asked Jenny to dance, but the night was young. Caroline would wear out eventually.

Not long after that, Bull asked Jenny to dance. I reminded myself that it was her nature to be cheerful and agreeable, but she seemed way too delighted at the prospect. Hopefully, she was only being polite.

Dusty finished his beer and began getting downright amorous. He was in the process of polishing my earring and my earlobe with the tip of his tongue when he whispered, "Troy said I haven't lived until you've sucked my balls. I know my dick isn't as big as Joe's, but my balls are cuter. Why haven't you done it to me, yet, Angel?"

I arched a brow. "It's a damn good thing you're still adorable after one beer. Keep drinking and you might find yourself getting downright homely."

He chuckled with fiendish delight. "If *you* keep drinking, Joe might get better-looking."

"I'm not drinking anything but straight Coke, and he looks fine to me," I declared. "Don't start picking on him now that Bull isn't around."

"I'm not picking on him," Dusty insisted. "He'll tell you himself how ugly he is. Won't you, Joe?"

"That's me, Big Ugly Joe," Joe concurred, taking a swig of his beer. "Horses love me, women fear me—or something like that. I forget how it goes."

Our remarkably attentive waitress brought Dusty another beer along with a smile that had me grinding my teeth. Fortunately, she didn't seem inclined to linger. I was already regretting my role as designated driver and would've killed for a Corona. Too bad none of my cowboys were in any condition to drive.

"That's a fisherman's saying," I told Joe. "'Women love me, fish fear me.' I've seen it on a T-shirt."

"Is that right?" Dusty seemed puzzled. "Do fish really fear you, Joe? Is it because you're so big? No, wait… That's why horses would love you—or maybe fear you, I dunno… I'll have to think about that. Or maybe it's women who might love you or fear you, depending on whether they were looking at your face or your dick. Some girls like those great big dicks—don't they, Angel?"

I shot him a menacing glare. "Dusty, do I have to punch you again? You leave Joe's dick out of this."

"But it's so fucking awesome." With a plaintive sigh, he picked up his beer bottle and began peeling the label. "I wish mine was like that."

"It wouldn't look right on you," I said firmly. "In fact, it's a little out of proportion on Joe. Can we talk about something else?"

Joe leaned back in his chair. "I dunno. Talking about my dick might get some woman to want to dance with me."

Between the two of them, I felt like tearing my hair out. "Maybe, but they'd have to be close enough to hear our conversation. Besides, in case you've forgotten how this works, you're supposed to ask *them* to dance—unless we've got some real liberated types here tonight." A swift perusal of the crowd suggested there might be a few. However, none of them seemed to be flocking toward Joe.

Troy and Caroline returned. This time, they actually sat down to rest. Bull and Jenny were nowhere in sight.

"But it's safer this way," Joe insisted. "If I wait until one of them asks me, then I won't feel rejected when they say no."

"Yes, but you might end up waiting forever," I pointed out. "Wouldn't you like to hurry things along a bit?"

"I suppose so. Maybe I need to practice some more." With a sigh, he stood and held out his hand. "Will you dance with me, Angela?"

"Sure, Joe." I made quite a show of batting my eyelashes. "I thought you'd never ask."

The other guys started whooping and clapping.

"Way to go, Joe!" Troy shouted. "Go get her, buddy!"

Chapter 23

WHEN WE REACHED THE dance floor, the band was playing a reasonably good rendition of George Strait's "I Cross My Heart," the romantic lyrics making me wish I'd been dancing with Dusty. Joe took me in his arms, which was a bit awkward seeing as how he was a good foot and a half taller than me.

I had to crane my neck to see his face. "Having fun?"

"I am now," he replied. "I've always wanted to dance with you."

"Really?" The stuff I was hearing from my normally reticent cowboys continued to amaze me. "Too bad we're so mismatched." I rolled my head from side to side, trying to work the kinks out of my neck. "I should probably be on stilts for this."

"Feels great to me." We danced several steps before he spoke again. "Any idea why Troy and Dusty are carrying on like a couple of idiots tonight?"

"You mean they're acting more idiotic than usual?" I was stalling. I had a pretty good idea what he meant, but it couldn't hurt to be sure.

"Yeah. Seems like every time they start teasing you, it's something about me. Then you tell them to shut up or hit them or kiss them. Mind telling me why?"

I should've come clean with all three of them, but it was kinda fun to keep them guessing, and I'll admit I was enjoying the banter. Romance wasn't the only thing my life had lacked since Cody's death. Joe might even get a kick out of the story. That way he could play along and we could really drive Troy and Dusty nuts. "You know I've sort of switched from Troy to Dusty, right?"

"I figured that," he said. "Especially since he's been sucking your ear off all evening. I'm kinda surprised that didn't happen a long time ago."

"Yeah, me too," I agreed. "Guess I was too blind to see it. Anyway, the night Goldie's foal was born, I was out in the barn with Dusty. Troy came in later, fussing at me for being with him. Turned out Dusty had already told him how things were between us and he was putting on an act. They gave me a hard time about being fickle and all, but eventually, they wanted to know who was the best—Troy, Dusty, or Cody—and while I was teasing them, I sort of let it slip that you were."

"The best what?"

Obviously, I wasn't the only one being cautious. "Um...lover."

"Well now, how in tarnation would you know that?" I'd seen that pleased-as-punch smile of his at least once before. He seemed even more pleased this time.

"You know what they say about bigger being better, don't you?"

"That's not necessarily true," he said. "But I get the idea. So you told them we'd...um...done it?"

"I let them think we had," I admitted. "I've been accused of a lot worse in my time."

"I never have," he said with fervor. "Thank you, Angela." He gave me a squeeze as a slow grin split his face from ear to ear. "I'm gonna play this for all it's worth—just wish I'd actually done it."

"Hey, now. I'm in enough trouble as it is. Don't you start too. We can always tell them we were kidding if things get out of hand, but for now..."

He chuckled. "They'll want to kill me."

"Is that a problem?"

"Nope. It'll be a blast. No one's ever been jealous of me in my entire life." He gave me a big kiss on the cheek and we danced on in silence for a few minutes. Joe was a surprisingly good dancer for someone who probably hadn't had much practice.

"Anything specific I should know about?" he asked.

This time around, I saw no need to pretend I didn't know what he meant. "Use your imagination. I didn't tell them very much except—" I stopped there, hesitant to explain further. Telling Joe was harder than I would've thought, especially since I'd seen him with his pants down—*and* kissed him.

"Except what?" he prompted, still with that same endearing smile.

Taking a deep breath, I blurted out all of it. "I said your balls were too big to get them both in my mouth at the same time, and that you look awesome when you're fucking."

His eyes grew round and he let out a low whistle. I'd seen *that* look before too. "So *that's* what they were going on about. Oh, Angela," he said with a chuckle. "This is gonna be so much fun."

I laughed right along with him. "Go ahead and enjoy yourself, but try not to make them too mad. They're already kinda sore. I don't want anyone putting a rattlesnake in your bunk."

He arched a suspicious brow. "You don't think that was an accident, do you?"

Relieved to have someone else to discuss it with besides Dusty, I needed no further encouragement. "How else would a snake get in the truck? That truck gets used nearly every day. It would be different if it had been sitting for a month. That snake had to get into it during the time you guys were unloading the supplies or it would have tried to bite Dusty on the way out there." Simply voicing that possibility made me miss a step. Fortunately, I didn't stomp on Joe's foot.

Regaining my composure, I kept dancing. "I can't understand how a snake could get into a truck without help anyway. I know they can climb trees and things, but into a truck? It's not like there were field mice in there for it to eat. Dusty still thinks his accidents were just that, but I'll have to admit this has me pretty worried."

"That's my fault for bringing up the idea," he said with a grimace. "But it does seem kinda suspicious. No one is *that* unlucky."

"No shit." On the other hand, Dusty had been very lucky to survive both of those incidents. The next time around, luck might not be enough to save him. Somehow or other, this "accident" business had to be stopped. "Any ideas on how we could find out who's behind it short of accusing someone?"

"Not really. Although, maybe if you moved Dusty out of the bunkhouse and into your bedroom, whoever's responsible might realize you don't intend to give him up without a fight—or stand quietly by and let anything else happen to him."

"Dad would throw such a fit," I said. "I wouldn't want to be responsible for him having a stroke."

"Okay, so you break it to him gently. But do it soon, before our perpetrator comes up with any more ideas."

"Perpetrator?" I echoed. "Geez, Joe, you sound like a police detective." Apparently all those reruns of *Law and Order* the guys watched had made an impression.

"Maybe we *do* need a detective around here."

"We should mention it to Bull. I'm sure he would claim to have been one at some point." According to him, he'd done damn near everything.

"Wouldn't surprise me a bit," Joe agreed. "Although I wouldn't believe it for a second. He's always trying to sound like a bigger man than he really is."

"Maybe he's compensating for that tiny dick of his. Whereas you never seem to put yourself forward for anything. Must be a confidence thing."

"Yeah, right," he grumbled. "Like I'm the most confident guy in the world."

"Naw, you're the strong, silent type." *Who happens to have an enormous dick.* Once again, I batted my lashes at him. "Women like that."

"Oh really?" he asked with a doubtful scowl. "How come none of them hang all over me like they do with Bull and Troy?" He glanced toward our table. "Or Dusty?"

"Hmm, good question. I'll have to think about that."

"You shouldn't have to think very long," he said. "I'm too homely to get noticed with them around. Bull may be a prick, but he's not bad-looking."

"If you like that shaved head thing," I conceded. "I've never cared for it myself. It makes his ears stick out."

"Yeah, well, my ears are still bigger than his."

"So is your—" I broke off there as a fiendish thought occurred to me. "Let me talk to Jenny and her friends. I'll set them straight on a few things. You're still one of the nicest of the bunch, even if you aren't the prettiest. Hopefully, one or two of them might appreciate that fact and at least act like they might want to dance with you. You're a pretty good dancer, you know."

"Aw, shucks, ma'am," he said with a grin. "I'll bet you say that to all your cowboys."

"My cowboys," I said dreamily, giving him a hug. "I've got some good ones, don't I?"

"I can't argue with that," he said. "That Troy is one helluva man with a rope. Have you ever watched him?"

I had enjoyed watching Troy do a lot of things, but I'd never actually seen him rope a calf. "Nope. I figured he was pretty good, though. I spotted that belt buckle right off."

"I'll bet that's not all you noticed," he said dryly. "He's about the handsomest man I've ever seen—and I don't enjoy admitting that, either."

"You don't think Dusty's cuter?"

"Maybe." He shook his head, chuckling. "I can't believe I'm having this conversation with you. I've probably said more to you in the past two weeks than I have in the past two years."

"I know, and I'm sorry about that, Joe. If I'd known about Rufus and his stupid rules a long time ago, things would have been different. I've had so much fun with you guys tonight, and, well... pretty much every day since Troy showed up. I guess we have him to thank for that."

"True, but it probably helped that you got to him before Rufus did. Otherwise, he'd have been cowed into submission along with the rest of us."

"I doubt that," I said. "He's a spunky little rascal—and he didn't know me when I was married. That might have something to do with it."

"Good point—although you being married didn't stop Rufus from lecturing us from time to time. Cody never said a word to any of us. Didn't need to, but you'd expect that to be the husband's job rather than the foreman's."

"Yes, and Cody *was* kinda possessive," I admitted.

The dance ended and I snuggled up against Joe's chest for another hug before letting go of him. He escorted me back to the table where Dusty sat with a redheaded Siren draped around his shoulders whom he wasn't lifting a finger to discourage. I'd sort of wondered what Joe had meant by girls hanging all over Dusty along with Bull and Troy.

Now I knew.

Jenny was in Bull's lap giving him a sip of beer while she toyed with his mustache. Surprisingly, Troy was alone for the moment. Rachel was still sitting at the end of the table, nursing a gin and tonic and looking miserable. I shot the redhead an evil glare and decided it was time to declare war. Tugging on Joe's hand, I somehow managed to get his head low enough to plant a big, wet kiss on his cheek.

"Oh, don't stop there," he pleaded, turning toward me.

I reached up and threaded my fingers into the soft, brown curls on the back of his head and gave him a good one, tongue and all. When I let go of him, Troy and Dusty were both staring daggers at me. I don't think Bull even noticed, but the redhead did. Apparently seeing this as evidence that Dusty wasn't taken, she began nibbling his ear.

Joe took his seat with a smug grin and a satisfied sigh. "It's so nice to be irresistible."

Dusty glowered at me and leaned his head away from the girl, offering her better access to the side of his neck. "Could you do that a little lower, baby?"

Ignoring him completely, I went over to talk with Rachel, hoping she hadn't heard our earlier conversation. She'd been raised on a ranch and knew better than to pay much attention to what a bunch of cowboys might discuss in a bar, but you never know about these things.

"Hey, Rachel," I said, pulling up a chair. "You need to come over and see my new baby. Jenny's stallion outdid himself this time."

Rachel smiled. "So she said. Nothing quite as cute as a foal, is there? I'll be sure to check him out before he gets much older." Rachel's Texas accent was even more pronounced than her sister's, which wasn't surprising since she'd been about fourteen to Jenny's six years of age when their family moved to Wyoming. "How've you been? I don't think I've seen you since Cody's funeral. You were pretty torn up at the time."

"Much better," I replied. "It took a while, though."

"You seem pretty happy now." Taking a sip of her drink, she darted a quick glance at the other end of the table where the others were laughing.

I wondered again exactly how much she'd overheard. "Love will do that for you."

"I'll take your word for it." Love never having been her strong suit, I was surprised she didn't laugh in my face.

"So what did Jenny say to get you to come here tonight?" I asked. "Threaten you with something dire?"

She shrugged. "Nothing really. She said she needed another person, although I don't see why. With me here, there are more than you need to each have a dance partner."

"But there are four men and four of us—oh, I see what you mean. Dusty isn't dancing."

"No, I meant the redhead. I'm kinda superfluous now."

"Yeah, well, the redhead is about to get her ass kicked," I said sweetly. "The one she's hanging all over is mine." Apparently, I was every bit as possessive as the guys.

"Really?" Rachel sounded surprised. "He's gorgeous, I'll grant you that—even if he *is* kinda young."

"Oh, he's pretty, all right," I agreed, smiling. I wasn't touching the age thing with a ten-foot pole. "Now if I could only get your stupid sister to fall for the right one, everything would be cool. I'm sure you've noticed she's doing it again—hanging out with the biggest prick in the bunch."

"She does have that history," Rachel concurred. "Which is why I moved to town when she married the second loser." Having no interest in ranching, Rachel had gone off to college to become a veterinarian. When their parents retired to Florida, she'd happily left the running of the family ranch to Jenny.

"The way I heard it, you wanted to be closer to your office."

"Yeah, well, don't believe everything you hear," Rachel said. "Her first husband was bad enough, but the second one was even worse. She may have finally reached the point where she couldn't stand being married to him, but you're right; her taste in men hasn't improved."

"Maybe I should tell her Bull is only here because he didn't want to waste his money on a hooker when he could get laid for the price of a drink."

Rachel dissolved into helpless laugher, which took years off her.

She wasn't a bad-looking woman, but she'd always seemed sort of morose where men were concerned.

"Oh God," she wailed, wiping her streaming eyes. "Jenny's sure to fall for him now."

I nodded. "Pretty soon she'll have him spoiled rotten and then wonder why he's impossible to live with. That mustache must have her mesmerized."

"Wouldn't surprise me a bit," Rachel said. "I've seen it happen before."

"I was hoping to pair her off with Troy."

She directed her gaze toward the other end of the table. "Troy is the really handsome, dark-haired one, right?"

"Yep. He's got plenty of *other* traits to recommend him too. I should know." I hoped my suggestive tone and the significant lift of my brow were enough to make my meaning clear without shocking her. Rachel had never been terribly excited about men in general, and I wasn't sure how well she would cotton to the idea of me taking on a boy toy. Then again, she hadn't heard the whole story. "Just not sure how ready he is to settle down."

Judging from the way her jaw dropped, my efforts to break it to her gently had failed. "You haven't slept with him, have you?"

"Now you're sounding like my father," I said, rolling my eyes. "He wouldn't like the idea, either—that is, if he'd known about it. Actually, I sort of decided I was already in love with Dusty, so I had to give him up."

"He doesn't seem to be too broken up about it," she observed.

I glanced over at Troy, who was laughing it up with Caroline. No, he didn't seem the slightest bit upset. "Trust me, he doesn't stay down for long. Twenty minutes, maybe," I added with a sly grin. "But that's about it."

She acknowledged this with a puzzled frown, but let it pass. "Who's that last one you were dancing with?"

"That's Joe," I replied. "If you'd get your buns down to the other end of the table, you wouldn't have to ask me all this. You need to talk with them, not me. And don't worry about the numbers. The redhead is about to become history. Come on."

Chapter 24

DUSTY WAS WELL INTO his third bottle of beer, and the redheaded chick was practically in his lap. He wasn't even bothering to encourage her anymore. She was doing just fine all on her own.

"Dusty, Dusty," I said with a slow wag of my head. "What am I gonna do with you?"

He looked up at me with a dreamy-eyed smile. "Take me home and suck my balls?" His speech was only slightly slurred, and if his rapt expression was any indication, the redhead might have been an inanimate object.

Not to mention grossed out.

"Eeeww! That's disgusting!"

She might think it was disgusting, but she obviously didn't hold it against him because she still had her arm around him—a circumstance I found particularly repugnant.

Oh yes, I was feeling *quite* possessive. Now that Dusty and I had each managed to make the other jealous, it was perfectly obvious where our true desires lay. The rest of the world could go hang for all we cared—but I still had to eliminate the intruder.

"Don't knock it 'til you try it, sweetheart." I bared my teeth in a mirthless smile. "If you want to keep that arm, you'd best be getting it off my husband." I was quoting Loretta Lynn, but this chick was probably too young and too drunk to realize that—or to figure out that Dusty and I weren't married.

"Hear that?" Dusty was still gazing at me with a beatific smile.

"She called me her husband. I think I like that. Angel, will you marry me?"

"Ask me again when you're sober, and I'll consider it."

Dusty gave the redhead a nudge. "Get up now, ma'am. You're sitting in my Angel's chair."

The girl hesitated just long enough to annoy me. Raising my right arm, I casually pushed up my sleeve. I'm not very tall, nor have I ever been what anyone would call intimidating, but she took the hint and scurried off like a scared rabbit.

Dusty didn't even seem to notice she was gone. "I love you, Angel. Take me home now. Please?"

"Not yet," I replied. "I haven't accomplished anywhere near what I'd hoped to tonight. Why don't you sober up and explain to Jenny what a mistake she's making—as soon as she comes back, anyway. Where is she?"

"I think she might have gone to the restroom," Caroline said. "I don't know where Bull is, but—"

A quick survey of the room was all it took to spot him. "Never mind. I see him. He's over by the bar, hitting on the redhead. Be right back."

I gave Dusty a quick kiss before heading off to find Jenny. I corralled her as she was coming out of the ladies' room.

"Dammit, Jenny," I snapped. "You've been dancing with the wrong guy." Pointing a surreptitious finger at Troy, I ticked off his attributes. "Bigger dick, fabulous ass, twenty-minute turnaround time, and unlike lightbulb head there, he's a real sweetie. You do the math."

"But isn't he the one you—?"

"Forget about me," I said with an impatient stomp of my foot. "Trust me, I don't need him anymore—haven't you been paying attention? So what if he doesn't have a handlebar mustache? Troy would probably grow one if you asked him nicely. Bull may have a gorgeous mustache, but he's a complete asshole."

"But—"

"But nothing. See for yourself. He's already gone off in search of easier game. Troy, on the other hand, is having a pretty good time with your friend Caroline, so you'd better get cracking. I brought two perfectly good cowboys with me tonight. Why you had to pick the one I'd just as soon have left at home is beyond me."

"Troy *is* handsome," she admitted. "Who's the other one?"

"That's Joe. He's a real sweetie, too. Plus, he's got the biggest dick you'll ever see without renting a video, although I probably shouldn't admit to knowing that from firsthand observation. Trust me, you could do a lot worse."

Scowling, she pursed her lips in a pout. "He's not very good-looking."

"But he's a helluva nice guy. Great kisser, too. You of all people should know looks aren't everything. Even Troy will tell you he gets away with murder because he's so damn charming. He knows it and uses it to his advantage. Joe might play on your sympathy a bit, but he's really quite likable. If he hadn't been so shy I might've fallen for him myself."

Jenny didn't seem convinced. "I'm sure he's wonderful and all that, but when you bring along someone who looks like the man of my dreams, what did you expect?"

Knowing what I did about Bull, I couldn't imagine he would resemble the man of anyone's dreams. Jenny needed to have her eyes checked.

"I *expected* you to learn from your previous mistakes. Cody never could understand why the really pretty girls always went for the biggest pricks. I've never understood it myself. Why *is* that? Can you tell me?"

All she did was stand there looking at me, her face as blank as a clean sheet of paper.

I threw up my hands in defeat. "Okay. I give up. The ball's

in your court now. I promised my guys I'd help them meet some women who weren't in it for the money. The rest is up to them—and you. Obviously I'm not much of a matchmaker. But please, consider yourself warned. Bull is not—and I repeat, *not*—relationship-worthy."

Jenny might've acknowledged me with a nod, but that didn't stop her from aiming a longing gaze at Bull. Resigned to her being a hopeless case, I stomped off to the restroom, washing my hands of the whole mess. I shouldn't have been surprised. My family hardly ever heeded my advice—even though my suggestions usually proved to be the best options. Most of the time, anyway.

As if I weren't already irritated enough, I made the mistake of noticing the other women in the restroom were all young, lithe, and beautiful. Bare midriffs flowed upward to tight, scoop-necked tops that clung lovingly to round, succulent breasts. Tight jeans hung low on hips that probably had no panties on them at all, unless they were wearing thongs. I sighed, shaking my head, before making the even more disastrous mistake of glancing in the mirror.

I must admit, I looked better than usual. My hair was twisted up in a clip as Dusty had suggested rather than in my usual braids. The deep cranberry shade of my V-necked top went well with my complexion. Like everyone else, I wore boots and jeans, and they didn't look half bad, despite my rather round figure.

But I was nothing compared to the other occupants of the room. Their torsos alone were longer than my entire body. I was undeniably older than any of them, and I had never been as stunning even when I was their age—not bad, but certainly not stunning. Did any of them realize how lucky they were to have been born beautiful?

Probably not.

Needless to say, I returned to our table feeling rather low.

Dusty sat there alone. At first glance he seemed as forlorn as I was. But he smiled when he saw me coming—that sweet, crooked smile that always warmed me all the way to my toes. Suddenly, I felt much, much better.

"Where'd everyone go? Home?"

He shook his head. "Dancing." Even our attentive waitress seemed to have neglected him; his beer bottle was conspicuously empty. Spotting the waitress, I waved her over and ordered another round. Dusty opted to forgo the beer and drink Coke along with me this time. Having placed our order, I turned my chair around to face him, running my hand over his cast.

"How long before you get this thing off?"

"Another three weeks," he replied. "I can't wait. It's been a total pain in the ass."

An amused smile played across my lips. "I'm sure it is, but at least it kept you close to home where I could see more of you."

I watched, fascinated, as Dusty's sensuous lips curled into a provocative smile. "You've seen a *lot* more of me, haven't you?" His gaze swept over me as though assessing every detail. His smile broadened, making me feel far more attractive than I had mere moments before. "I've seen a lot more of you too. I don't suppose we could go somewhere more…private, could we?"

"What? And leave everyone else to fend for themselves?"

Dusty seemed to have sobered up considerably in the past fifteen minutes, leading me to wonder if he'd really been quite as drunk as he'd appeared. "Caroline already went home—said something about her babysitter not wanting to be out very late—which leaves Jenny and Rachel to take care of Troy and Joe." He glanced over his shoulder at the dance floor. "I don't think they'd mind too much if we asked them nicely. I don't give a shit what happens to Bull."

"He, um, followed your little friend over to the bar." I nodded in their direction. Apparently she'd transferred her attentions with no difficulty whatsoever and was now draped over Bull like a second skin. "By the way, did you enjoy having her hanging all over you?"

"Not really," he replied. "She was pretty, but she's not my Angel." With a cunning grin, he added, "My Angel would never say sucking my balls was disgusting."

"Never." I agreed with him wholeheartedly, although it was something I'd never actually done prior to that evening. "There isn't a single thing about you that's disgusting, Dusty. Not one single, solitary thing."

"I'm glad you feel that way," he said. "Hold that thought."

I glanced up as our friends made their way back to the table, noting that they still weren't paired off the way I thought they should be. Jenny was partnered with Joe, and Troy was escorting Rachel. It was all wrong; their heights didn't even match up right. Rachel was actually a shade taller than Troy while Jenny hit Joe at about the same level that I had. I shook my head in disgust. These people were enough to drive any self-respecting matchmaker to drink. However, I refrained from comment, saying instead that Dusty was getting tired and I probably ought to take him home.

To my surprise, this didn't seem to be a problem. "I'll take the others home if they want to stay longer," Jenny offered. "Or Rachel could do it. We drove separately."

The knowing lift of Troy's brow made it plain I hadn't deceived him for a moment. He knew precisely why I wanted to leave. "Tired, huh? It's not *that* late."

"*Sick* and tired," Dusty amended, never once taking his eyes from my face.

"Hmm…tired of waiting, maybe," Troy suggested. "Myself, I think I'd like to stick around a while longer." He glanced at Rachel. "Would you mind taking me home?"

I know how *I* would've replied to that question if I'd been in her place—especially since I'd already done it once. But Rachel? I wasn't sure.

She beamed a radiant smile at him. "Not at all."

Joe wasn't even mentioned, which made me wonder whose house Rachel planned to take him to. I seemed to have missed something somewhere. However, one glance at Joe made it patently obvious he wasn't ready to leave, either.

Still, I had one more cowboy to account for. "Think you could make sure Bull has a way home too?"

Dusty's grin suggested he knew something the rest of us didn't. "I don't think you need to worry about Bull. That redheaded hooker will see that he gets home all right—although he'll probably have to pay extra for the ride."

"Hooker?" I squeaked in astonishment. "You mean she's—"

Dusty nodded. "Sure seemed that way to me. I guess she thought I might be desperate enough to pay since I couldn't dance—or she thought I was, I dunno…unattached, maybe?"

"Well, shit," I exclaimed. "If that's the case, I'm not leaving you alone again for a second." Dusty was much too attractive for anyone to think he would have to pay for sex—broken leg or no. That girl was either incredibly stupid or she wasn't much of a hooker—especially since ball-sucking was one of the least disgusting acts a prostitute might be called upon to perform. She couldn't have known Dusty had won the cutest balls award in our contest, but *still…*

I giggled wickedly. "He's going to end up paying after all."

"Serves him right," Dusty said. "Let's go home, Angel."

―⁂―

Dusty must have truly been tired because he fell asleep on the way to the ranch. Granted, it was a fairly long drive and the beer may have been partly responsible, but he had to be exhausted from dragging himself around all day with a cast on his leg. I had an idea he'd been conking out fairly early these days, kinda like I did when I was pregnant.

I'd seen him asleep before, but still felt the need to glance over at him from time to time, watching him as he slept. Mark Chesnutt's cover of "I Don't Want to Miss a Thing" was playing on the radio. I knew exactly what those lyrics meant now. I didn't want to fall asleep—I wanted to watch him until the sun rose and he stirred, blinking the sleep from his eyes. I wanted to see him do whatever he did first thing in the morning—even if it was rubbing his dick or scratching his balls.

I'd never given Cody the chance to mess with his version of morning wood. I nearly always woke up first—reaching for him, massaging his back, pulling off his underwear, and going for his ass, his tiny sighs and groans telling me how pleased he was to be awakened in that manner. I would push him onto his back to stroke his cock, feeling it stiffen even more beneath my touch.

My God, how I missed that.

After we turned off the highway and onto the bumpy, pitted road that would take us home, I drove more slowly, trying not to wake him.

I wanted to take Dusty back to my room that night—my own bed, in my own house. I wanted to keep him there until morning and stay in bed late, making love with him in a slow, lazy, Sunday morning sort of way. I wanted to fix breakfast for him, watch him eat it, and then make love with him all over again. If he fell asleep, so much the better. I would keep watch over him, ensuring that no harm would ever come to him. Nothing bad could happen if I was there to prevent it. I was his guardian angel—he'd said so himself—and I couldn't fail him, because if I did, I'd be failing myself.

The song ended and I turned off the radio, not wanting to hear anything else that might break the spell. The last time I'd driven down this road with a man was the day I'd picked up Troy. What a day that had been! He'd done so much for me, brightening my life and giving me back my soul. I owed him so much for that.

So very, very much…

I'd have never known what a great guy Joe was if not for Troy.

He would've gone right on staring at the ground whenever I was near, rarely speaking and certainly not pleading with me for hugs and kisses. Dusty might never have declared himself if he hadn't found me in the bunkhouse inhaling Troy's scent. What if he'd seen me just a few seconds later, never realizing what I'd been doing? Would he have ever said a word to me? Would he be safer now because of it or would he be in even greater peril? I'd lost one man before—surely I couldn't lose another, could I? Would God really do that to me, or was it my own fault? Was I some kind of bad luck charm, causing accidents to happen to the men I loved the most?

If so, then all three of them—Troy, Dusty, and Joe—were in danger, because I loved them all. Each in a different way, perhaps, but I would be devastated should anything bad happen to any of them. I would see it as my fault and never be able to give my heart to anyone again, knowing they might be at risk because of me. It made me want to take them back to my house so I could keep them out of harm's way—away from rattlesnakes and wild horses and any other threat to their safety. No doubt they would laugh and accuse me of being silly and paranoid.

Except Joe. He'd been the one to see the pattern and bring it to my attention—even before the rattlesnake incident. Knowing there might be a problem hadn't helped prevent that occurrence. Perhaps I was to blame for not risking a confrontation with Bull and Rufus. I could discount my father and Calvin. Dad didn't have the physical capability to wrestle with a snake, and Calvin was deathly afraid of them.

Perhaps if I were to let my suspicions be known, the accidents might cease. Suspicion was much less dangerous than outright accusation, but the trick would be to do it without making a bad situation worse.

The solution to that dilemma kept my mind occupied for the remainder of the drive. However, despite my best efforts, I was no closer to an answer.

Chapter 25

I MADE NO PRETENSE of dropping Dusty off at the bunkhouse. I parked my truck in the garage and woke him up. If we ran into my father on the way to my room, so much the better. I was getting tired of all the clandestine bullshit. I loved Dusty, and I saw no reason to hide that love anymore—at least, not from my father. Rufus might notice Dusty's absence, but he wouldn't necessarily know where to look for him—although he might have been able to make a pretty good guess. With Bull off somewhere with his expensive pussy, Rufus was the only one I needed to be concerned about. The way I saw it, regardless of who might be responsible for the accidents, Dusty was safer with me than alone in the bunkhouse. And he would've been alone because Rufus and Calvin slept on the other side of the mess hall—Rufus in the foreman's private room and Calvin in the cook's quarters, away from the other men.

If Dusty was surprised I'd brought him up to the main house, he kept quiet about it, busying himself instead with the task of getting out of the truck without breaking another leg. I flipped on the kitchen light and held the door open for him while he negotiated the two steps up from the garage.

Despite Troy's insistence that it wasn't all that late, it was nearly one thirty. Dad had apparently gone to bed. Even if we'd elected to go to the bunkhouse, we probably wouldn't have been disturbed for at least two hours, perhaps even more if the guys didn't come straight home after Cactus Bill's closed.

But I wanted more than a few hours. I wanted all night and into the next morning with Dusty—and the next thirty or forty years after that. I might even get it, seeing as how he'd asked me to marry him. I hadn't given him an answer yet, but when I did, it would be a resounding *yes*. That is, if he remembered asking me. I would have to check on that to be sure.

As he paused in the doorway, it occurred to me that Dusty had never even been in the kitchen before. He'd only been in the office, which was off to the right of the front hallway. Since the back door was inside the garage and not visible from the bunkhouse, Troy had always come in that way whenever he'd visited me. Dusty never had, which made this moment seem almost as significant as if he were carrying me across the threshold on our wedding day.

The kitchen was the heart of any house, and family members entered through that door. Thankfully, Dusty seemed no more out of place there than Dad, Cody, or the boys would have been. He already belonged. For him to head straight to the refrigerator for a snack would have been perfectly natural.

And that's exactly what he did.

"Sorry, Angel," he said. "But I'm starving. I don't suppose you have any more of that chili, do you?"

Here was my lover, the man I'd been dying to get my hands on all evening, asking to be fed before I ripped his jeans off and had my wicked way with him. It might have been perfectly natural, not to mention endearing, but it was funny as all get-out at the time.

"Sure do," I replied with a giggle. "Dad doesn't know how to make a small batch. There's always enough for an army—although it never seemed like too much once Cody and the boys got into it. It's there in that big green bowl."

I realized then just how little I knew about Dusty's likes and dislikes. Sure, he liked chili—I'd never known anyone to turn their nose up at my father's version—but would he eat it cold or would he warm it up? Would he drink beer with it, or would he want water or even milk? I had no idea what to expect. I hadn't lived with anyone completely new since the birth of my second child, and while figuring out what a new baby will eat is always a learning experience, milk and cereal are generally a good place to start. I didn't have a clue what Dusty liked. Granted, I was the one who brought home the groceries and occasionally helped Calvin with the cooking, but his specific preferences were a mystery.

"Why are you looking at me like that?" he asked.

Obviously, I'd been staring. I shook my head in an effort to reset my brain and clear my thoughts. "No reason. Just wondering how you want it."

"In a bowl, hot, with grated cheese on top, and a glass of milk." His tone and expression implied that as far as he was concerned there was no other way. He might as well have added the "Well, *duh*."

"Sorry." I flapped a hand. "Just a question. You'll have to fill me in on the stuff you like."

"I'm not hard to please. I mean, if it was a bowl of chili in *my* refrigerator, I'd probably stick a spoon in it and eat it cold." He grinned. "Seems a bit presumptuous at the moment, though."

"I see your point." I took the bowl from him and set it on the counter. "Have a seat and I'll fix it for you."

Turning a chair sideways, he sat down, stretching his legs out in the middle of the floor. I wondered if this was another quirk of his until I realized it was simply a matter of maneuverability. With his leg in a cast, he would have a hard time getting up if he tucked his legs under the table.

My hands were shaking as I put some chili in a bowl and stuck it in the microwave, and even more so when I poured a glass of milk. Granted, bringing a new man into my home was worth a few butterflies, and the prospect of making love with him might've had something to do with it, but I shouldn't have been so nervous. After all, Troy had visited me several times, and I hadn't been anywhere near this rattled. I was doing my best to seem nonchalant, but my awkward movements must have given me away.

"Angel," Dusty said. "Are you having second thoughts about all this?"

So he'd noticed. *Imagine that.* "What do you mean?" I was stalling, of course. I knew precisely what he meant. I wasn't fooling anyone, not even myself.

I set the glass of milk on the table beside him. "I don't know… It seems strange having you here."

"You aren't gonna give me that you're-just-a-hired-hand-and-I'm-the-rancher's-daughter spiel, are you?" His tone made it clear just how disappointed he would've been with me if that were the case—although no more disappointed than I would've been with myself.

"That isn't it at all," I replied. "But there's something unsettling about all this. I feel like I'm"—I broke off as it dawned on me what the problem was—"replacing Cody."

Without any warning, exhaustion suddenly overcame me, and I leaned back against the counter staring dumbly at him, completely ignoring the microwave when it dinged. Troy was different—he'd been a fling, a temporary affair that was bound to end sooner or later. But I intended to marry Dusty—to share my life and the running of the ranch with him. Future decisions would be made based on how well we could discuss important matters—rationally, with clear heads and open minds.

I'd grown into the idea with Cody, but this was different. Dusty was an adult, not some kid right out of high school whom Dad had taken under his wing to educate him on how things were done on the Circle Bar K. I had no idea what his own thoughts were on the subject. My love for him was reason enough to bring him into my house, but once we were married, this would be his house, his ranch, his life, just as much as it was mine. No, the problem wasn't the hired hand versus the rancher's daughter thing. My concerns would have applied to anyone I married.

I was beginning to understand why Dad thought Rufus, with all of his knowledge and experience as foreman, would be such a good choice. Dusty had worked for us for several years, but I had no idea what his opinions were. Would he leave the running of the ranch to me, or would he take a more active role? Would he defer to me in most matters, or would he attempt to usurp my position, relegating me to the role of a mere housewife—which was something I'd never truly been, not even when Cody was alive. I did my housewifely chores, of course, but Cody had always understood that while he would share ownership with me eventually, the ranch belonged first and foremost to my father and subsequently to *my* side of the family. I hadn't had the opportunity or the inclination to discuss this with Dusty as yet. It hadn't seemed important until he sat there in my kitchen, waiting for me to make one of the more important decisions of my life.

Replacing Cody. This was different from starting out in life as a young couple, learning as you go along. This was more like a big company suddenly losing its CEO and having to choose a new one— one that the board of directors hoped wouldn't run the company into the ground, or embezzle from the pension plan, or fire all the workers and hire his own relatives. I sincerely doubted that Dusty would do any of those things, but while he might be a fabulous partner for me, was he the best choice for the ranch?

I refrained from saying anything further for fear of offending him. Instead, I took the chili from the microwave and fixed it the way he'd asked me to.

I could almost feel his speculative gaze on me. Had I already offended him? He didn't appear to be angry—puzzled perhaps, but not angry. He couldn't possibly have read all the thoughts racing through my head, couldn't have known even half of what I was thinking, but he somehow managed, quite perceptively, to key on the most important issue.

"You're thinking the replacement won't measure up to the original. Have I got that right?"

I summoned up a smile. "In some ways, you surpass him entirely. But in other ways... I simply don't know."

"I'll do my best, Angel," he said gently. "And I'll love you. I can't promise you any more than that. I'm not perfect and I'm sure Cody wasn't either, although you may think that now. When he was alive, you would've been more likely to admit to his faults, just like anyone else, but now...well, he's gone and..." He finished his sentence with a shrug.

I knew exactly what he meant. I'd probably romanticized my marriage a great deal in the years since Cody's death. Perhaps I remembered things differently, but given the circumstances, that was understandable. I'd loved Cody, and he'd been taken from me without warning, just when our children were nearly grown and our future together seemed bright. The ranch was a thriving concern, Dad had been in better health, and aside from the day-to-day details, there had been no worries. Not like there were now.

"I'm dreaming about the good old days?" I suggested, arching a brow. "Is that it?"

"Something like that," he replied. "But don't underestimate the future, Angel. It might even be better."

"You're right." I was so tired, the stuffing seemed to drain out of me as I took a seat at the table. "What about you? Are *you* having second thoughts?"

"I'd be lying if I said I didn't," he replied. "No one can ever be completely certain about anything. One day you're riding high and the next you're flat on your face with a mouthful of dirt. But right now, with the way I feel about you, I believe it's worth the risk. My heart's been broken before, and I've been kinda shy about giving it to someone again.

"Maybe that's why I fell in love with you. You were married and unavailable. I could love you as much as I wanted and never get hurt. But it *did* hurt. When you'd smile at me I'd feel better for a while, but then I'd be miserable because I knew a smile was all I'd ever get from you. And now, well…now I can have it all. It might be kinda scary, but I'm willing to take the risk because you're worth it—worth risking my heart and soul for. I love you so much I can hardly stand it."

"I love you too." I smiled, glancing down at his bowl. "So why don't you, um, hurry up and eat that so we can go to bed?"

He made a face but dug his spoon into the bowl anyway. "I know what it is," he said with a sage nod. "You only love me for my body. Right?"

"You betcha—although there are plenty of other things I love about you."

"Such as?"

I didn't have to think very long before making my reply. "The way you make me laugh is one, along with that impish expression when you're teasing the hell out of Bull. The way you don't panic in the face of disaster. You can be stuck in a truck with a rattlesnake under your foot and you still don't lose your sense of humor. The way you allow yourself to be vulnerable—letting your heart go, even though it might cost you dearly. Finally admitting how you felt about me, even knowing it might not be worth the risk. I like that. The courage it took for you to say something at last was remarkable, and it made what you feel for me seem that much stronger."

I reached across the table and gave his hand a squeeze.

"I love the way you make me feel when I touch you, the way you're not afraid to let me look at you, the freedom you give me to say whatever I wish. The way you don't fuss at me for giggling all the time like some men might. The way your body responds to me. I like knowing I can reach for you anytime and you're already anticipating it, already craving it. I like the way you want me the way I am—not younger, prettier, or thinner. You told me I was beautiful. You make me feel that way, and you make me feel loved." I smiled at him again. "Is that enough, or should I keep going?"

I'd already stopped him in mid-bite a couple of times. At that rate, he was never going to finish that chili.

"Keep going," he replied. "I'm not done eating yet."

I laughed. "Dusty, if I keep going, I'll have to resort to describing the various parts of you and why I like them. You wanted to know other things, didn't you?"

"Yeah. Keep going." He took another bite.

"Okay. You're honest, hardworking, trustworthy, and loyal. You have the cutest smile I've ever seen. I love your curly hair, the curve of your shoulder, the line of your hip in a pair of jeans—and out of them. I love the way you wanted me to smell you. Did you know I've been sniffing at you for years? I could never understand why you wore cologne. It seemed unnecessary, but I liked it. I used to walk behind you just so I could catch a whiff."

The smile he gave me said it all. "I wear it for you, Angel. Only you."

I nearly choked on the lump in my throat, needing a moment to recover before I went on. "Do you remember when we delivered that foal together last year? Afterward, I was standing beside you, leaning over the stall door. The foal was adorable, but you were even more so. You were so close I could smell you and feel your heat. All I wanted was for you to put your arm around me and give me a hug. But you didn't. I figured it was because I was too old or not attractive enough or something."

He swallowed another mouthful of chili, somehow making that simple act seem overwhelmingly erotic. "I remember that night, and believe me, I wasn't thinking about how old you were—or that you weren't pretty enough to suit me. I hate to sound indelicate or unromantic, but you nearly got nailed. It took every ounce of self-control I had not to rip your jeans off and take you right there—whether you liked it or not."

His big blue eyes were riveted on my own, scorching me with their heat. Quite suddenly, those jeans he'd spoken of needed to come off—badly. They were too hot, too confining. My nipples threatened to wear holes in the cups of my bra. I wanted—needed—his hands on me, and I longed to caress every inch of him with my entire body. He took another mouthful, sliding his tongue across the underside of the spoon, an act that stole my breath and made me squirm in my chair.

"What's the matter?" A sensuous gleam shone in his half-closed eyes. "Getting hot?"

"No," I gasped. "Hungry."

He held out the spoon. "Want some of this?"

I shook my head. "I want some of *that*." I pointed at the bulge in his groin, noting that the button-fly of his jeans was being tested to the limit.

A slow, devilish grin curled his lips. "Help yourself. It's yours for the taking." He leaned back against the chair, stretching out his legs.

I'd partially undressed him once before, but with his leg in a cast, I wasn't sure how to go about getting those jeans off him—at least not with any speed. Not that I needed to remove them *completely*…

Kneeling between his knees, I popped open the top button and nearly swallowed my tongue when I realized he wasn't wearing briefs.

"You okay, Angel?"

"I'm fine—I think. You, um, be sure to finish your milk. We need to get this leg healed."

"Don't worry, I will," he purred. "What are you going to have?"

"Not sure," I replied as the second button went. "But there seems to be *something* wet in here."

He shifted his butt in the seat. "I dunno. Feels more like a rock—and you know you can't get water out of a stone, don't you?" His slow, teasing drawl was certainly making *me* wet. My mouth was a different story.

"You just watch me," I told him. "I'll bet I can do it."

The third button followed the previous two, and I got my first glimpse of the soft, blond curls those pants had been hiding. He was carrying his cock up against his belly, but off to one side, and I pushed back the flap to reveal it in all its hard, succulent glory. Where it lay against his stomach, the hair was wet and sticking to his skin.

Leaning forward, I nudged his penis aside with my cheek to lick the damp slickness from him. "See? All the water I need."

"Okay," he admitted. "You really *can* squeeze water out of a stone. But would you like something extra to go along with that? Something sweet and warm and creamy?"

If I hadn't known better, I'd have called my reply an orgasm. Sure felt like one. Either way, it took me a moment to recover my wits.

"I dunno," I said with a slow wag of my head. "If you really think you can come through a cock that tight, you go right ahead and try it. But I bet you can't."

"Watch me," he said. "You suck hard enough, and I'll fill you right up."

I sat back on my heels, scratching my head in a mock bewilderment. "Correct me if I'm wrong, but as I recall, I was supposed to take you home and suck your balls, not your dick."

Dusty's gut-wrenching groan made me smile. Two could play this game…

"Ooh, hard choice. But I've been a good boy. I ate all of my supper and drank all my milk. Can't I have both? Huh, Angel? Pretty please?" His pleading expression could've seduced a nun.

Chewing my thumbnail, I let out a resigned sigh. "I suppose I *could*—although I can't even see your balls yet." I popped open the two remaining buttons. "Now, where *are* those little devils?"

Wiggling his butt, he thrust his hips forward, making his cock sway back and forth. "They're in there, waiting for you—but they're getting kind of impatient."

"Poor babies," I said. "Don't worry, your Angel will find them and make them feel *so* much better."

I found them, all right, but I didn't use my hands or my fingers in the search. Kissing the uppermost part of his scrotum, I sucked in, creating enough of a vacuum to hold on as I pulled, and out they came. If his openmouthed reaction was any indication, no one had ever sucked Dusty's balls out of his jeans before. Come to think of it, I couldn't recall having ever done it myself.

Still, if anyone had ever deserved to win a "Cutest Balls" award, it was Dusty. Smooth and firm within his soft, furry scrotum, they were truly worthy of being called the family jewels. Leaning closer, I licked lightly around the outer edge, his cock pulsing against the side of my face anytime I inhaled as if about to give in to temptation and suck them. I went on teasing him, drawing back from time to time, simply admiring the way his cock and balls were framed by those dark blue denim jeans…

Whoa, momma…

After a bit, I got up to retrieve a dish from the table.

"What's that?" he gasped.

"Shh… You'll see," I promised. "But not yet."

I picked up where I'd left off, licking, teasing, and gradually wetting his entire scrotum with a combination of my saliva and his cock syrup.

"Angel, I'm gonna come if you don't stop."

Opening my mouth as wide as I could, I placed it against his balls and inhaled. Both of his nuts popped into my mouth.

Dusty let out an "ahhh-h-h-h…" the memory of which I would undoubtedly cherish until my dying day. Running my tongue over the underside of his scrotum, I continued to tease his balls while gently sucking them away from his body.

When I reached up to cup his cockhead in my hand, he shuddered, sending more juice gushing onto my palm. Grasping his cock, I slid my fingers over his skin. His own lubrication was almost enough, but not quite, and I wanted this to be good—not the slightest bit uncomfortable for him. Moving by feel alone, I took the lid off the dish and scooped up a dollop of soft butter and slathered it all over his cock.

Glancing up, I saw the same expression of awe mingled with ecstasy I'd seen on his face that day in the bunkhouse. I wanted to be able to see that at least twice a day for the rest of my life.

"Oh God," he gasped. "You're really gonna do it, aren't you? Right here in the kitchen?"

I couldn't reply—couldn't even nod without hurting him—so I gave him a quick thumbs-up with my buttery right hand. Wrapping my fingers around his cock, I slid them lovingly up and down his quivering shaft. As I leaned into him, inhaling his masculine scent, my core contracted, sending the moisture that had been building up inside me out with a whoosh—along with another mini-orgasm. I had to stifle a chuckle. There I was trying to get him off, and I'd already flown off into space twice before he ever left the launchpad.

Not that it would take much longer. His breath came in quick, hard gasps as I fucked him relentlessly with my hand.

"Angel," he cried out suddenly. "I'm—" He stopped as his words were replaced with inarticulate grunts as his nuts spasmed inside my mouth. Releasing his balls, I rose from the floor, going for his hot, buttered dick just as it let loose like a geyser. The first spurt hit me on the chin, but I was able to suck him into my mouth in time to get a mouthful of butter-flavored semen. I allowed him a few seconds of recovery time before licking him clean.

When I finished, I stood and reached for a napkin to wipe the butter from my face and hands.

Dusty closed his eyes and sighed. "Troy wasn't kidding, was he?"

"About what?"

"He said I hadn't lived until you'd sucked my balls." He gazed up at me with a mixture of adoration and gratitude. "He was right."

I smiled. "I'm glad you agree." I glanced at the clock. "Two o'clock is *way* past my bedtime. Are you ready for bed now?"

"I-I think so," he replied, a dazed expression in his eyes. "Let's see now… My stomach's full and my dick's empty. Is there anything else I should do?"

"You might want to pee and brush your teeth. Aside from that, it sounds like you're good to go."

He frowned. "Don't you want me to, um, do you?"

As befuddled as he seemed, I wasn't sure he was up to it. "Think you can?"

His eyes widened. "Are you kidding me?" Apparently my taunt had cleared his head better than a whiff of ammonia. "Might need someplace to lie down, though. Not sure I can nail you on the kitchen table. Not tonight, anyway."

"I know just the place." I shot him a wink. "Follow me."

Chapter 26

GETTING INTO BED WITH Dusty was like a dream come true at the end of a very long and extremely eventful day.

Granted, I was tired, but just as my taunt had revived him, the sight of him on my bed had a similar effect on me. He'd been irresistibly sexy lying on the bunk in the tack room, but he seemed to belong here in my room. Like I'd spent every night of my adult life in bed with him.

I hadn't of course, nor was I replacing Cody. I was simply moving on. Cody would understand, just as I would have understood his need to find love with another woman if I'd been the one to die.

Pushing those morbid thoughts aside, I slid into Dusty's embrace, pressing kisses to his lips as I sifted my fingers through his hair. Oh yes, I was dreaming. Dreaming of the days and nights ahead with this wonderful man. There would be problems to unravel and other obstacles on the road ahead of us, but together, we could solve anything. I was sure of that now. Nothing could stand in our way.

Well…maybe two things did. Dusty's accidents for one. Would they cease when I openly acknowledged him as the man I loved? I wasn't sure. Somehow, I thought they might, but as determined as those efforts had been—if indeed they *were* intentional—I couldn't be sure.

The other problem was that same old nagging suspicion that someday Dusty would decide he wanted children and trade me in for a younger, more fertile woman. This was one fear I could confront, and I needed to do it now, before our relationship went any further.

"Comfy?" I asked.

"Very," he replied. "I could get used to this."

"I hope you do." I sucked in a breath and held it for a second. It was now or never. "You know I—well, there's something we haven't talked about. I'm not sure how to say it other than to just come out with it. If you think you're gonna want kids someday, you might want to rethink being with me. Aside from the fact that I'm probably too old to be having babies, I had a tubal after Chris was born. There won't ever be any little Dustys running around the ranch. Are you okay with that?"

He was silent for a long moment. "I gave up on that idea a long time ago," he finally said. "I pretty much had to."

I could understand him giving up on the idea simply from knowing my age, but he couldn't possibly have known I'd been fixed unless Cody or Troy had told him, which I very much doubted. "What do you mean?"

"You know those balls you think are so damned cute?" He plunged on ahead without waiting for my reply. "They don't work. I had the mumps when I was sixteen." He winced at the memory. "Went straight to my nuts, and you want to talk about something painful. I thought I was gonna die. Anyway, I wound up sterile, but at least I'm not impotent."

My jaw dropped. "Damn. Wish I'd known that. I mean, I'm real sorry that happened to you and all, but I've been beating myself up over not being good enough for you because I couldn't have your children. If I'd known I wasn't the only one in this duo incapable of reproducing, I wouldn't have been quite so hesitant."

Dusty stared at me with surprise. "I would've thought the fact that I'd never bothered to use a condom might have been a good clue."

I snorted a laugh. "True, but I've been feeling this way since way before the use of a condom became an issue. And even when it was, I didn't give it much thought. I'd already told Troy he didn't need to worry—although looking back, I probably shouldn't have trusted him to be free of disease. Guess I should've been more careful. Either way, the need for birth control was the farthest thing from my mind that first time with you in the bunkhouse. If I'd thought about it at all, I might've assumed you knew something from talking to Troy or Cody—although I can't imagine why either of them would've mentioned it."

"They didn't. But, like I said, I knew it didn't matter." He caressed my cheek with a fingertip. "And it wouldn't have mattered even if I wasn't shooting blanks. I love you, Angel."

Bone-melting kisses followed, preventing me from professing my love in return.

Not that any declarations were necessary. Dusty knew how I felt. I didn't need to tell him. Not with words, anyway.

I trailed my fingertips from his neck to his shoulder, then down over his chest, grazing his nipple on the path to his hip. Would I ever tire of touching him?

Never, never, never…

His sigh tickled my ear as his kisses took a similar path along the contours of my own body, although he was obviously not content to merely graze my nipple with his lips. Surrounding my tingling flesh with the wet warmth of his kiss, he suckled my breast, occasionally swiping his tongue over the taut bud, reminding me once again of the direct connection between my breasts and my core. The ache deep inside me cried out for his attention, but I uttered no protests, made no attempt to encourage him, simply reveled in the effect he had on me. I welcomed that pain and the flood of moisture that followed.

Dusty's kisses moved on down the slope of my chest to my waist before moving up to the crest of my hip. Once there, he eased me onto my back. His lips found their way to my mound, his tongue delving into the places that begged for his touch. Lifting my leg over his head, he settled between my thighs, kissing my wet folds as though seeking the source of that dampness—coming close to easing the ache, but never quite reaching it.

Moonlight shone through the stained glass of my window, illuminating his hair, altering its hue, first blue, and then green with a splash of crimson. Those soft blond curls were the only part of him I could reach. I let them sift through my fingers, wishing I could touch more of him and yet somehow feeling content. The intensity grew steadily, rapturously, ecstatically.

I hovered there, waiting for the stroke that would send me flying, but it never came. He backed off and moved up beside me.

"I want to fill you with cream before I finish that," he said.

Again, I made no protest, perfectly willing to let him play me like a well-tuned guitar, the way I'd played him in the kitchen.

He rolled onto his back, taking me with him. "Mount up, sweetheart. Time to save that horse and ride your cowboy."

I hummed with pleasure. "I thought you'd never ask."

Placing a hand on his chest, I rose slightly before backing onto his dick. Capturing his cockhead with my pussy lips, I eased backward until I had him inside me, then sat up to drive him in the rest of the way. The emptiness inside me now banished by his presence, I leaned back to enjoy it, pivoting on his cock, drawing my knees up and using my weight to achieve the deepest possible penetration.

Absolute perfection.

"Beautiful," he whispered. "My beautiful Angel." Palming my breasts, he thumbed my nipples, driving me ever closer to the point of ecstasy before sliding his hands to my hips. "Ride me." To further illustrate his meaning, he took my hips in his hands and lifted me slightly, then pulled me down. "Mmm…yeah, like that…hard and fast and deep."

Lifting me again, he slid me up his shaft then dropped me back down on his prick.

The rebound effect was incredible.

Following his example, I tried it myself.

"Holy shit, that's good." Not that this was anything new because it *all* felt good. So incredibly, mind-blowingly good…

Circling my hips, I swept my slick inner walls with his cock, only then realizing I hadn't quite reached the pinnacle of ecstasy. Not yet. Not when that simple movement could ignite even more fireworks.

Dusty let out a groan. "That's it. Use it…use my dick like a fuckin' *spoon*…"

The spoon analogy made me giggle, but it also gave me an idea. "Hold on."

I'm still not sure how I did it, but I somehow managed to turn around until I was straddling his right leg. With more freedom of movement than ever, I was able to generate even more force as I rocked up and down on him. Picking up speed, I let him have it for all I was worth.

Dusty was panting now, his upward thrusts meeting me on each downward stroke. "Oh, God. Fuck me, baby. Fuck me *hard*."

Gripping my upper thighs, he pulled me down on him one last time.

Every pelvic muscle I possessed contracted, doubling me over as a deep, guttural groan escaped my lips—a sound I'd never heard myself make before. Seconds later, Dusty's breath seemed to catch in his throat, only to come out with an explosive exhale. I clutched blindly at his leg as he pumped me full of cream.

His spurts had barely subsided before he began tugging at my hips. "C'mere and sit on my face. I need to finish what I started."

I wasn't sure I could move, let alone do something requiring that much coordination. Nevertheless, I was willing to give it a try. After extricating my foot from beneath his left thigh, I turned around. "Didn't hurt your bum leg, did I?"

"Oh God, no." He dragged me up over his chest until I was straddling his head, then held me poised above his face. "Hot, creamy pussy. Mmm…" With that, he sat me down, teasing my labia apart before sliding inside to fuck me with his tongue. At that point, I couldn't decide which felt better, his tongue or his dick.

Probably his dick, but this is pretty damned good.

Easing me up slightly, he bathed my clit with his tongue, sending lightning bolts of ecstasy ripping through me. Gulping in a breath, I grabbed the headboard and held on for dear life. My head was already spinning, but when he latched on to my clitoris and sucked, I saw stars.

As primed as I was, I didn't think it would take much more than twenty seconds for me to come.

It took ten.

With a rasping moan, I lurched forward as my body imploded. Dusty held me right where I was, relentlessly licking my clit until I finally let go of the headboard and keeled over sideways. I don't believe I moved a muscle that wasn't orgasmically connected for the next ten minutes.

"Holy sheep shit," I muttered when I could speak again. "You're gonna be the death of me."

"No way," he said. "I might let you go forty years from now, but not one second before."

All I could say after that was "Mmm."

Later on, I got up to pee and put on my pajamas before crawling back in bed with him.

"Pajamas? Seriously?"

"Get used to it, big guy," I said as I pulled the blankets up over us. "You can take them off anytime you like, but I'm sleeping with them on."

"Okay," he grumbled. "If you insist. Not that I have any room to talk. I always wear a T-shirt and boxers to bed. Then again, I'm usually in a bunkhouse with a bunch of guys. I hardly ever sleep in the nude."

I reached down to lay my hand on his naked cock. "I dunno… This feels pretty good. Guess that's what you get for being such a slut and leaving off your undies."

He put his arms around me and dropped a kiss on my forehead. "Yeah, well, I could probably get used to that too."

Lying in the circle of his arms, I drifted off while listening to him breathe, feeling his warmth, and inhaling his scent. He was mine now, and no one was going to take him from me. Ever.

I woke up sometime during the night, thinking I heard a car in the drive, but dismissed it as probably being Jenny or Rachel bringing the other guys home. I rolled over to go back to sleep, wondering briefly if they'd had as nice a time as Dusty and I had.

Naw, I decided sleepily, *probably not nearly as good.*

I must have fallen asleep because I was in the middle of some sort of idyllic dream when a noise right above my head had me as wide awake as flicking on a switch.

The unmistakable sound of a pistol being cocked.

Chapter 27

I FROZE, BARELY TAKING a breath as I opened my eyes a slit. What little light there was cast swirls of color over the face of someone standing over me, holding the cocked pistol to Dusty's head. I didn't know if Dusty was awake or not, but I was taking no chances. Erupting from the bed screaming bloody murder, I knocked the startled intruder's hand aside just as the gun fired.

Whatever I said probably wasn't the least bit coherent, but I did shout it at the top of my lungs.

"Get out of the way, girl," a male voice hissed at me. "I need to kill his sorry ass."

"No!" I fell on top of Dusty, doing my best to shield him from this maniac, whoever he was.

"Don't protect him, sweetheart," he urged. "Not after what he's done to you. You protected the other one, too, didn't you? He didn't deserve it, either. Now get out of the way. If you don't want to watch, you should leave, honey. I'll take care of him. Believe me, it'll be a pleasure."

Honey? Sweetheart? Who would be calling me that? It couldn't have been my father. The voice sounded so strange, not like anyone I knew—more like that of a young man whose voice couldn't decide whether to be soprano or baritone. None of the men on the ranch were anywhere near that age. Who *was* this?

My heart pounded like a bass drum. I could feel as well as hear the pulse in my ears, and my hands and feet turned to ice in an instant. My brain wasn't working very well, either. I was terrified and couldn't think of a single thing to do to keep this from happening.

"I've waited too long," he went on. "Too late. It's my fault. I should have been watching more closely and kept you safe. I'm sorry this happened to you, sweetheart. I blame myself for it. Myself and him. You aren't responsible. We are. And he'll pay, just as I have, just as the other one did. Now move."

I found my tongue at last, saying what was first and foremost in my mind with what wits I had left. "Who are you? Dusty hasn't done anything wrong. I love him. I don't want him dead."

"You don't know any better." He sounded almost apologetic, like a father remonstrating with a beloved child, but the voice... the voice was all wrong. It was too youthful, too pure... "You're too young to know. I trusted them, but they betrayed that trust, and so did he. He has to die, honey. Has to."

Again, he sounded so patient and calm as he explained why he needed to kill the man I loved. How could he ever hope to convince me? The idea was ridiculous, laughable.

But I wasn't laughing.

I was trapped in the middle of a surrealistic nightmare. This couldn't be happening, couldn't possibly be real. I was still asleep, and if so, I desperately needed to wake up, because I couldn't see any way out.

"No," I whispered. "*No*."

"You don't understand what he'll do to you, darling. He'll take you and hurt you, slit your throat, and leave you to die in a cold, dark alley. I can't let that happen, honey. Not again. I couldn't live with myself if I let it happen again. I can barely live with myself now."

"What do you mean, let it happen again?" I clutched at that tiny phrase like a lifeline. Perhaps he had me confused with someone else. "I've never been hurt like that—never. And even if I had, Dusty wouldn't have done it; he loves me."

He let out a hearty laugh. "Yes, yes, that's what they told me too. 'We like her,' they said. 'We'll take good care of her.' And like a fool, I believed them. They were my friends. They wouldn't lie. Not to me."

"Angel." Dusty's voice sounded from behind me, quiet and steady, letting me know for the first time that the bullet hadn't hit him.

It's about time. I was slightly pissed at him for leaving me to wonder for so long. For all I knew, I might have been protecting a corpse.

"Do what he said and move out of the way."

"And let him kill you?" I squeaked. "No way. I'm staying right here."

"He's right, you know," the other man said from the shadows. "You should move. You should listen to him. He knows what he's done. He understands the penalty."

Although he stood in the shadows, I could still see the faint gleam on the barrel of the gun silhouetted against the darker outline of the open doorway.

"Angel," Dusty repeated, more firmly this time. "Get out of the way. The gun might go off again. I don't want him to shoot you by mistake."

"Angel?" the voice from the darkness inquired with a curious inflection. "Her name isn't Angel." When he laughed again, the hair prickled at my nape. "You see, sweetheart, he doesn't even know your name. How can you protect someone like that? Listen to me, listen to your brother. You know I'm right. He's bad. They're *all* bad. I know I failed you so long ago, honey. I let the others live after what they did to you, but I've kept you safe since then.

"Until *he* came. I stood it for a long time. You seemed happy enough, but then one day I heard you screaming. I knew he was there with you, hurting you, and I couldn't let him get away with it the way the others did. He had to die. I killed him, just as I'll kill this one. The first one was easier, though. This one is much harder—like a cat with nine lives." He chuckled at his own joke. "But even cats aren't impossible to kill. You have to be persistent."

I keyed on what was apparently the most pertinent point in what he'd said, trying to ignore the fact that he seemed to be confessing to Cody's murder. "I don't have a brother. What's your sister's name?"

"Silly girl." His quiet laughter grated on my nerves like the screech of fingernails on a chalkboard. "Always a silly, giggling little girl with long, shining braids. My lovely Adrian. So sweet, so loving, so trusting. I said I'd look after you, and I have. The nasty men can't come near my girl. I've made sure of that—or tried to. I can't watch you all the time, though." His tone altered slightly, as though deepening with regret. "Too many of them…had to scare them…had to make them stay away. But you seek them out, don't you?" His voice changed even further, becoming more accusing with each word he spoke. "You fight me every step of the way. You must *want* to die."

Something in his voice finally struck a chord. Suddenly, I knew who it was—had really known all along. I sat up, leaning forward, trying to see him, to reason with him.

"Rufus," I said gently. "You aren't my brother. I don't have a brother. I'm Angela Kincaid McClure. I'm not your sister."

"You're lying." He spat the words at me. "I know who you are, and I can't stand quietly by watching while they turn you into a fucking whore." I heard the pistol cock again. "Maybe you need to die too."

Dusty yanked me backward just before the gun went off. The bullet shattered the glass in the window behind me. Rolling me over the top of him, he flung me onto the floor on the opposite side of the bed. I heard Dusty's cast hit the floor as he moved to attack Rufus with nothing but his bare hands. Shouts and running footsteps sounded in the hallway. Scrambling to my feet, I groped for the lamp on the nightstand, although I wasn't sure if light would help or not.

I was still debating this question when someone else who apparently thought differently bellowed, "Turn on the light, Angie!"

I flipped the switch just as Dusty launched himself at Rufus, using his cast like a club to knock Rufus's feet out from under him. Unfortunately, the momentum robbed him of his own footing, and he flipped over in midair like some bizarre karate leap gone terribly wrong, landing facedown on the floor. Rufus fell in the opposite direction, only to be pounced upon by Joe and Troy.

Where my father was in this melee, I had no idea, but I could hear him shouting. "Damnation! What the devil is going on here? Are you all drunk?"

Troy wrestled for control of the gun, banging Rufus's knuckles on the floor in a vigorous attempt to get him to drop it. Apparently beyond feeling any pain, Rufus held on despite everything Troy was dishing out.

Joe was more direct. Seizing Rufus by the hair, he yanked his head back and flattened him with a roundhouse punch to the jaw that knocked him out cold.

I ran around the end of the bed to where Dusty lay prostrate on the floor, his legs tangled up with Rufus's and his peachy little buns aimed right at the doorway. As I might have predicted, my father chose that particular moment to peer into the room.

"Good God, girl!" he thundered. "What the hell are you doing with a naked cowboy in your bedroom?"

The sheer irrelevance of his question struck me as hysterically funny. Dissolving into helpless laughter, I collapsed on the floor next to Dusty, who seemed to be recovering from his spectacular fall and was attempting to rise.

"Fixing to marry him, I guess." Still shaking with a mixture of laughter and relief, I took Dusty's hand and helped him to sit up.

"Fuck!" Joe swore from out in the hallway, rubbing his bruised knuckles.

"That too," I agreed, smiling at my darling Dusty. "Every twenty miles and twice whenever we get to wherever we decide to go on our honeymoon."

"I guess I'll take that as a yes," Dusty said, obviously recalling his proposal. "Although it sure took you long enough to tell me." A carnal gleam lit his eyes as he appeared to realize what I'd meant by that. "How about we go somewhere like—oh, I dunno—Brazil, maybe?"

"Think you're up to it?" In his current state, he didn't appear to be capable of much at all.

"Maybe not, but I'll die trying," he promised.

"Don't say that!" I exclaimed with a shudder. "I've had a hard enough time keeping you alive as it is."

On that sobering note, I figured I'd better explain the situation to my father, who undoubtedly thought Rufus had been attempting to break up some sort of drunken orgy.

I nodded toward Rufus's inert form. "Dad, Rufus pretty much confessed to killing Cody, and he's also been trying to kill Dusty. Apparently, all this is because of something that must've happened to his sister." I paused as another thought occurred to me. "Anyone have any idea how he knew Dusty was here with me? I mean, he might have guessed it on his own, but—"

"You can blame Bull for that." Joe leaned heavily against the doorjamb, still massaging his hand. "He called Rufus wanting a ride home and let it slip that you and Dusty had left the bar together hours ago. When Rufus came looking for one of us to go after Bull, he realized Dusty wasn't in the bunkhouse. He went back to his room, saying he'd go and get Bull himself. I didn't think any more about it until I heard that shot coming from the house. Troy and I ran up here as fast as we could. Fortunately, Troy knew where to look for you since he'd…um…been here before. Sorry we didn't get here sooner, but we'd both gone to bed already and had to at least put our boots on."

Chalk it up to my agitated state of mind, but it was only then that I realized neither Troy nor Joe had on anything but boots and briefs and also that Joe had a hickey the size of a quarter adorning the base of his neck. No wonder Dad had thought we were all drunk.

"You did great," I assured them. "Of course, Dusty was doing pretty well on his own." I hugged him tightly. "You saved *my* life this time, didn't you? I guess that makes us even." Actually, I was still one up on him since that first shot would have undoubtedly killed him if I hadn't spoiled Rufus's aim. However, I chose not to mention it.

"Sort of," he replied. "But I think it means you belong to me now."

"Now, there's a moot point if I ever heard one," I declared. "I—"

I didn't get the chance to complete that sentence because at that precise moment, the phone rang.

"Miss Angela," Bull said when I answered the phone. "Is anyone comin' to get me? I called the bunkhouse again 'cause I was so rattled I forgot to tell Rufus to have them bring me some frickin' clothes when they came, but nobody answered the goddamn phone."

"Well, Rufus *was* coming," I said. "But he's been…delayed. Mind telling me why you need clothes?" I had to bite my lip to keep from laughing out loud. Bull sounded pretty desperate, and for some inexplicable reason, I didn't want him to think I was laughing at him.

First time for everything…

"That girl I was with turned out to be a goddamn hooker," he exclaimed. "I didn't have the money to pay her—although I didn't tell her that until after I'd done her. I just figured she'd drive me home and I could pay her ass then, but you know what that stinkin' little cunt did? I got out of her car to take a piss, and she drove off and left me there with nothing but my shorts and my boots. The little shit got my clothes, my wallet, and my hat—although she threw my wallet out the window after she took all the money I had left. Now, why would she do a thing like that? I woulda paid her. Hell, I *always* pay."

"Okay, okay," I soothed. "Where are you?"

"The police station," he replied. "The cops picked me up and wanted to charge me with indecent exposure until I told them my story. Now they're just keepin' me here until someone comes after me."

Closing my eyes, I took a deep breath. "Let me get this straight. You told the police you'd stiffed a hooker and they're letting you *go*?" Somehow the justice of that scenario escaped me.

"Dammit, I didn't tell them she was a frickin' hooker." By this time, he sounded more impatient than desperate. "I told them my girlfriend dumped me—I mean, it happened to Troy, didn't it? It could happen to me too."

I was about to point out that he actually had to *have* a girlfriend before she could dump him, but somehow managed to refrain from commenting. "I don't suppose any of the police can hear this conversation, can they? Because if so, they're gonna know you lied."

"They already do," he said. "But they thought it was so goddamned funny, they didn't have the heart to lock me up—said I'd already gotten what I deserved. You know, I think the cops around here must be in cahoots with the damned hookers. I mean, why else would they side with her instead of me? They ought to be lookin' to arrest her butt for prostitution and for stealing my clothes instead of lockin' my ass up, doncha think?"

Honest to God, the more he talked, the deeper he dug the hole. "Okay, Bull. Let me speak with one of the officers."

The phone popped and crackled in my ear as he apparently set it down. "Hey," he shouted. "Could one of you guys come talk to my boss?" I heard a chair screeching on the floor as though someone had jumped to their feet rather abruptly, followed by brisk footsteps. "Now, you watch your mouth," Bull said in a loud whisper. "This ain't no piece of ass. This is a lady."

I had to press my hand to my mouth to keep from laughing as the officer took the phone.

"Yes, ma'am?" he said with barely concealed amusement.

After counting to three to regain my composure, I said, "I don't suppose you'd consider giving him something to wear and keeping him overnight, would you?"

"Are you kidding? If we could've stood listening to him, we'd have arrested him. If it's all the same to you, we'd like to get him out of here."

"Actually, I have someone else here who needs arresting. Our foreman just tried to kill one of my ranch hands…and me. He's also admitted to killing my husband two years ago."

That certainly got his attention. "We'll be there as soon as we can. And we'll bring that other one with us."

I could almost hear his unspoken question as to why it was that, having had a perfectly good murderer around to dispatch him, Bull had somehow managed to stay alive. Until that moment, I would have been hard-pressed to come up with a reply, but I knew the answer now. As far as Rufus was concerned, Bull was the model cowboy. I didn't particularly care for him in general—and certainly not in the romantic sense—and despite his language, he had always shown me the respect due to a lady, albeit in his own inimitable way. Rufus had never had anything to fear for me where Bull was concerned.

I thanked the officer and hung up the phone, turning to survey the room. "Seeing as how everyone else is here, we should probably have a meeting or something. Where's Calvin?"

"Oh, you know Calvin," Joe said. "He's probably still in his bed, snoring to beat the band. It'd take more than a pistol shot a hundred yards away to wake him up."

I gave an involuntary shudder. "I'm so glad you guys were home when Bull called. Otherwise, things might have turned out a lot differently."

"I was doing all right without them," Dusty insisted as he hobbled over to sit on the side of the bed. "I could've taken him."

"Sure you could," Troy said with a smirk. "Right after Angie sat on him long enough for you to get up. That was one helluva crash when you hit the floor. I guess it's a good thing your dick was soft or you'd have broken it when you landed."

"I did bruise my nuts," Dusty admitted, rubbing his groin. "Otherwise, I probably could've gotten up quicker."

"You hurt your cute little balls?" I exclaimed, horrified at the possibility. "Let me see." It was as good an excuse as any to get my hands on him again. Not that I truly needed an excuse.

"I'm going back to bed," Dad announced. "This is too much excitement for an old man. Let me know how things turn out."

Apparently if I was planning to marry Dusty, Dad considered it okay for me to check out Dusty's groin injury, although he obviously had no intention of standing around to watch while I did it. Joe and Troy, however, had no such qualms and stood by, snickering.

"Why don't you ask her to kiss it and make it better?" Troy suggested as I took Dusty's scrotum in my hand to inspect it for damage. Just what I would have done if I'd actually found any bruises I had no idea, but for some reason it seemed important for me to give him my immediate attention. Actually, Troy's suggestion wasn't half bad. I didn't think Dusty would like it very much if I were to put ice on it, for example.

"Why don't you go fuck yourself?" Dusty shot back. "She's doing a fine job without any help from the likes of you."

"Ooh, he's a bit testy, isn't he?" Troy commented—he could certainly be a sarcastic little shit when the spirit moved him, but that was part of his charm. "I guess that's the thanks I get for saving his ass. Must not have gotten laid before Rufus came barging in, huh?"

"Just goes to show what *you* know," Dusty said with a smug grin.

"Oh, I get it," Troy said with a knowing nod. "It's because she hasn't sucked your balls yet, and now they're too sore. Too bad, Dusty. You know, you haven't lived until Angie's sucked your balls."

"You must not have gotten laid tonight, either, or you wouldn't be in such a pissant mood now, would you?" Dusty retorted.

"Well, it's for sure nobody sucked my balls," Troy admitted. "And I—"

"Speaking of sucking," I interjected, glancing over my shoulder. "Joe, would you care to tell us what happened to your neck?"

Blushing a fiery shade of red, Joe stared at the floor, his fingers unerringly touching the spot in question. "Jenny wanted to pretty me up some. Said this was more…decorative."

"You must not have shown her your dick then," Troy said with a knowing grin. "She wouldn't have said you needed decorating if she'd seen that."

I had an idea she would've tied ribbons around his dick—once she recovered from the shock. I hadn't completely recovered myself. That first glimpse nearly had my eyes popping out of their sockets. I couldn't help wondering how long it would take Jenny to get used to it.

Maybe never.

"No, I didn't show her my dick," Joe growled. "I just met her. You don't do something like that the first time you meet a woman."

This time I had no hope of controlling my giggles. "Troy does. I saw his before we even got out of the truck." I'd jacked it off too. Truth be told, I'd never seen an ejaculation with that much force behind it before. Apparently his sperm cells were as spunky as the rest of him.

Joe stared at Troy in patent disbelief. "Do you mean to tell me that as good-looking as you are, you *still* have to resort to whipping out your dick to impress a woman?"

Troy shrugged. "Hey, you use whatever works for you."

It had certainly worked in my case—although to be honest, I'd been more taken with his ass.

The implications were obviously beginning to sink into Joe's befuddled mind. "Damn… With my dick I could've had—"

"—all the pussy you could possibly want," Troy finished for

him. "I can hear them now: 'Oh, Joe,'" he said, pitching his voice to a girlish falsetto. "'My pussy is so hot and empty. I need your big dick to fill it up and stretch it 'til I scream.'" He paused, grinning. "Or something to that effect."

Troy was certainly on a roll. All the excitement must've had his testosterone and adrenaline levels soaring—either that or he was still a little drunk. I was okay with that, though. Given the serious nature of the evening's events, we all needed a bit of comic relief.

"Well, shit," Joe swore. "Who knew?"

I cleared my throat. "That might not work with every woman, Joe. It might get you arrested."

"You should ask them first," Dusty suggested. "That is, if you could ever get the nerve to actually say something like that."

I couldn't see it happening myself. Joe wasn't the type to toot his own horn, much less brag about his dick.

"You could make it a regular part of introducing yourself," Troy said. "Hey, baby. I'm Joe Knight." With a suggestive flick of his brow, he sidled up to Joe, sounding like some god-awful prick of a lounge lizard. "Wanna see my sword? It's really huge."

Joe gave Troy a shove and he staggered sideways, laughing his head off and nearly crashing into my dresser.

We probably could've carried on like that all night, but Rufus was beginning to stir. The thought of him getting his gun back and going on another shooting spree didn't appeal to me at all.

"Hey, guys," I said. "Think you could tie him up with something and make sure that pistol isn't where he can reach it?"

"Sure you don't want to kick the living shit out of him before the cops get here?" After all the banter, Troy's expression was far more serious than I would've expected.

I stared at Rufus, lying there in the hallway. "I can't say it hasn't crossed my mind, but I think I'll pass. He's been in hell for years. Nothing I could do to him could possibly make him feel any worse."

"Might make *you* feel better, though," Dusty said.

"I don't think so," I replied, turning to gaze lovingly at him as he sat there beside me, unabashedly nude with my hand still caressing his sore crotch. "Besides, that's your job now."

Dusty sat up straighter, his brow rising in surprise. "Full time? You mean that's all I have to do? Not rope calves anymore? Not mend fences?"

"Trust me, it doesn't work that way," Troy told him sadly. "She'll still make you work."

I aimed a withering glance at Troy. "It's different when you marry the boss and own the ranch." I turned back to find Dusty smiling at me, which wasn't surprising since I had moved on from his balls to caress his stiffening rod.

"C'mon, Joe," Troy said with a scowl. "Let's get Rufus tied up and get out of here. If I have to stand around watching her playing with Dusty's dick much longer, I'm gonna have to go fuck something." He sounded downright jealous, which was something I hadn't had to deal with in my entire life. I had no idea how to handle it—except with that cluster fuck thing.

Fortunately, Joe had a suggestion. "What about Rachel? You probably could've gone home with her, you know. You're so damned cute you can get away with anything."

Joe's problem-solving skills were beginning to impress me. I thought perhaps he might make a good foreman.

Troy gave his chin a thoughtful rub. "Yeah. I could've fucked her. I mean, I liked her. Caroline was prettier, but Rachel was very nice—good dancer too. Hmm…" The wheels were turning visibly in his head. I couldn't recall having ever seen him think that hard before. But then I hadn't known him for very long.

Joe chuckled. "I'd be willing to bet she's never had anyone like you in her life."

I certainly never had, so it was a safe bet Rachel hadn't, either. Troy was unique—both in looks and in temperament.

"I can't remember her ever having a boyfriend," I said. "You might actually be the first. She's a veterinarian, so she could probably afford to keep you. Play your cards right and you could be a real boy toy if you wanted. She even has a swimming pool. You could lie around the pool during the day and fuck her brains out at night."

Troy's expression brightened considerably. "I'll have to think about that."

With incentives like that, Troy might not even stick around until Dusty could ride again. What with Rufus going to jail—or a mental hospital, which was more likely—pretty soon I wouldn't have any cowboys at all, especially if Joe got together with Jenny.

I'd be left with Bull and Calvin.

Shit.

Chapter 28

JOE AND TROY MANAGED to get Rufus tied up without too much trouble, and I helped Dusty get dressed before the police got there. Fortunately, we were spared a visit with Bull. The police dropped him off at the bunkhouse before coming to get Rufus.

Rufus.

In his own crazed mind he'd been protecting me for years—whether I'd needed his protection or not. I'd missed out on so much because of him, and my husband had lost his life. I couldn't help wondering what my life—and Cody's—would've been like without so much interference. Cody had been a wonderful husband, but I'd never had the chance to have fun with all the cowboys we'd employed. We could have had barbecues and barn dances. Midnight rides on the range. Closeness and camaraderie, if not actual sexual contact. Simple hugs or a pat on the back would have been preferable to never being touched at all.

I'd loved most of the men who'd ever worked for us—each in his own special way and some more than others—but I'd cared about them nonetheless. Loved their goofy looks, their stubbornness, and their vulnerability. I didn't so much regret the lack of romance as I did missing out on their friendship. Perhaps that's why I had loved Cody so completely. From my perspective, he was the only man on God's green earth who found me attractive and lovable and worthy of his friendship. We truly had been best friends as well as lovers—laughing at life's humorous moments as well as heating each other's blood with a carefully aimed glance.

The similarity between Cody and Troy was simple yet so subtle I hadn't put it together before. Both had come from outside Rufus's range of influence and were therefore unaffected by his strictures. After Cody's death, I'd been so stifled by those rules it was no wonder I'd gone overboard with Troy. Given the way I felt—as evidenced by the fantasy that had carried me away so completely—it was a wonder I'd kept my hands off him for even as long as I did. Believing that men found me unattractive in general might have had something to do with that, but apparently I'd been wrong about how they felt.

So completely and utterly wrong...

Rufus came to after they'd tied him up and the look in his eyes when he saw me nearly tore my heart out. I'd never seen such an expression of pain and anguish. No doubt he was convinced I'd betrayed him. After he'd "protected" me for so long, I thanked him by sending him to jail. He never said a word to me or to anyone else, but went quietly, barely heeding the officer who read him his rights.

Perhaps he was simply exercising his right to remain silent, but I'd expected ravings or recriminations—protests of his innocence at the very least. The complete and utter silence was even harder to bear. No, I wouldn't have taken my revenge on him for what he'd done or what he'd tried to do, even though he'd killed my husband. Rufus must've believed Cody deserved to die for hurting me. In actuality, Cody's only fault had been that at least one time—although I couldn't figure out precisely when—he'd made me scream in ecstasy loud enough for Rufus to hear it. I couldn't help wondering how short Cody's life would have been if we'd been less discreet.

I'd learned to climax quietly when our children were small and easily disturbed, but as they grew older and spent less time at home, I must've gotten more vocal. I'd begun to express my feelings more than I ever had before—especially since Dad had gotten so hard of hearing we could have been pounding the walls in the next room and he wouldn't have heard us.

If I'd kept quiet, Rufus would never have heard me and would've had no reason to suspect Cody of harming me. My climactic cries must've sent him right over the edge. What Dusty had done was far less provoking, but perhaps Rufus's mental condition had deteriorated to the point that it took less and less to set him off. He'd been content to arrange for Dusty's death to appear to be accidental rather than a cold-blooded murder, but the realization that Dusty was with me in my bed had apparently been enough for him to snap again. I had no way of knowing why Rufus's deranged mind had connected me with his sister, although he *had* mentioned her braids and her giggles during his rant. When I'd been able to believe Cody's death had been an accident, there was nothing to blame it on except perhaps bad footing for his horse or whatever might have spooked it. I wondered how Rufus had killed him. He'd never said. Cody had apparently fallen from his horse and smashed his head on a rock. I could accept that. No life is charmed, no one is immune from accidents, but knowing that a loved one was murdered changes a person.

A few weeks went by. Dusty had his cast removed and was pronounced fit to return to work by his doctor. We were still short a man, so there was no reason for Troy to leave unless he wanted to. The job was his for as long as he wanted it. I thought perhaps he would leave, but he chose not to, although his reasons weren't quite what I expected.

"I have nowhere else to go," he said quietly. "And you need me, so I'll stay for now. I might move on after I get a little money saved up, but not yet."

I did need him, but I wondered if he didn't need us even more. Apparently he hadn't considered becoming Rachel's boy toy to be a viable option, although I was fairly certain he'd never brought up the idea whenever she was around.

I spent more time with the men—going out occasionally, talking with them, and getting to know them better than I ever had before. I learned that Calvin's family had all been killed in an accident, and that he'd never let himself get close to anyone again because he couldn't stand the thought of losing someone else. I could relate to that, and we had a number of long talks about it. Discussing it sooner would've helped us both, but better late than never.

I even got to where I could tolerate Bull. Beneath his bluff bravado and foul speech were enough insecurities to astonish anyone. Without Rufus there to tell him what a good job he did, he seemed to wither a bit, and he was quieter, just as I was. That experience had changed us all.

I promoted Joe to foreman, and I believed it was a good choice. He started dating Jenny in earnest not long after that, and I had high hopes for their future happiness.

Chris and David came home from college over the Thanksgiving holiday, and though I'd told them about all that had happened, there were details they wanted to know, so I had to relive the whole thing, rattlesnake and all.

Chris looked at me with Cody's eyes and said, "Mom, it's not your fault. You didn't make Rufus insane. Someone else did that long before you ever met him."

The insightful little rascal hadn't even heard me say I had placed a portion of the blame upon myself, but somehow he knew. Cody might be gone, but he'd given me a couple of great kids.

After that, I threw myself into the preparations for a truly memorable Christmas, decorating the house, the barn, the bunkhouse, and anything else I could find. I even went out to the highway and tied a big red bow around that cottonwood tree. The men were busy getting the cattle settled in for the winter, so I spent a lot of time by myself, even getting all of my stained-glass orders done in time for Christmas.

We all got together at the house for a Christmas Eve party, planning to have Christmas dinner in the mess hall the next day so there would be enough room for all of us to sit down without being crowded. Calvin was so excited about having a real Christmas with the family he got downright tearful. Joe hung mistletoe all over the place and kissed me every chance he got.

"Jenny will get jealous," I warned.

"Don't worry," he said. "She gets plenty of my kisses. She can spare a few for you."

Perhaps he'd been saving them up the way Dusty had.

The mistletoe had an added effect, one I never would have expected, which was a rather chaste kiss from Bull. After a while, the men began to talk more among themselves and the boys were off in their rooms playing video games. Feeling the need to commune with our typically white Christmas, I went out on the porch alone.

The air was breathtakingly cold with a sky so clear the moon and stars seemed even brighter than usual, and moonlight sparkled on the surface of the snow like a million tiny stars. I stood there, shivering, looking up at the sky and thinking how small and insignificant all of our troubles truly were. In the greater scheme of things, they meant nothing at all. The universe would go on, the stars would still shine whether we were there to see them or not—whether we were happy or not, whether we loved or hated or were callously indifferent to one another. The stars couldn't make a difference in our lives. It was up to us to determine how we would live and whether we made the effort to find happiness.

I'd been out there for several minutes when Dusty joined me, his cup of spiced cider steaming in the cold night air. "Hey, Angel. Are you frozen yet?"

"Almost." I let it go with that, not being able to think of anything else to say. Not that I minded. On a night like that, voices seem to intrude on the stillness, the peace somehow disturbed by them.

"You seem awfully quiet tonight," he remarked, echoing my thoughts. "Something bothering you?"

"Maybe," I replied. "It's hard to say exactly."

He set his cup on the porch rail. "Want to talk about it?"

"I would if I understood it myself—well, maybe I do, but it's still hard to explain."

"Try me." He stood behind me, holding me close in his embrace. "I'm a pretty good listener. I'd have to be to put up with Bull."

I smiled. "I didn't think you ever actually listened to him."

"I don't always tune him out. After all, we misfits have to stick together."

"Misfits?" I twisted around to look up at him. "What on earth do you mean by that?"

"It's what most of us are. That's what you get for having a bunkhouse. Most ranches don't have them anymore." He nuzzled my neck. "Didn't you ever wonder why none of us ever went home for Christmas? Sure, there's always work to do, but it's mainly because we don't have any place else to go."

I stood there, shivering in the cold, trying to process what he'd said. He was right. Even with the extra time I'd spent with the men, I still didn't know everything about them. Not even Dusty. "No, I didn't. But obviously I should have."

"I remember when Joe first came here looking for a job. According to him, the prospect of having a place to sleep and food on the table was an amazing improvement over trying to scrape out a living at a lousy job and driving back and forth from a dingy apartment in an old rattletrap of a car. That bunkhouse seemed like a palace to him.

"You've always taken such good care of us, making sure we had anything we needed. Joe still talks about the time you took him to the emergency room and waited while he got that bad cut stitched up. And when I broke my leg—" He paused, squeezing me even tighter than before. "I knew how much you cared. I could see it in your eyes."

"I would've done a lot more if Rufus hadn't run me off. He never thought I should be out there 'coddling' you guys."

"Trust me, we knew how you felt and we appreciated what you did for us. We would've done more to show it, but Rufus's threats kept us quiet. Other than a simple thank you, we weren't going to do or say anything to jeopardize our jobs. We were much too happy here to ever do that. After the thousand things you'd done for us, we couldn't give you anything in return, except loyalty and hard work."

"You guys certainly did that. After Cody died and Dad began to fail, I was afraid everything was going to fall apart. You men kept it together." I didn't mention Rufus. He'd done a lot, but this wasn't about him.

"We didn't want this ranch to go down the tubes any more than you did," he went on. "Joe will tell you he's never had any money in the bank until now. We all do, except maybe Bull. But it wasn't only the money or the roof over our heads we needed. Deep down, we're all here because we're trying to avoid facing up to something."

I was pretty sure I knew what Dusty's reasons were. I wasn't so sure about the others.

He pressed a kiss to my neck. "I've been hiding from love ever since I discovered I couldn't father a child. Then I came here and fell in love anyway. Joe's been doing his best to avoid women too. Neither one of us felt like we had anything to offer, and of course good ol' Rufus made us believe it even more. That's why we're all here, because we don't have families and don't believe there's a snowball's chance in hell we ever will."

"I had no idea." Although I should have, especially after what Troy had told me about Rufus's lectures. He'd said it was enough to make them all want to ship out on a freighter or go live in a whorehouse—either to avoid the idea of love entirely or to find a woman who, for the right price, would pretend to love anyone.

"Calvin's here because he's afraid to lose another family. Bull's here because he's never been able to get a decent woman to give him the time of day and most people don't like him. We're *all* screwed up. Rufus wasn't the only one."

"But there's nothing wrong with any of you," I protested. "Maybe Bull has some issues, but I love you all so much. Surely to goodness I'm not the only one who could feel that way."

"I'll admit to having learned a few things in the past few months. But tell me, Angel. Have *you* learned anything?"

"What do you mean? What should I have learned?"

"Simply that we all love you just the way you are. Even if I wasn't shooting blanks, you wouldn't have to have my children to make me happy. You don't even need to make Christmas dinner. Before you and I got together, all any of us wanted was to hear your laughter and see you smile. And me, well, I love you so much it scares me. I always have."

I couldn't say the same to him. When we'd first met, I still had a husband I was very much in love with. And then there was Troy…

"I may not have loved you for as long as you've loved me, but I wish I'd known how you felt before I picked up Troy."

Would things have turned out differently if I had known the truth?

Possibly, although not necessarily for the better. Rufus might have actually succeeded in killing Dusty. I tried not to dwell on that possibility. Losing one husband to a crazy foreman was more than enough for one lifetime.

"That's water under the bridge now," Dusty said. "Speaking of Troy, do you think he'll stay on?"

"He said he would for now, but I don't think he's ready to bury himself here. We might even lose Joe to Jenny before long. Then where would we be?"

"Stuck with Bull and Calvin?"

"Maybe. I certainly can't see Bull leaving." I shot him an admonitory glance. "You won't be able to pick on him like you used to."

"I know." His groan indicated precisely how difficult that would be. "At least I won't be living in the bunkhouse with him."

"True. But Calvin isn't getting any younger. We may have to hire some new cowboys."

Dusty chuckled. "If you bring home any more like Troy, we may need to have a talk."

I put up a hand. "I promise. Only ugly or obnoxious cowboys—as long as they can rope and ride."

"Ugly is good. Not sure they need to be obnoxious."

Given Dusty's trials and tribulations with Bull, I really couldn't argue. "You don't need to worry, Dusty. You're all I want. I don't need anything else."

"Hmm… Well, if *I'm* all you want or need, I guess I oughta return this." With a sly smile, he reached into his shirt pocket.

"Return what?"

"Your present," he replied. "Although it *is* part of a package deal. I sort of come along with it." Taking my hand in his, he slipped a ring onto my finger. When I held up my hand, it sparkled back at me like a jewel from heaven.

"It's beautiful—and so are you, Dusty. This is one package deal that doesn't have any drawbacks." I wrapped my arms around him and hugged him as hard as I could. "I love you so much."

The kiss he gave me warmed the cockles of my heart—if not the rest of me.

He must've felt my shiver. "Let's go inside and get you warm."

Chapter 29

Dusty took a seat on the sofa near the fireplace, draping his arm around my shoulders when I curled up beside him.

"Happy?"

"Incredibly." I followed my reply up with a kiss intended to show him exactly how happy I was. Unfortunately, I still had a confession to make. "There's just one thing I need to clear up. Troy, you need to hear this too."

Troy was leaning against the mantel, staring into the fire, but he looked up when I called his name. "What's that?"

I took a deep breath and spilled my story. "I never did it with Joe. I have no idea whether he's better than either of you. I just didn't want to have to hurt one of you by choosing the other."

"And how did it help to tell us Joe was better than both of us?" Troy demanded. "It made us both feel bad, and Joe rubbed it in every chance he got."

"Sorry about that, but he was tickled to death to at least be able to *pretend* he could outdo you guys. He's not what you'd call self-confident when it comes to dealing with women."

"He oughta be," Dusty said. "With a tool like *that*…"

"Yeah, well, it's a nonissue because, like I said, I wouldn't know."

"I'm not gonna ask which of us is better," Troy said, indicating himself and Dusty. "Although I'm guessing it's Dusty."

"You both had your moments," I hedged. "But without putting too fine a point on it, sex is better with someone you love."

Troy heaved a sigh. "I can't argue with that." He plopped down beside me. "Guess that explains why you two are so lovey-dovey tonight—unless it's the eggnog. That's some pretty strong stuff."

I patted his knee. "Among other things."

"Holy shit! When did you get *that*?"

Clearly, he'd noticed my ring. "I dunno...about five minutes ago?"

"We should celebrate—maybe drink a toast with some more eggnog."

"Mmm-hmm." Leaning closer, I traced the outline of Dusty's ear with the tip of my tongue. "Or maybe we could have some hot buttered rum."

"Sounds great! Didn't know you'd made any."

"I haven't," I replied, still nibbling Dusty's ear. "I was just thinking about it."

"Oh. Well, if you decide to make it, I believe I'd like a cup. I've never tried it before."

"It's pretty tasty," I said. "Although to be honest, I wasn't planning to drink mine from a cup." I paused for effect. "I was thinking about dipping Dusty's dick in it and then licking it off."

Troy let out a groan.

"Not too hot now." Despite his teasing tone, passion flared in Dusty's eyes. "You wouldn't want to raise blisters on me, would you?"

I shook my head. "It'll only be warm enough to make your blood boil."

Troy cleared his throat. "Don't suppose you'd consider making that a party of three, would you?"

"Nope."

"That's all?" he demanded. "Just 'nope'?"

"Yep." I kissed Dusty again, using as much soft, wet tongue on him as was humanly possible.

"Shit!" Troy exclaimed. "We've got to get the two of you married, and soon. The temptation is killing me."

Bull was on the other side of the room playing checkers with Joe, but Troy's outburst got his attention. "What? You two want to get married?"

"That's the plan," Dusty replied, frowning. "I thought everyone knew that."

"Goddammit, of course I *knew* it," Bull declared, leaping from his chair. "What I'm askin' is do you wanna get married right now?"

I should have known... I made no reply but held my breath, waiting for him to continue.

"Because I can marry you." Puffing out his chest, he announced, "I'm an ordained minister of the Church of the Holy Evangelical Society for the Spiritually Deprived."

"Depraved, you mean," Dusty muttered.

"Might be legal in Nevada," I admitted. "Not sure it would be binding in Wyoming."

"Oh no!" Bull waved his arms expansively. "It's good anywhere, even at sea. I performed a marriage between two sailors once."

"I thought the captain was supposed to marry people at sea," Troy said with a frown. "Why couldn't he do it?"

"Because it was two *guys*," Bull explained. "It might not have been all that legal back then, but it sure as hell made them happy."

Dusty's expression was so innocent a halo should've been hovering above his head. "Is that your goal in life, Bull? Bringing joy to the gay men of the world?"

Trust Dusty not to let that pass without comment. I glanced over at my father, noting that he and Calvin had, thankfully, both fallen asleep in their chairs and were serenading us with a chorus of loud snores. Joe stared at Bull, clearly dying to hear his reply.

"Someone has to," Bull declared. "I mean, how happy could they be when they've only got each other? I don't know a single goddamn hooker who'll touch them."

"Bull," I said, fighting back the laughter that threatened to overwhelm me. "They only want each other. That's what makes them gay."

"I never could understand that," he said with a shake of his head. "How could any man live without pussy to fuck? It's unnatural."

Troy pounced on that one like a duck on a June bug. "Holy shit, Bull! You said fuck in front of Angie. Joe, you're the new foreman. You should fire him right now, on the spot."

Bull blushed to the roots of his hair—or he would have if he'd had any. "I'm so sorry, Miss Angela." His wide-eyed, stricken expression was downright comical. "Don't know what came over me. Please don't fire me on Christmas."

"No, we won't fire you, Bull," I said, trying desperately to sound sincere when inside I was giggling harder than I ever had in my life. "And while it was very kind of you to offer to marry us, I think we'll stick with the more traditional ceremony. There are legal issues to be considered—future ownership of the ranch and all. I'm sure you understand."

"No problem," Bull said. "I'm only tryin' to help."

"I know you are. Don't worry about it." Rising from the sofa, I gave his arm a quick pat before heading out to the kitchen.

"Hey, where are you going?" Dusty called after me.

"To make some hot buttered rum. Want to come along?"

Dusty was on his feet in an instant.

"Oh God, she wasn't kidding, was she?" Troy's voice sounded sort of strangled—like it had been choked off way down deep in his throat. "I should never have thrown in the towel. I should have kept coming up to your room every night and begging—on my knees if necessary."

"Wouldn't have done you any good," Dusty said. "I was way ahead of you from the start. You just got the ball rolling."

"Yeah," I called back to him, "the hot, buttered rum balls. So tasty, so delicious, so—"

"I know," Troy groaned. "I'm trying to forget. So, Dusty, has she—?"

I couldn't see Dusty's expression because I was rummaging

around the kitchen in search of the proper ingredients, but I heard his reply.

"Oh yeah," he said. "All the time."

I glanced at the doorway just as Bull darted into the kitchen right behind Troy. "Has she what?"

This, I had to see. Momentarily abandoning my quest for brown sugar, I turned around and leaned against the counter.

"Sucked his balls," Troy replied in the most matter-of-fact tone imaginable.

Following a gasping breath that should've choked him, Bull aimed a slack-jawed gape in my direction. The suggestion that he try sucking a few balls himself might've triggered a more astonished expression, but frankly, I didn't see how.

Having witnessed Bull's reaction, Troy obviously intended to play it for all it was worth. "Honestly, Bull, you haven't lived until Angie's sucked your balls. Just ask Joe."

"Joe?" Bull's normally loud, ringing voice was barely a whisper. "She fucked Joe too?"

"Oh yeah," Troy said. "She did us all the night Rufus was arrested. What did you think set him off like that? He caught us cluster-fucking her in the bunkhouse and wanted to kill the whole fucking lot of us."

Troy was a bit drunk on the spiked eggnog or I doubt he would have ever said anything of the kind. However, the effect his lie had on Bull was such a treat I didn't give a damn—despite the fact that my reputation was taking a major beating.

"I don't believe it." Bull must've regained enough of his composure to be struck by the inherent unlikelihood of such an event. "Miss Angela, you haven't really—"

"She jacked me off in the truck the day she picked me up," Troy insisted. "She likes to fuck. Trust me, she's not the proper little princess you all thought she was. Are you, Angie?"

"Oh no." Tossing a devilish smile at Troy, I added, "I did him every twenty miles and twice when we got here."

Bull swallowed hard and attempted to wet his lips with a tongue that had to have been as dry as a desert during a twenty-year drought. "And Joe?"

"Oh yeah." With a nonchalant wave, I resumed my search for the brown sugar; otherwise, I probably couldn't have kept a straight face. "He's an absolutely awesome fuck. You should see him in action. He's really quite impressive."

Bull didn't say a word.

Having gathered the necessary items, I measured the ingredients into a saucepan, turned on the burner, and began stirring the aromatic concoction, waiting for the other shoe to drop.

Joe sauntered into the kitchen, smiling. "Why, thank you, ma'am. It's nice to know I'm appreciated."

"I know he's got a dick big enough to satisfy a horse," Bull said, his voice sounding rather strained. "But are you saying you like that too?"

I took in a deep, shuddering breath before replying. "Gives me chills just thinking about it. Too bad Jenny's claimed him now. I'll never get the chance again." With a sigh of regret and a slow wag of my head, I went back to stirring the rum.

"What about Dusty?" Bull was grasping at straws now—desperately. "I thought you were going to marry him. What's he got to say about all of this?"

"Oh, she's mine *now*," Dusty insisted, indicating the ring on my left hand. "But that was the night she made her choice, which was why I was up here fucking her brains out when Rufus came gunning for me."

"What's so goddamned special about Dusty?" Bull demanded.

I still hadn't decided whether he actually believed our crazy story, but the note of jealousy in his tone suggested that he did.

"Just the sweetest, most succulent cock and balls I've ever tasted, that's what." I wasn't lying, either. "Now if you'll excuse me, I'm going to soak them in rum and get drunk licking them dry."

"Rum balls!" Troy shouted. "Let's have some rum balls!"

"I thought that was bourbon balls," Joe mused, rubbing his chin.

"Maybe so, but I prefer rum." I gazed at Dusty with lust-filled eyes. "Sweet. Hot. Buttered. Rum."

Dusty's lips curled into a sexy grin as he unbuckled his belt in a blatantly sexual fashion, his hungry eyes never leaving mine for so much as a second.

"Fuck!" Bull bellowed at the top of his lungs. "I missed out on that because—"

"You were off fucking a hooker," Dusty said as he unbuttoned his jeans. "I guess you should've come home with the rest of us that night. Now if you'll excuse me, there's something I've got to do for my Angel."

The veins in Bull's head and neck looked like they were about to blow. "Fuck!"

Joe cleared his throat. "That's twice you've said that word in front of the boss now. One more strike and you're—"

"Of all the goddamned, motherfuckin' bullshit I've ever heard in my whole fuckin' life…" Bull ground out the words as he raked a hand over his head. If he'd had any hair, he probably would've yanked out a handful.

"Out!" I yelled with glee.

Bull was struck dumb after that. I would enlighten him later, but at the moment, peace on earth was infinitely preferable to his blustering. I set out several punch cups and ladled some of the rum mixture into one of them.

"Here, Dusty," I said. "See if this is the right temperature for you."

Bull watched goggle-eyed as I held the cup, not anywhere near Dusty's mouth, but closer to his waist. Dusty dipped a finger into the warm, buttery concoction and slipped his hand inside his open fly. The little slut wasn't wearing any underwear—again—and judging from his pleasurable sigh, the temperature was perfect. He ran his tongue over his fabulously kissable lips, provoking a delighted giggle from me.

Bull let out a screech, then stomped from the room without another word.

Troy stared after him with awe. "Jiminy Christmas! For once in his life, he's actually speechless." As he turned around, Troy's expression went from wonderment to wicked in the space of a heartbeat. "I also thought he'd never leave." With a smirk, he swaggered toward me as that big, silver calf-roping belt buckle flashed open with a touch of his fingertips. "Mind if I try some of that?"

I nodded toward the pan on the stove. "Help yourself. There's plenty more. Dusty and I are heading upstairs."

"But it's Christmas!" Troy protested.

"You bet it is." Dusty put his arm around my shoulders. "And I've got a present to unwrap."

Troy heaved a sigh and glanced at Joe. "Care to join me?"

"Sure," Joe replied. "Just don't put any rum on my balls. Jenny wouldn't like that."

"I don't blame her." I gave Troy the once-over. He was a nice guy, and he was gorgeous. Why was he alone on Christmas Eve? "We've gotta get you a girl, mate."

"I have one in mind," Troy said. "Think it's too late to call Rachel?"

"Probably not. If you wish her a merry Christmas now, you might get lucky on New Year's Eve."

"True." Not bothering with the ladle, Troy poured the remainder of the hot rum into two of the cups. He handed one to Joe, then took a sip from his own. "Not bad. Might taste good on Rachel too."

"Remind me to give you the recipe." I winked at Troy. "Well… good night, guys. Merry Christmas."

Joe held up his cup in salute. "Merry Christmas to all…"

"And to all a good night!" Troy downed his rum in one gulp, making me glad I'd only heated it enough to melt the butter.

Chuckling, Dusty gave me a squeeze as he steered me toward the stairs. "I'm betting some of us will have a much better night than others."

"Probably so," I whispered. "Just don't let Troy hear you say that."

"Too late!" Troy sang out. "Better give me that recipe now, Angie." He wiped his mouth with the back of his hand. "I'm gonna need it."

Read on for a sneak peek at the next book
from Cheryl Brooks

Cowboy Bliss

Coming soon from Sourcebooks Casablanca

Bunkhouse cook wanted.
Experience preferred.
Must love cowboys.

"You're looking for *who*?" The eyes beneath his dark, forbidding brow were an indeterminate hazel, yet I'd never seen a more intense gaze.

"Mr. Douglas," I replied. "Calvin Douglas. He's supposed to work here. This *is* the Circle Bar K ranch, isn't it?"

"Yeah. He's here. Just never heard him called 'Mr. Douglas' before."

Anyone else would have smiled at that point, but his expression didn't soften in the slightest. From beneath the brim of a dusty brown cowboy hat, his eyes bored into me like a pair of drills, setting off an attack of nerves that made my hands shake and my throat go dry. He was precisely the kind of man I tended to shy away from.

Who am I kidding?

I shied away from all of them.

"M-may I see him?"

Getting out of my car had already taken most of the courage I possessed, even with Ophelia by my side. A mix of German shepherd and several other breeds, Ophelia had been rescued from an abusive home and taken to the shelter where I had worked as a volunteer during my senior year in high school. Usually, she was fairly timid and tended to cringe at loud noises. But she could turn into a fierce, growling protector whenever she thought I was in danger—as several suspicious characters I'd encountered while out walking near the park could attest. Surprisingly, she didn't growl at this man.

Obviously, she didn't consider him a threat.

I disagreed. I couldn't even look him in the eye, much less argue with him.

Not that he was arguing.

He nodded toward a long, one-story building near the enormous barn. "He's in the kitchen fixing dinner."

That occupation certainly fit with what little I knew about my grandfather's old Army buddy. According to the letter I'd received from him, their friendship had begun in boot camp and continued on through active duty. Calvin had served his unit as a cook, while Grandpa became a combat soldier. While I could only guess at Calvin's current state of health, Vietnam and Agent Orange had certainly left their mark on my grandfather. Grammy had been pregnant with my mother when Grandpa was drafted and had no other children even after he returned. Five years later, unable to deal with the way the war had changed him, she divorced him and remarried. As Grandpa's only child, my mother wound up being the one to deal with the mood swings and poor health that were the legacy of his tour of duty.

Although Grandpa wouldn't talk about the war, I'd seen the scars and witnessed the sickness, both mental and physical, that had only worsened with the passage of time.

All that was over now, and his ashes had been scattered in the Tetons as he'd requested. When his demons got to be too much for him, those mountains had been the only place he could find peace. I had often wondered why he'd never gone there to live, but I suspected even they were only a temporary fix. No doubt he became immune to their effect after a while, just as he'd become tolerant of so many of the drugs used to control his illness.

The tall cowboy tipped his hat in a gesture that struck me as being more dismissive than polite and went back to the barn without another word, leaving me to find the kitchen on my own. I watched him go, wondering what his story was, why he had been so abrupt and unfriendly.

Not that it mattered. I wouldn't be there long enough to find out anyway. I was simply there to fulfill yet another of my grandfather's dying wishes.

"Come on, Lia," I said, giving my dog a pat on her broad head. "Let's do this and get going."

I wrapped my coat more tightly against the chilly wind. Grandpa had died the first of September. No doubt autumn in Wyoming would've been fine weather-wise, but with so many things to do in the aftermath of his death, I wasn't ready to pack up and go before winter set in. Even he had suggested I wait until spring to scatter his ashes.

"Go in April," he'd advised in one of his more lucid moments. "The weather will be better then." As cold as it still was in the mountains in late April, I wished I'd waited until July.

I stared at the building the cowboy had indicated, unable to decide which of the three doors led to the kitchen. Scanning the roofline, I spotted a wispy vapor rising from a vent above the door near the center and headed toward it.

Grandpa had come to live with us when I was a child, and since his bedroom and mine shared a wall, I often heard the rattling of my closet doors as he pounded away on the old manual typewriter he'd inherited from his father. I had always known he corresponded with someone on a regular basis, I just hadn't known who he was writing to until I read his will.

To be honest, I hadn't expected the address to be current, but my letter to Calvin Douglas had received a reasonably prompt reply. In it, he thanked me for informing him of Grandpa's death and offered his condolences, stating that he hadn't heard from his old friend in more than two years.

I climbed the two steps up to a small wooden landing. In response to my knock, a tall, rail-thin man with sparse gray hair opened the door. "Tina Hayes?"

I nodded, holding out a hand that was still trembling from my encounter with the cowboy. "You must be Mr. Douglas."

"Calvin," he corrected. He looked even older than Grandpa had when he died, but his handshake was firm and at least he was smiling. Smiling men had become something of a rarity in my life. I'd become accustomed to Grandpa's wild-eyed glares, his doctor's solemn mask, and then there was the funeral director's grave countenance. Even the lawyer hadn't smiled much.

"Thanks for your directions," I said. "I might not have made it here without them—even with the GPS on my phone." I'd driven across the country with Grandpa's ashes in a box in the trunk and Calvin's letter taped to the dashboard. Having lived in Kentucky all my life, Wyoming's vast open spaces and rocky terrain were completely foreign to me. Now that I'd finally seen the Tetons in person, I wished I'd found the time to accompany Grandpa on some of his trips out west. Unfortunately, school and work had always gotten in the way.

Always too busy.

And now it was too late.

"Those fancy gadgets don't help much out here," Calvin admitted. "Come on in. Dinner will be ready shortly."

"I hadn't planned on staying that long." I hesitated. I had no desire to sit down to dinner with a bunch of rowdy cowboys—if the one I'd met was any indication, they wouldn't want me to—nor did I want to seem rude.

I'd had no idea how this meeting would go. Calvin hadn't heard from Grandpa in two years. A lot had happened in that time, and none of it good. Surely he wouldn't want to hear all the gory details. I certainly didn't want to talk about them, especially over dinner.

"Do you really think I'd let John Parker's granddaughter come all this way and not stay for dinner?" Narrowing his eyes, Calvin gazed at me from beneath bushy gray eyebrows and shook his head. "Ain't gonna happen, young lady."

I caught myself smiling for the first time that day.

Calvin apparently took my smile as acceptance of his dinner invitation. "That's more like it. In honor of your visit, I'm making my famous chili and corn bread." He shot me a wink. "It was your granddad's favorite, although I work with better ingredients now than I did when we were in the Army."

I had the strangest feeling this man knew my grandfather better than anyone. I'd never noticed him having a preference for that particular meal. But then, perhaps none of us made chili the way Calvin did. What sort of things had they discussed in those letters? I hadn't a clue, but I'd found three full shoe boxes of them in Grandpa's closet after the will was read.

A will that instructed me to do what I was about to do now.

"Sounds great." Several moments went by before I found the words. "I guess you're wondering why I'm here."

He shook his head. "Not really. You have something to give me, don't you?"

I nodded. "In his will, Grandpa asked that I give you back the letters you'd sent him, and these." I handed him the two small boxes I had tucked in my purse.

Tears filled Calvin's eyes. "He saved my life, you know. Saved a bunch of us." He opened one box and then the other. "He got this one for saving us, and this one for nearly dying in the process."

I blinked back a few tears of my own. "A Purple Heart and a Silver Star." I shook my head slowly. "I never even knew he had them."

"John was like that. Never one to toot his own horn. Kinda shy, really."

That description also fit his granddaughter. However, I kept that tidbit to myself.

Calvin slid the two medals into his pocket, then went back to his stove and began stirring a huge pot of chili. The heavenly aroma of chili combined with baking corn bread soon had my stomach growling, making me very glad I'd agreed to stay for dinner.

Voices from the next room broke the silence, accompanied by the scuffling of booted feet and the scrape of chair legs on the wooden floor.

"That'll be the men coming in for dinner," Calvin said. "Go on into the mess hall and have a seat."

Mess hall. I wondered what the dining room had been called before Calvin took charge of the kitchen. "Can I give you a hand?" I didn't want to admit that being the lone woman in a room full of men brought out the nervous Nellie in me like nothing else could.

"Sure." His smile suggested he either understood my reluctance or at least acknowledged the reason for it. "I'll dish up the chili if you'll get the corn bread."

Grateful for a task to occupy myself, I took off my coat and laid it on a chair next to a small corner table, then snatched up a pair of slightly singed oven mitts. One by one, I removed two cast iron pans from the oven, each of which was divided into seven sections containing round loaves of lightly browned corn bread.

"Smells great," I said. "Love the pans."

Calvin snorted a laugh. "Keeps the men from fighting over who gets the most. Everybody gets two."

"Nothing wrong with their appetites, huh?"

"It's practically a full-time job keeping them fed." He grinned. "Kinda like keeping the hogs happy."

"I heard that!" someone shouted from the mess hall. Good-natured laughter followed.

"You boys get on in here and grab a bowl," Calvin called back. "Or should I just pour the chili in the trough?"

"We're coming." After more scraping of chairs and scuffling of boots, the men descended upon the kitchen.

I should've turned around and smiled, but I simply couldn't face them. I'd be gone in an hour anyway. No need to make friends with everyone. Not that I *could*…

Apparently, Ophelia wasn't interested in making friends, either. With a whine, she darted between me and the stove, sending me stumbling backward only to slam into a rock-hard body and be gathered up by a pair of strong arms.

Acknowledgments

My sincere thanks go out to:

    My loving husband, Budley

    My handsome sons, Mike and Sam

    My pals from my nursing days

    My wonderful readers

    My talented critique partners, Sandy James, Nan Reinhardt, and Tia Catalina

    My keen-eyed beta reader, Mellanie Szereto

    My supportive agent, Melissa Jeglinski

    My longtime editor, Deb Werksman

    My amazing blog followers

    My fellow IRWA members

    My insane cats, Kate and Allie

    My normal cat, Jade

    My barn cat, Kitty Cat

    My trusty horses, Kes and Jadzia

    My peachy little dog, Peaches

    And every woman who has ever dreamed of riding a cowboy

About the Author

A native of Louisville, Kentucky, Cheryl Brooks is a former critical care nurse who resides in rural Indiana with her husband, two sons, two horses, four cats, and one dog. She is the author of the Cat Star Chronicles series, which includes *Slave*, *Warrior*, *Rogue*, *Outcast*, *Fugitive*, *Hero*, *Virgin*, *Stud*, *Wildcat*, and *Rebel*. Her self-published works include one erotic romance novel, *Sex, Love, and a Purple Bikini*, one erotic short story, *Midnight in Reno*, and the erotic contemporary romance series, Unlikely Lovers, which includes *Unbridled*, *Uninhibited*, *Undeniable*, and *Unrivaled*. She has also published *If You Could Read My Mind* writing as Samantha R. Michaels. As a member of The Sextet, she has written several erotic novellas published by Siren/Bookstrand. Her other interests include cooking, gardening, singing, and guitar playing. Cheryl is a member of RWA and IRWA. You can visit her online at www.cherylbrooksonline.com or email her at cheryl.brooks52@yahoo.com.